A Secret In Ash Brooke

A Secret In Ash Brooke

A Novel

By

Dutch Rhudy

Copyright © 2013 by Dutch Rhudy

Colophon:
Cover Illustration Copyright © 2013 by CHL, L.C.
Cover Design by Dutch Rhudy and CHL, L.C.
Editing by GVJD Copy Writing Service
Published by Classic Haus Limited, L.C.
Printed and Distributed by CreateSpace

A SECRET IN ASH BROOKE
First Edition: February 24, 2014
Copyright © 2013 Dutch Rhudy
Written by Dutch Rhudy
10 9 8 7 6 5 4 3 2 1

A Secret In Ash Brooke

A Secret in a small town is hard to hide. Her perilous Secret must be kept at all costs.

Chapter One – Martin home from the service

I felt uneasy as the bus approached my home town, it turned on The Boulevard. How much changed since I joined the service? I'm drawn home, because I love my home. Now that I'm here, what do I do, where do I go? Are my emotions confused? I have no one to come home to.

Martin Thomas Hurston is an avid newspaper reporter and amateur sleuthhound. In a quest to improve his skills, he befriended Detective Roland Pease, Ash Brooke's top investigator. Roland, who can never pass up a free meal, took Martin under wing to mentor.

Mr. Nascent offered Martin an expensive luxury apartment, anchored in the quiet west end of the industrial district. In lieu of rent, Martin is appointed manager of the newly renovated Menton Building. Across from his Liberty Street residence, sits a small garment mill.

To gain access to their leased storage area. Ella Thornton, the mills supervisor, often met Martin at the Menton Building. Her daily routine followed a precise schedule which never varied. Ella also belongs to a strict church. Her manner of dress, demeanor, and activities are most suited for a member of her congregation.

While practicing the facial recognition lessons Roland taught him. Martin studied Ella's face each time she visited the storage area. An affluent widowed tenant in his building, often invited Martin to join him at the theater. The resemblance of Ella to the soloist, who sang during a pause in a choreographed routine, captured his imagination.

After several months of study and research, Martin is sure the chorus girl and Ella are identical twins. After Roland joined the investigation he negated Martin's suspicions. Ella would never be caught dead near such a place. Martin continued his pursuit to prove a correlation between Ella and the chorus girl Rosie, until he is shunned by Roland.

Certain his gut instinct is correct, Martin followed each incriminating trail. His obsession continued to grow until he believed Ella and Rosie are the same person. Every lead and attempt to discover her well guarded secret, only prove to reinforce the impossibility of his suspicions.

Martin's investigations sealed one simple fact, Ella does not leave the garment mill, until after Rosie is on stage. It is impossible for them to be the same person. Or is it? One person cannot be in both places at the same time. Or can they?

Martin's quest to solve this puzzle started after he returned home during World War I. The bus passed his former employer's newspaper and dropped him off at the street corner. Glad the lights were still on, he rushed to the paper.

I hope Mr. Blaine still owns the place.

Busy at work behind his aging roll-top desk, hearing the front door handle squeak, John Blaine peered over his horn-rim glasses. He grumbled as the intruder entered.

Who is bothering me at this time of night?

The rusty old bell swung from a curved tin strap atop the door, and made a dull clink as the door shut. John leapt from his chair.

"Well, if you aren't a sight for sore eyes, welcome home Martin."

"Just stepped off the bus Mr. Blaine; figured you would still be here working."

"The presses roll in the morning, you remember how the night before goes."

"Sure do Mr. Blaine."

"Seeing as you are home, are you ready to return to work?"

"I hoped you held the position for me Mr. Blaine."

"Everyone is gone off, fighting the war. I have a girl typesetting, and two young boys running the presses."

At first, Martin did not recognize the unusual lingering scent mixed with the familiar aroma of printers ink.

Must be perfume.

"A lot has changed while you were away fighting for our country Martin. Women working in factories, driving trucks, running half the businesses in town. Some troublemakers are making strong demands, wanting to run the whole show. It's not right Martin, not right at all."

"You'll get over it Mr. Blaine. Someone needs to keep Ash Brooke running while the men are away."

"They are a great help with the war effort, but many have taken jobs women should not be doing, like in the munitions plant."

"Can't argue with you there Mr. Blaine."

"Will you stop calling me Mr. Blaine; as of now you are back on my payroll."

"Right-e-o J.B., you got it, and thanks Homer."

"You want fired before you start?"

"Sorry J.B., just testing the water."

"I'll test your water right out of here if I hear you call me that again."

"Yes Sir, will not happen again J.B. - Is your old cot still in the paper room? I need a place to sleep tonight."

"No need Martin, let me get the key to Mark's

apartment. It is exactly as he left it; if you do not mind staying in town."

"I promise not to touch any of his things."

"You may take anything you desire Martin. He has no family to claim his effects. Mark seemed to like you best of all. I'm sure he would want you to have his few keepsakes."

"I'll start looking for a place to live in the morning."

"You'll have to go hunting on your own time, I expect you here at seven AM sharp. Busy day tomorrow. You may use Mark's apartment for nine days, before the new owner takes over the building."

"Thanks J.B."

Mr. Blaine returned to work at his desk. Martin tapped his cap and stepped outside. He glanced down the street; the once bright street lamps now burn dim, cold, and uninviting. The entertainment district appeared deserted. He turned to walk up the trash littered sidewalk.

Mark's living quarters are two blocks east of the newspaper. The feed store vacated the property a week before Martin joined the service. An old tattered sign, advertising a new movie house, still hung inside the plate glass window; the red 'Coming Soon' line, faded to pale orange.

Looks like the place has been vacant the entire time I was gone.

A new permanent sign erected over the front door spelled out, 'Burrows Air Chute Company.' A card tacked to the door stated. 'Help Wanted – Applications available across the street at Miller and Crofts.'

Weary from the long bus ride, Martin trudged the three flights up to Mark's small rooftop apartment. The harsh afternoon sun blistered the dark green paint and time caused it to peel. He brushed the curled flakes covering the lock, unlatched and pushed the door open.

The stale feed store smell trapped inside hit him in the face. Martin is the first person to step foot in Mark's apartment in over three years. He let the door stand wide open, and raised the only two windows to help release the musty air.

After he enlisted and called to serve, Mark covered what few sticks of hand-me-down furniture he owned. Not much dust accumulated, less than Martin expected. He lifted a framed picture upright, which lie face down on the dresser. Mark's late mother and father.

A tear rolled down Martin's face as he thought about his own late parents. He laid the picture down and uncovered the overstuffed chair and bed before washing up. Rusty liquid poured from the tap for several minutes before turning clear.

Figures; the water heater is off.

A truck passed below the window, diesel fumes drifted through the apartment and out the door. Martin shut himself in for the night, allowing the familiar aroma of the feed store to reclaim its rightful home.

Martin had a hard time trying to sleep, and lie uncomfortable in Mark's bed. He could not shake the memories of the years he and Mark worked together. Scenes of battle and fallen comrades overcame his every thought. Soon, exhaustion took its toll and Martin fell fast asleep.

A loud whistle gave him a start. He jumped out of bed shaking and reached for the rifle he no longer carried. He laughed at himself, then checked his wristwatch. More rusty water poured from the tap. He nicked his face shaving when another factory whistle blew a call to workers.

Pleased with his clean appearance and having his old job back. Martin hurried to arrive at the Ash Brooke Citizen ahead of J.B.

Perfect timing.

Chapter Two – Martin meets the typesetter and starts work

Martin propped himself on the newspapers narrow window sill ledge. An old city bus drove past, piloted by an older woman. It left a choking trail of black diesel smoke, then stopped at the next corner.

A flurry of women dressed for work poured out. After the bus pulled away, a nearby factory horn sounded three penetrating blasts. Several ladies crossed the intersection in haste. One girl, who did not look more than around sixteen, came down the sidewalk toward Martin.

She paused at the corner of Mike's Diner and checked to see who might be around her. Martin sensed her fear of seeing a lone man standing and watching her.

"Hello, I'm Martin Hurston, just waiting for J.B. to arrive."

A distant bell rang as she approached, causing her to pause for a moment.

"I work for Mr. Blaine, he's late."

Martin noticed the impossible to remove ink stains on her fingers.

"You must be the typesetter J.B. Mentioned."

"Why yes, one of my many duties. Oh, I'm sorry, I am Luella, Luella Crolloff."

As Martin began to speak, J.B. rapped on the window and unlocked the front door.

"I'm glad you are here early Martin. I need you to run up to the hardware store and buy a new handle with lock for the back door. Make sure you tell them to cut me four keys. Broke my last key off, trying to get in."

"Yes Sir J.B., on my way."

"Luella, here is today's copy, keep the right galley on page three open."

"Will we be running Mayor Detjen's public service announcement again Mr. Blaine?"

"Not this week, set an official notice about Burrows Air Chute Company moving into the old feed store. Folks must come to claim whatever they stored in the building before next Monday."

"Seems crazy to me Mr. Blaine, making soldiers jump off observation balloons."

"They claim it will save more lives Luella."

Mr. Blaine went to his desk, and Luella got busy setting type from the many sort cases lining the east wall. Martin returned from the hardware store with the locking door handle and extra keys Mr. Blaine sent him to buy.

"Would you like me to install the new lock J.B.?"

"No, go set it down on the side table in the paper room and come back."

J.B. motioned for him to pull a stool up beside him. He stared up at Martin, peering over his glasses while rubbing the sides of his jaw. Martin experienced J.B. doing this many times over the years. Especially when contemplating how he wanted to say something important.

When young Martin started working for Mr. Blaine, he was assigned to a secluded street corner to sell papers. He sold more than anyone else who worked that area. J.B. called him into the office, and after sizing him up, offered Martin a better location.

The last time Martin found himself fidgeting on the stool. J.B. pulled him off the streets and placed him on salary, working inside. Martin learned many aspects of the newspaper industry, and worked hard in each department.

He was due for another advancement before the war started. When word of a pending war reached Ash Brooke. To serve their country, he and his friends rushed to enlist early. J.B. rolled his chair back, stood up, and set his hand on Martin's shoulder.

"Martin, the paper is in trouble. Circulation is the lowest in fifteen years."

Martin swallowed hard, his thoughts raced, the only job he really knows well, and J.B. cannot afford to keep him.

Is he closing the newspaper?

Mr. Blaine continued.

"We have no journalists, and only two young boys gleaning story material. Most of our current articles are submitted by irate women about their trials in the factories."

An older woman entered the newspaper and marched right up to J.B. waving a handful of handwritten papers. Mr. Blaine motioned for Martin to go to the back room.

"Attend to that handle Martin."

"Oh; you scared me. Slow down Martin, I almost dropped the chase."

"Sorry Luella, J.B. sent me to replace the back door lock."

"Mr. Blaine only wanted you out of the front office while Jessica tore into him."

"What ever for Luella?"

"It all started after Mr. Blaine accepted two of her articles. She showed up one Tuesday morning and dallied around until Mr. Blaine went to lunch. She claims he invited her out to dinner. He says she followed him to the diner to talk about having her own column."

"J.B. has a hard time saying no to someone, so he must have given her a chance."

"He convinced her a column was hard work, but would

consider reviewing her articles. Many were published, and ever since, Mrs. McRabe thinks she is his star reporter. She brings in several stories each week, but Mr. Blaine rarely finds something worth printing."

"That's too bad; J.B. said the paper is shorter than normal now. I better get this lock on."

Martin disappeared into the paper room to install the lock. The open door allowed the light to expose the deplorable condition of the main press. Saddened by its appearance, Martin started cleaning the important guide rails.

He was so busy working, he did not hear Jessica leave, or sense J.B. standing in the doorway watching him. Mr. Blaine is well aware of the run down condition of his valuable equipment.

He also knew Martin cared about the presses as much as he did, a true asset to the newspaper. Mr. Blaine was torn, and stood their grieving in his thoughts.

What good is a press with nothing to run on it?

J.B. returned to his desk. Propped his head face down, with both hands on his forehead; eyes closed in deep thought.

Before Martin left for the service, J.B. sent him out to work with Mark Adams, his star reporter. When Mark's mother died, J.B. offered him the apartment over the feed store. The war drew Mark to serve as an in-the-action news correspondent for the Ash Brooke Citizen.

Mr. Blaine shuffled his feet under the desk. Martin had a natural nose for news, and proved an excellent writer. He had not made up his mind whether to promote Martin as a reporter, or keep him in-house as a journalist.

Now I need him in here and working the streets.

Mr. Blaine drug his hands slowly down across his face, looked up and pulled a photo from a pigeon-hole in his desk. He stared at Mark's image for a long time before placing it in his leather keepsakes folder. Without rising from his chair, he turned and called for Martin.

"Pull that chair over here and take a seat Martin."

This shocked Martin. J.B. usually said to sit on a stool.

"Sure thing J.B., what's up?"

"I perceive how much you love that old press, care for it like your own. Nobody here to tend to things like you did since the war started."

"I will get her back in shape in no time J.B."

"I know you will Martin. However, we have more pressing issues at the moment. I need you outside as a reporter and in here. Nor can one man do the work of four, all by himself."

Martin's thoughts dwelt on the possibility of the newspaper closing down, and offered Mr. Blaine his support.

"J.B., how long have you been struggling with one girl and two young boys? You have managed to hold down the fort and keep things humming. I am back now and willing to work extra hard, we can do it, you'll see."

Mr. Blaine smiled, probably for the first time in years.

"Martin, when I started this newspaper back in eighty-two, I did it all. I was mighty proud of that lead single sheet issue too. I worked harder than I ever did in my entire life. The paper grew, and continued to grow to employ many hard workers.

"Our subscribers expect the same quality publication they have become accustomed to. The war turned everything to nothing but turmoil, grief and complaints."

"We'll get those readers back J.B., you just wait. It will be like the old days, no need to shut down the presses."

"What? Shut down? Oh no Martin, I am not expecting to close up shop. I thought of reducing the number of pages again for lack of content."

"So you're not firing me on my first day back? I sensed you were trying to figure out a way to break the news to me. Just tell me what you need done and I shall hop right to it."

"That is what I hoped to hear Martin. If you are ready to wear four hats, there is a meeting starting in half an hour over at the old wire works. Those demanding women should be good for a scoop. Then check out the progress on the new trolley."

"Yes Sir J.B., you will not be disappointed."

"Be back here no later than two, when the presses roll."

Chapter Three – The presses roll

Martin filled several pages in his notebook, before reaching the proposed trolley site. On his way back to the newspaper, he met his old friend Detective Roland Pease. He befriended Martin before the war, after he learned Martin wanted to advance his sleuthing skills."

"I got word you arrived home safe. Ready to pick-up where we left off?"

"Not yet Roland, I'll be busy at the paper. But as soon as we are caught up, I will hunt you down. We can run through some refreshers and tackle something new."

Martin arrived early, surprised to hear the presses running, and startled by their rough labored sound. Absent was the customary, rhythmical melody, which formerly produced beautiful music in his ears.

He saw J.B. in the back with the boys, struggling with a frayed paper feed strap. Martin instinctively knew they only had precious few seconds before the pick-up engaged. He ran to assist. His experience of working with these older machines on a tight schedule paid off.

He folded back the strap and clamped the jaws, just as the pick-up snapped the next roll. The new young workers failed to set the axle tension properly, and the fresh cylinder almost back-lashed beyond recovery.

J.B. spun the friction wheel, to prevent a time consuming re-threading of the presses. He took one side of the press and Martin the other, twisting knobs, turning screws and adjusting levers. The presses began to hum their merry tune, just like the old days. J.B. smiled at Martin.

"She's still a little discordant, but starting to sound sweet as ever."

The high noise level prevented a proper introduction. However, no words need be spoken. Martin motioned for the young boys to join him at the controls. He touched his ear, to indicate they should listen to the machines.

He turned a knob slightly in one direction, then back the other way, which made the sound of the press change. He had the boys do the same thing, adjusting the machines until they sang a prettier tune.

Martin taught the boys to listen close as the chorus sounds blended, and allowed the presses to sing. He also instructed each boy how to make the several fine adjustments, until they heard the pleasing music of happy presses.

The run completed, the presses were powered down and abandoned without being cleaned first.   J.B. introduced Martin to the boys. Freckle-faced Kent recently turned fifteen, and Jerome neared his seventeenth birthday. No time for further conversation.

Papers needed to be delivered.   The boys busied themselves loading the carts, pulling the heavy load behind them as they hit the streets.   Mr. Blaine grabbed an armload and left the building right behind them. Luella immediately started breaking down the galleys.

Martin was appalled at seeing her placing the type back in the cases, without cleaning them properly. She only wiped the galley faces with a dampened rag.

"No wonder your fingers are so stained."

Before she pulled another galley, Martin donned a leather apron and began washing down the type bed. Luella turned to comment on what he was doing.

"No, stop, you'll get ink on the side of the blocks."

Martin grinned and held up his clean fingers.   He

removed a galley and carried it to the end of the cases. Luella frowned and followed right behind him. She appeared upset when he slid open a deep drawer in the last case, which faced the rear paper room wall.

Not used in years, the tin liner was almost empty. Martin cleaned and refilled the basin from an overhead tank; to a line of indentations showing the full mark. He set the galley down on the upper bath tray.

After dipping a soft brush in the cleaner, he scrubbed the type until it sparkled. After dunking the tray in the bath solution several times, he set the chase on the drying rack above.

"I prefer to put type away directly from the galley, saves having to study each face. Re-casing goes faster this way."

"Yes, I know, but we cannot waste so much type cleaner, there is a war going on you know."

Martin grinned sheepishly.

"I just returned home from the war."

"I know that too Martin. Mr. Blaine filled me in. He also stated you were worth your weight in gold, but don't let him know I told you what he said."

"I'll finish washing the galleys for you before I start on the presses; that way J.B. will have to complain to me."

The two boys returned and shoved the empty carts in the corner. Jerome dropped a few scribbled notebook pages on J.B.'s desk. They snatched the large single cart of newspapers and dashed back out the door. The cart bounced across the threshold, then the door slammed shut.

After cleaning the galleys for Luella, Martin went to wash the presses down. A process which normally used a considerable amount of cleaner to do properly. Martin was never wasteful of the cleaning fluid, he used large trays to recover that which did not evaporate.

An old drum he prepared as a settling basin, to filter the fluid for reuse, was missing from the loading dock. He looked around, and found no metal drums anywhere. J.B. normally had trouble disposing of them, and now none were to be had.

Martin took a walk up and down the alley, to scrounge up as many discarded glass bottles as possible. They would hold the waste, but he did not figure a way to place the flat layers of screening inside. Their tiny necks were too small.

J.B. returned carrying a couple of newspapers and plopped down at his desk. Kent followed within a few minutes, his right pants leg torn from the cuff to his knee. His right sleeve ripped open, showing a good scrape on his shoulder.

"Mrs. Annie's dog again Kent?"

"Naw Mr. Blaine, lost my pants clip, and got caught in the chain going between Bing's store and the diner. Fell against that rusty old coal chute."

Kent handed J.B. a leather pouch, then ruffled through his pockets, passing him bits of paper with notes scribbled on them. Kent left by the back door, and Luella bid Mr. Blaine good evening and shot out the front door to catch her bus.

"As soon as Jerome gets back, we can go eat dinner at the diner."

"Sounds great, I'm starved, but don't they close at seven J.B.?"

"They save a plate or two for us late comers who sneak in the back door."

While waiting for Jerome, Martin inquired about the supply of cleaning fluid, and brought up the water heater to Mark's apartment.

"Here is the key to downstairs, the switch for the heater is behind the blue panel. You have time to run up and turn it on."

"I don't think I should do that unless I am there J.B., the unit has been off for a long time."

"You always think clearly Martin. The cleaning fluid

costs a little more, but it's not scarce. I put a curb on using it due to how fast the kids wasted it."

"What happened to my separator barrel, so I can use the cleaner over several times?"

"Everything made of metal, not bolted down, is collected for the war effort. Best keep the empty barrels inside. I'll order a fresh supply in the morning, you will be needing it soon."

Jerome kicked the door open, to pull the large cart through. After moving the two small carts out-of-the-way, he pushed the biggest cart into the corner. Then tilted the small cart up on the large cart and rolled the remaining cart tight against them.

"Got rid of them all today Mr. Blaine, collected for last month from the butcher, and old Mr. Snyder signed back up."

"That is wonderful news Jerome."

He set his collections bag on the desk and asked if J.B. read the notes he dropped off earlier. He had another wad of scrunched up papers he handed to J.B.

"I came in the door only a minute before you did Jerome. I will look over your notes tonight."

Jerome had a disappointed look on his face as he left the building for home. J.B. searched around on his desk, picking up the crumpled scraps of paper the boys placed on it. He shoved all of them in the leather pouch he carried home every night.

J.B. rose from his desk and placed the collection bags in his safe, and after spinning the dial announced.

"Let's go eat."

Martin pulled the shades down as J.B. locked the front door. Before exiting the back door, he pulled the main power switch to the equipment and doused the lights. A lone street light near the intersection reflected from pools of rainwater puddled in the alley.

"Jerome tries his hardest to come up with a

newsworthy story. He has this habit of bringing me a few notes when picking up another paper cart. He stands towering over me and waits, giving the impression of an air of urgency about them. Jerome wants me to stop what I'm doing and read them right away."

The cook at the diner spotted Mr. Blaine and Martin coming and held the back door to the kitchen open for them.

"Almost gave up on you tonight Mr. Blaine; Mr. Hurston, so glad to have you home, I'll tell Maggie you're here."

Martin rolled his eyes.

"I'll surprise her tomorrow."

Although he had no such intent, and would avoid her if possible. Maggie came rushing from the kitchen. J.B. got a kick out of seeing her trying to corner Martin to prevent his escape. Her nasal voice and constant chatter irritated half the town.

Martin was always attentive and pleasant to her, even if it meant biting his tongue. Mike, owner of the diner, followed a minute after Maggie to rescue Martin. She brought J.B. his regular order; a slice of meatloaf, peas and mashed potatoes.

Mike brought out a steak, pan fried potatoes, and a side dish of green beans for Martin. J.B.'s mouth watered at the sight of the perfectly seared beef.

"Where did you get a steak from? You don't serve steaks here."

The chef overheard J.B.'s bellowing clear back in the kitchen and started laughing. Mike began to rib J.B. mercilessly.

"Mr. Blaine, we 'recently' added steak to the menu you never read; oh about two and a half years ago now. You tried one and said it was tough, dry, and way to expensive."

"Oh yeah, so I did, I remember now."

Mike shooed Maggie back to her cleaning the dining

area, then left his back room diners alone to eat in peace. J.B. winked at Martin, opened his folder and handed the scraps of paper to him to peruse.

"The ones signed Minot are from Jerome. Kent never signs his, but sometimes draws a bugle on them. Probably because his last name is Horn. I hope you can make something newsworthy out of this mess."

Maggie came into the room, acting busy while keeping her eye on Martin until he finished. She collected the dishes and disappeared in the kitchen. The lights in the front diner section went out. This was their cue to escape before Maggie accosted Martin again.

Martin found the boys little tidbits most helpful in tracking down leads. He followed up on each of them, then went out to dig up more articles. He spent the next week wearing all four hats, in preparation for the next issue.

After the newspaper hit the streets with information about the new Burrows Air Chute Company; most folks who had items stored in the old feed store came to claim them. Mr. Burrows invited Martin to remain in the upstairs apartment while the buildings early renovations were underway.

Mr. Burrows felt it provided a valuable measure of security, as the flimsy aging doors and windows were replaced. He chose sturdy steel doors and new casement windows. Martin still worried, because places to live were scarce, and he found no nearby openings available.

From the comments J.B. made about the women, Martin was unsure about whether he should agree with them or not.

Shall I present the positive side of their organizing, or view them as J.B. does, as troublemakers? Taking the lady's side may prevent a strike.

He decided to play it safe, this time, and write the articles concerning their position as neutral as possible. Not taking either side of the issues at hand. His expertise at only showing the positive points of both sides, eventually paid off. A fair new agreement resulted.

Martin rose early each morning to work at the newspaper, cleaning and restoring the machines and office fixtures.   Several weeks lapsed before they sparkled, returned to their former glory. Jerome and Kent learned to have greater respect for the presses, and for Martin.

He took a professional interest in their leads; much more than J.B. ever did, and gave the boys credit for the articles he wrote from their tips. While out canvassing the area for stories, Martin often crossed paths with the boys, who now would pass their notes to him.

Seeing their names in print, as the source of the stories. Allowed Martin to teach them how to sniff out newsworthy events, and provide better details.   In the evening, Martin donned his journalism hat and assembled the stories for the upcoming edition.

Martin often worked with Jerome or Kent separately, when building a story from their notes. He did most of the legwork and interviews himself; but felt they would learn faster, if they watched what items he included, and how he worded each story.

Chapter Four – A new apartment

The Menton Lumberyard storage sheds once sat behind a row of industrial buildings. The largest housed their massive box manufacturing facility. Others, now razed, served as a hardware store, a sales office, and an equipment maintenance garage.

The lumber sheds burned down a decade before Martin entered the service. A candy company leased the bottom floor of the main structure for a couple of years. Afterward a group of artists rented the whole building.

They renovated the upper floor, creating unique little loft type apartments. Over time, they joined the twenty small lofts to form eight spacious living areas. When the war started, they abandoned the building to go serve their country.

A close friend of Mr. Blaine's, Thomas Nascent, purchased the huge box factory. He speculated owning a saloon with several upstairs rooms; strategically located between the new movie house and theater, would prove to be a wise investment.

A non-drinker himself, Mr. Nascent failed to follow the news regarding the new laws concerning the establishment and sale of alcohol. He continued to move forward with his plans. As the extensive renovation neared completion, he found no saloon keeper interested in leasing his building.

No one would take the chance with the proposed Eighteenth Amendment on the docket. He did manage to rent the building to a local company for their annual Christmas party; and to a private individual for their gala

News Years Eve celebration.

His wife Clara, joined the Womens' Christian Temperance Union, and was active in the promotion of womens suffrage. With the Eighteenth Amendment ratified two weeks into the new year, Mr. Nascent chose to let the building sit vacant.

To help recover his ongoing expenses, while waiting for a tenant; he temporarily leased the large front room, as storage space to the garment mill across the street. He stopped by the newspaper often to run various ads regarding his fancy building.

While in the newspaper talking to Mr. Blaine about running a whole page ad, offering it as an inn and coffee house; J.B. mentioned Martin's need of an apartment.

"With Burrows Air Chute Company opening, Martin could guard the building for you, until you get it leased."

"Yes, a splendid idea. Mr. Burrows talked of him a couple of times. I doubt anyone will be interested until after this dreaded war is over and the men return home. I'll bring the keys to you tomorrow."

After seeing the size of the apartments, Martin became deeply concerned about what Mr. Nascent may ask in rent. At work the next day, he discussed this with Mr. Blaine.

"J.B., I toured those lofts and I'm afraid I will never be able to afford such luxury."

"Tom did not mention to me what he expected to charge; he will be at the diner in about an hour. Wait until he is finished eating, then pop in and feel him out."

Martin followed up on a lead and almost missed Mr. Nascent. His late arrival turned out for the best. Thomas sold another building on the other side of town for a sizable sum of money. Martin called down the street.

"Mr. Nascent, please wait up."

A light sprinkle turned into rain so they ducked back inside the diner.

"Elegant apartments in your building Mr. Nascent, but

I'm afraid they are more than I can afford on the salary J.B. pays me."

"Nonsense Martin. From what John tells me about you, I should pay you to stay in the place."

"I wouldn't go quite that far Mr. Nascent, J.B. overstates a lot of things. I must move this weekend and all the places are taken by women who stay in town close to their jobs."

"Yes, they pestered me to death as well, wanting me to let four to a room. I cannot guarantee how long you can stay Martin, I have the building up for sale or lease. I doubt if anything will happen before the war ends."

"I understand Mr. Nascent."

"You can call me Tom."

"Yes Sir, I mean OK Tom."

"I have an idea Martin. I live on the other side of town, and rent out storage space downstairs to the garment mill. Living upstairs, you can let them in whenever they receive a shipment of goods or need to retrieve materials."

"I would be glad to handle those tasks for you Mr. er, Tom."

"Hey, you can also manage the payment transactions for me as well."

"Speaking of payment, what about the rent? I don't make very much money."

"Can you afford twelve dollars a month Martin?"

"If I plan to set enough aside, sure, that will work Tom."

"I will give you credit toward the rent to handle the garment mills storage, and a little extra for keeping the place clean. Your month's rent will never go over ten dollars."

"That's mighty generous of you Tom, thanks."

"Oh, tell John to cancel my ad. I have some thoughts to consider for a few weeks."

Martin selected the front corner apartment with the large west facing windows. No one has lived in them since Mr. Nascent renovated the building. Martin only needed to clean up the construction debris, and a little dust off ledges before moving in.

Jerome arrived just after lunch, as promised, to help Martin move in. Jerome let out a long loud whistle.

"Wow, will you look at this place."

Kent joined them as they passed the newspaper. Together they moved everything from Mark's apartment. Martin placed most of Mark's things in another empty room, to decide later what should be done with them.

The low mounted living room window faced north, and provided the right amount of daylight for evening work at his desk. Across the street Martin had full view of the sidewalk, where it ran in front of the garment mill.

His bedroom window faced west. Unobstructed by other buildings, the entertainment district, several blocks away, appeared close. The newly renovated building provided a sharp transition from the industrial style factories to the east.

Martin heard a bang and clumsy footsteps climbing the stairs.

"Here, let me help you with that Kent."

"I got this desk chair from Mr. Burrows. There are several unclaimed items left in the feed store. He shoved the better stuff, left by owners after the deadline, in a back room. He said you should hurry and come over."

Kent walked right in, like he owned the place. He led Martin through a maze of long tables and strange looking machines. Mr. Burrows was in the storeroom.

"Hi Martin, I am glad you came. I hate to see some of these items get thrown away. I'm keeping this twenty-drawer cabinet and those two short desks. If John can squeeze these tall cases in at the newspaper, I'll keep them set aside until you find a place for them."

"Great, they're in wonderful shape. I will hurry to clear space for them, and thanks Mr. Burrows."

"Here are some things I'm sure you will be interested in Martin."

Mr. Burrows opened a tall cabinet and inside were two typewriters. One antique with parts missing, but the other was almost new, not a scratch on it. On the top shelf were several reams of paper, spare ribbons, and a whole pile of unused notebooks.

"Thanks Mr. Burrows, I've always wanted one of these."

Mr. Burrows pointed across the room to a slate board.

"Several file drawers are hiding behind those chalkboards. Help yourself to anything else you want, it's all yours. Monday, whatever is left goes to the dump."

Kent noticed two floor lamps in the corner and asked Mr. Burrows for them. Mr. Burrows glanced at Martin, who nodded it was OK. Kent grabbed the lamps and ran to the newspaper office. He brought back a paper cart, to help bring their haul to Martin's apartment.

Martin wrapped the typewriter in an old pair of drapes, cradling it like a baby. He trotted home and set it in a safe place before returning to help Kent with the larger items. Jerome happened by right before dinnertime and pitched in to help.

With all the space downstairs, the boys moved the accumulation to Mr. Nascent's building; except what they were supposed to leave behind. Kent stayed behind to sweep out Mr. Burrows storeroom.

Martin did not have a use for everything the boys collected. So as he had time, he planned to clean up the better items, and repair the broken things. To donate to good homes, rather than get tossed in the city dump.

The next week kept Martin busy making space in the newspaper for the cases Mr. Burrows provided. They did not fit in the front room as planned, being either a foot too long or an inch too deep. The back area was already overcrowded. But they were a perfect fit in the enclosed end of the loading dock.

Chapter Five – Martin meets Ella

With Martin's help, Jerome and Kent were fast becoming avid reporters. They spent many nights in Martin's apartment, learning how he compiled each column for the newspaper. This saved Martin hours of work, and allowed him to spend more time working as a journalist.

Living directly across the street from the garment mill turned out perfect. He learned the timing of the various factory horns in the area. They became his personal cue to leave for work in the morning.

Martin met many of the sewing machine operators as they came to and from their jobs. On Friday evenings, before their whistle blew marking the end of day. He would place the restored storage items from the feed mill out on the sidewalk.

No sooner than he had items ready, the women snatched them up. Many of the ladies who lived in town, benefactors of these gifts; brought Martin special baked treats from their home kitchens on Monday mornings.

He learned most of their names, and looked forward to conversing with them. Knowing he was a reporter, several informed him before newsworthy events took place. Many of these advance leads were the type normally only discovered after the fact.

Martin became a friend of the garment mill employees, which led other factory personnel to trust him with inside information. Martin often presented his articles in a positive light, favoring the workers.

J.B. preferred the masculine or business owners side of the story. So many published items remained neutral; until J.B. realized that standing up for womens rights greatly increased circulation. Ad revenues rose also, especially from businesses catering to the heavy female population.

Martin met Miss Thornton on a professional level, when Mr. Nascent first introduced them. He informed Ella, manager of the garment mill, where Mr. Hurston worked, and instructed her to call him for access to the building.

Ella instinctively knew how busy he would be at the newspaper. So if she needed access, rather than bother him at work, she kept a vigil. Martin often passed the garment mill when out and about following leads.

Likewise, Martin was just as considerate of her time. If a materials' delivery truck passed the newspaper, he would meet her at the Menton Building door. This arrangement worked out well, and drivers need not wait for Mr. Nascent to arrive from up north.

Martin ensured the entire building was always kept sparkling clean. The material deliveries for the garment mill produced a considerable amount of dust. This settled everywhere, and on the few remaining broken items obtained from Mr. Burrows.

To help keep this hard to clean area of the building pristine. Martin chose to place the next garment mills shipment in a back storage room. This secure area, designed to hold beer kegs, is divided from the rest of the building's interior.

A pair of double doors served as a side utility entrance, and gave Ella ready access. Martin would give her the keys to these doors the next time she required entry. Ella still must continue to locate Martin until they consume the front room inventory.

Roland, Martin's detective friend, stopped and yelled from his car window.

"Hey Martin, did you keep that steel frame of wood box drawers from Burrows?"

"Sure did!"

"Save them for me, I'll go borrow dad's pick-up truck and be back in a few."

Martin hung around for a bit after the delivery truck pulled away. Rather than waste time doing nothing, he scooted the last few items from the feed store to the middle of the room. All these items had broken welds, and he did not own the proper repair equipment.

He locked up and started walking toward the newspaper, when Roland came rumbling down the street. That old truck left a trail of blue smoke all the way from The Boulevard. He stopped at the front door.

"Shut that thing noisy stinking thing off before you kill someone."

"Sorry Martin, she ran fine until I turned on the highway."

"There are a few junk items left inside. Would you take them to the dump or give them away to someone who can fix them? Better yet, while you are there, leave that old truck at the dump too."

Martin helped Roland load his pick-up with everything left from Mr. Burrows. He started the truck to leave, and the old clunker purred like a kitten. But that only lasted until he passed Pottery Row and turned on The Boulevard. Blue smoke drifted east from the Klein Avenue overpass as he crossed on the highway.

Ella caught Martin as he was leaving for work, she needed to check their recent inventory delivery against the invoice. She had a look of worry on her face, until Martin handed her the keys to the side entrance. He then showed her where he placed the new shipment.

The side doors worked out well for Ella, and avoided the two steps up to the raised walk, in front of the building. The side entrance was in a straight line to the garment mills service door. Mr. Deckett, owner of the mill, was most pleased with this change. This allowed his stock workers to collect materials without hunting for Mr. Hurston to let them in.

Mr. Nascent had meetings nearby, so stopped to check his building often for the first couple of months. He only asked for five dollars in rent at month's end. After seeing how immaculate Martin kept the place, he waived collecting the rent.

Tom normally stopped at least once at the end of each month, or to eat lunch with John at the diner. Several months elapsed before he was down on Liberty Street again. He made the trip this time to talk to Martin, and found him at the newspaper.

"Hey Tom, long time no see. I keep your rent at the apartment."

"Do you have time to sit and talk Martin? Not here, in private."

"Sure do, is the apartment OK."

Mr. Nascent and Martin walked from the paper down to the Menton Building. They only exchanged casual conversation, and talked about some remodeling work or new construction they passed along the way. Martin unlocked the front door and they went inside.

"Come on upstairs Tom, no place to sit down here."

"You have this place fixed up neat, and the downstairs is spotless. But where is the garment mill's storage?"

"I put their latest shipments in the back room storage area. Easier to keep the place clean, and less damage around the front entrance."

"That was a great idea Martin. I like to work at a desk by a window as well."

"The light is perfect, just enough without being too bright."

"I stopped by to let you know I decided not to sell this building. I am still trying to lease the downstairs, it would make a grand diner."

"So true Tom, yes, especially now, with three more factories open, the diners are all packed solid. Some of the factories are even rotating their dinner shifts."

"I held off advertising, because I worried about the garment mills inventory. You have already solved that problem for me."

Tom stood to look out the window.

"Another bus load of service men returning home Martin. With the women staying in town during the work week, the men without families have no place to stay."

"For sure, apartments here in the city are mighty scarce Tom."

"Since I am renting one out, I thought perhaps I could rent out the others. I am also considering changing them back to a smaller size. Not yours of course, or the one across the hall from you. Sure would help out the returning soldiers."

"Seems like an awful lot of expense to go through Tom. I know from talking to the women across the street, several of them no longer kept their homes or large apartments to return to. They will need family size apartments, many are sharing a room with four other women."

"So Martin, you think it is better to rent to a married couple, rather than a single man or two?"

"Single men can get mighty wild Tom. If you only rent to married couples, I feel you will have less problems, damage and complaints. Also it will free up the smaller apartments for the single servicemen."

"I believe you are right Martin. I shall ask John to run an ad."

"No need Tom, I've received several requests concerning the apartments. If you advertise, you have less control than if I inform those couples who are seeking a larger place. Or better yet, let me select a few tenants you will be pleased with.

Chapter Six – Martin appointed apartment manager

Tom and Martin move from the couch and overstuffed chair, to his desk. Where Tom opened his briefcase and spread out, sorted and re-stacked some papers.

"I don't want you to be shocked when I show you these figures Martin. Much consideration and comparison with other apartments have gone into determining the rent. I'm not greedy, but I do have to cover the expenses involved in making them available."

Tom handed Martin a sketch of the second floor showing each apartment. Even though Martin is in and out of them several times cleaning, he never realized each were a different size.

"The four rear apartments are priced lower than those facing the street, and the two smallest even less. Turn the sheet over Martin and study the back, then tell me what you think."

Martin flipped the paper over and studied the figures. The line items display the room sizes in square feet, and the rents charged by many of the apartment owners in the immediate area.

"I had no idea those tiny places rented for so much Tom."

"And they are going up fast Martin. I want you to check my competition for yourself first hand. I'm sure you will agree, the rental amounts I intend to charge are more than fair."

Tom handed Martin another paper, this one showed the rental rates he will request.

"You don't have a figure written in the box for my apartment Tom."

"Yes I do Martin. Right here."

Tom pointed to a tiny number twelve he jotted in the corner, scratched through with the number five below. It is in the same place as the other apartment numbers are written.   On this drawing, number five is Martin's apartment.

"You are way too kind to me Tom."

"How would you like to be my manager Martin?   To execute the rentals in the manner we spoke of earlier."

"I can handle that easily Tom, and select who my neighbors will be as well."

"I wasn't finished."

"Sorry Tom, I didn't mean to interrupt."

"You have done a splendid job and kept the whole place looking wonderful. That is why I have not collected any rent from you. Now is your chance to earn a little extra. You manage the apartments, collect the rents, take the deposits to Center Bank; and I will pay you a dollar for each rent collected and deposited."

"I don't expect you to pay me Tom. With how little you are charging me, I'll be glad to do those tasks for you."

"No, I insist."

"Still way too much Tom. However, since you insist, make it a quarter, and keeping my rent at five dollars."

"You got a deal Martin, except you don't pay rent, it's included."

The two men shook hands, and walked back to the newspaper. Tom hopped in his car and drove off. John got a little miffed he didn't stay long enough for lunch.

"I thought for sure Tom would want to talk to me over dinner. He mentioned possibly needing an ad run in this weeks issue."

"He changed his mind J.B., plus he is late for an appointment; up on the far north side, beyond Clopton Hills."

After work, Martin began super cleaning each apartment, in preparation of renting them out. He spoke with Ella to ask which mill employees are married. However, she is reluctant to disclose private information about anyone.

Martin already met several of the women, and those who collected the items from Burrows he offered. While working at his desk, he made notes to himself, naming the women who wore wedding bands.

From his list, he chose two who remained in town during the weekends. He spoke to them privately after they got off work. He learned the mill paid less than Martin's own meager salary.

What Martin thought would be an easy job, with the scarcity of living quarters, renting out the apartments soon proved to be a monumental task. He decided to check area rents, only to convince himself that Tom truly is offering a fair price.

Every apartment owner he spoke with received a high premium, some more than double of what Tom was asking. He also learned that companies frowned on those in management positions, rooming with the employees they supervise.

Martin took this as a hot lead and while out working as a reporter, spoke with several women managers. Although many of them stayed in town during the work week, they had homes and families to return to on the weekend.

Martin found it hard to locate anyone in management who relinquished their permanent home. More service men returned each day, so Martin persisted in his quest. From his bedroom window, he noted the increased activity in the amusement area.

He also watched them drop their wives off at the old and new factories. Many men also drove newer style cars. Martin, who did not own a car himself, walked down to where they congregated after dropping their spouses off at work.

After speaking to several men looking for work. He met George, son of the bank manager for the largest bank in Ash Brooke, Center Bank. This was the break Martin needed. He just arrived home from the service, and returned to his position as loan officer at the bank.

His wife Marie is a manager at the new department store only two blocks north. She stayed with her parents while he served his country, and they were actively seeking a newer apartment. Not sure they wanted to live in the industrial area; the proximity to the bank and department store enticed them to come take a look at the apartments.

The beautiful renovations to the exterior, made the Menton Building appear out-of-place in an industrial area. Situated at the far west end, closer to the entertainment district, away from the noise, provided the incentive to select an apartment.

George and Marie chose unit number four, directly across the hall from Martin. They expected the rent to be much more than Tom requested, so immediately grabbed the place before someone else could beat them to it.

Once they got settled in, Mr. Clepstein introduced Martin to an élite class of possible tenants. Douglas Dentmar, owner of the newest factory in town became the next tenant. Being a widower, he took the smallest front apartment. From the east window in number eight, he could see the back of his new building.

It did not take long for professional businessmen to learn about these luxury class apartments at paupers prices. Within a week of renting the second apartment, all remaining vacancies were filled.

Due to their status in the community, it was not uncommon to find interior decorators and art dealers visiting the new tenants. They asked Martin to obtain permission from the owner, to upgrade the renovations even further.

Martin contacted Tom about their requests. After explaining to Mr. Nascent who they were, and gave each of their names; poor Tom almost fainted. Recovered from the shock, he informed Martin, other than the widower; he knew each of their families well.

"I'll leave you in charge Martin. You are far better at this than I am. Whatever you approve for them to do is acceptable to me."

Unsure of what their plans may entail, and being busy at the newspaper. Martin posted a sign on the bulletin board in the hallway. Renovations permitted after submission of drawings and approval by management.

To his surprise, each tenant who desired to upgrade their apartment, provided professional, highly detailed blueprints. They outlined not only the work to be performed, but the contracting companies who will do the work. Each recognized for being meticulous, and expensive.

The contractors were in and out in no time. Noise was kept to a minimum, and their craftsmanship immaculate. The work vehicles and moving vans delivering materials and new appliances, were considerate as well. Each using the west side vacant lot, not to block the street.

Within three weeks, daily activity returned to normal. The tenants held a small open house party to show off their apartments to one another, and invited Mr. Nascent. Tom could not believe a tenant would put so much money into a place they only rented.

Less than a month later, Martin found a set of blueprints and an artist's rendering slid under his door. The tenants pooled their resources and requested upgrading the side entrance, stairs and hallway. The plans showed a new rich façade at each door, including his own apartment.

Martin called a meeting among the tenants who proposed these changes to the building. He had a gut instinct, there is an underlying motive to their madness. He also concluded something of this nature should be discussed with Mr. Nascent.

Chapter Seven – Martin upgraded to building manager

Shortly after the war ended, hundreds of soldiers returned home to Ash Brooke. Women became accustomed to working and enjoying the fruits of their labors. Jobs were scarce, so many of the men became interested in opening their own businesses.

Construction started on two new stores between the Menton Building and the entertainment district. More requests about leasing Tom's first floor began pouring in. The possibility of whom Tom may lease to, became a serious topic among the tenants.

Martin confronted Tom with the renovation request made by the tenants. They took this extra step to show Mr. Nascent how easy it is to add posh elegance. This work would make his property more valuable, and attract higher class clientele.

They feared the paltry rent Tom requested for the space, would cause the first floor; originally designed as an upscale saloon; to be leased out as a diner catering to factory workers, and excessive noise and problems would soon follow.

Tom was busy leasing his properties on the north side of town. Pleased with everything Martin did for him in the past. He ceased all advertising for the first floor of the Menton Building.

"Martin, I'm turning the matter of leasing the first floor over to you. You have full control of all that takes place. Whatever you say goes, you are now my building manager."

"I'm not sure if I have enough contacts to find a suitable tenant for the first floor Tom."

"No hurry Martin. I know everything will work out just fine."

Mr. Nascent was privy to information he did not disclose to Martin. He figured Martin would learn in due time, as the course of events unfolded. Tom was certain Martin would strike a far better deal than he is capable to imagine; and gave him some lease figures to work within.

To ease tension, Martin informed the tenants, Tom canceled the advertisement to lease the building. Turned out a good move, as the tenants put a plan together, to preserve this end of the industrial district, and cater to élite clientage.

Toward their goal, with the help of the bank, they acquired the three lots west of the Menton Building. They also purchased two lots across the street, next to the garment mill. If their plan is successful, they intend to buy the mill, should it ever come up for sale.

Unbeknownst to Martin, the tenants previously made an offer to Mr. Nascent to buy the building. For whatever reason, he chose not to sell. He told them he would ask Martin in the next week or so, to manage the affairs of the building for him.

The tenants pooled their resources to lease the first floor, but waited for over a month before talking to Martin. Their attorney took this long to draw up some example long-term lease forms for Martin to study and present to Mr. Nascent.

When he approached Tom with the contracts, he reminded Martin that he left everything in his hands, to do what he thinks best. This was not at all like the Tom he knew.

Perhaps he is just overly stressed with his other

buildings. I'll talk to J.B.

Mr. Blaine always offered good information and sound advice. He thought it best if Martin ran the agreements past his attorney. Martin made several notes while talking with J.B., then made an appointment with John's lawyer.

All three contracts were most agreeable, placing no expenses of any kind on Mr. Nascent, which the lawyer said was most unusual. His only concern; a clause appearing on each, allowing them to use the building for other enterprises; should the restaurant plan fail.

The lawyer carefully reworded the open-ended clauses, making them tighter, and combined the three agreements into a single long-term contract. The new contract included the duration, renewal clauses and financial terms. The tenants deemed the new contract more lenient, and offered better terms, than those they requested. They immediately agreed to the deal.

With everything in place, the tenants brought in their contractors. To make slight modifications and turn the saloon into a posh restaurant. They hired the services of a five-star managing firm to set-up and run the fine dining establishment.

The company tried to get the tenants to reduce their standards, claiming the area is unsuitable for a five-star restaurant. One designer stated.

"A four-star would have trouble making a go here George. Who in this area can afford such extravagant meals and prices?"

The tenants intended for the restaurant to have very few customers at first. Their plans were only a small part of their vision. They had much larger goals in mind. They knew the establishment would grow and keep pace as further improvements were carried out.

Area diner owners learned the new restaurant chose not to cater to factory employees. So both the mid-town and Mike's diner expanded. Despite their larger sizes; they were unable to feed everyone who desired to eat lunch out rather than brown bagging.

Mid-town diner expanded again, taking over the first floor of two adjoining buildings. Relief came when construction on another new factory began. Two more east end lunch kitchens opened, to provide for the employees of existing and the new factories.

Word spread of the fancy dining place for the affluent. As business grew, the tenants added a new red-carpet main entrance, bordered with silk ropes and gold fringe. A valet service moved cars to a tree lined parking lot, on the west side of the Menton Building.

The realization of their dream began to unfold, as the entertainment district followed in suit, upgrading their establishments and slowly raised prices. The theater performed extensive upgrades and offered higher quality shows.

Diners of higher social prominence visited the restaurant and theater more often. The area west of the industrial district gradually turned more formal. This invited a few lower priced restaurants to open north of the entertainment district, on Klein Avenue.

Those businesses west of Vine Avenue tried to maintain their old world flair and low prices. However, as the east entertainment district continued to improve, the west end went steadily downhill.

Visitors to the theater and restaurant preferred not to drive through the industrial area, nor would they arrive via the rough western route. A few of these patrons held public office, and persuaded the city officials to improve a small alley-like service drive.

The officials pushed hard enough to get the alley repaved and extended. From the new shopping district on Simmons Parkway to Liberty Street; right in front of the valet parking lot. The tenants divided their lot across the street, and donated it to the city to widen the new road.

To add charm and beauty to this new route. The tenants provided the funds to include a planted island between the two lanes. They also added trees along the border of the right-of-way all the way to Klein Avenue.

Later, they extended the row of trees to Coventry Road. The excitement tapered slightly during a disruptive construction period along Simmons Parkway. Once they completed the new shopping center, business ran as usual for several years.

Mr. Nascent, who left everything to Martin to handle, rarely ventured south to check his building. Although somewhat well-to-do himself, he could only afford to treat his wife to dinner at the restaurant on rare occasions.

To repay Tom for his favors and graciousness. Martin often invited he and his wife Clara to special events held at the restaurant. The tenants insisted on hosting his sixtieth birthday party, and surprised him with his favorite duo.

Gus Van and Joe Schenck, the comic vaudevillian team. Arrived two days before their scheduled performance at the theater; to entertain Tom and Clara for his birthday. They also received a gift of theater tickets to see Gus and Joe's newest vaudeville routine.

Chapter Eight – Martin frequents the theater

Martin enjoyed the theater, and was fortunate to become close friends with the widower, who lived in number eight. Doug lived alone and often invited Martin to join him for dinner, and take in the theater.

After the other tenants learned how he loved the theater, they kept Martin well supplied with tickets. Anyone who needed to find him on a Friday night, knew he sat in the tenth row, center loge. If Doug did not attend, Martin invited Roland or J.B. to take his seat.

Roland, Martin's detective friend, was not one to turn down the opportunity for an exquisite meal at a posh restaurant. Martin deemed it the least he could do, for all the free lessons Roland taught him.

He also provided exclusive newsworthy details about interesting cases over dinner. Martin's interest in detective work as a hobby, plus free meals, gave Roland the incentive to teach Martin the various aspects of crime investigation.

Martin continually practiced each of his lessons; and tried to capture the type of things Roland instructed him to keep an eye out for. He often followed interesting individuals to study their unique daily routines.

Being a reporter, Martin already kept immaculate notes. Now he carried a second notebook, where he maintained a record of suspicious suspects. A separate page was used for identifying possible important clues, for a specific aspect he was studying.

He paid particular attention at the theater on Friday

nights, to study the performers choreographed steps. Martin enjoyed the opening chorus best of all. Over time, he learned the entire routine and in which order each performer moved through their paces.

Martin continued his observations, studying the skits and play that followed. He discovered that most of the chorus line performers, were also actresses in the opening vaudeville show and the main program.

"The girls are amazing Doug. I wonder how they learn all those lines, skits, and perform the changing choreography steps so well."

"I trod the boards when I was in high school. Never got very good. Dropped little theater before they yanked me off the stage with a hook."

"You were probably much better than you admit."

"If you caught my act back then, you wouldn't think so. Before I forget, stop by my apartment tomorrow morning. I finally finished the ad copy I wish to run in your paper."

"May I pick it up early on Monday instead? My apartment is a shambles right now."

"You can stay with me while they redo your apartment."

"They have my bedroom finished already. Tell the tenants thanks for me. I never expected you fellows to pay for renovating my apartment."

"After everything you have done for us, it's the least we could do. Hope you like the design."

"I love it. The style your architect came up with is better than perfect. G'nite Doug."

Martin did not have the opportunity to check with Roland, as he practiced his detective hobby. He developed a bad habit, finding inconsistencies in people's normal everyday lives. To him, everyone became suspect of something secretive.

He carried these unfounded suspicions all week, and now he applied these crazy notions to the theater performers.   Martin was enthralled with the lead singer and her wonderful voice. The music started, so he shifted his primary focus to her routine.

The more he studied the opening choreography and tried to follow her steps, the more puzzled he became. Feather boa's and large fans always obscured her face, until the moment she burst forth in song.

From attending the theater so often, Martin discovered little nuances in when the lead singer performed her two solos. The customary routine, included a solo near the end of the opening choreographed number.

During a short comedy skit by performers, the prop crew changed the scenery behind the curtains.   She performed her second solo before Act I of the play, and to exit the stage, followed the curtains as they opened.

Every third month or so, when Friday lands on the fifth week. Two skits and a vaudeville routine replace the play. On these dates, the lead singer sang her second solo between the first two skits.

Martin discovered the girls who dance in the choreographed numbers. Appear at different times in the plays, skits or vaudeville routines; all except the lead singer. He thought it odd the star soloist never appeared in any other show.

This prompted Martin to engage his sleuthing skills to figure out why.   After several attempts to follow her movements during the choreographed number, he only became increasingly more frustrated with himself.

What on earth can I be missing?

He spent over a month, arriving at the theater early to study the performers, as they parked and went inside. He watched carefully for her starting place in the chorus line, and when she stepped out of the line. As a last resort, he called Roland for help.

Roland first worked with Martin to cure his problem of finding inconsistencies in everything. He then listened to his present dilemma about the choreographed show. Also how the lead singer just appeared on stage, sang her two numbers, then disappeared.

Martin invited Roland to the theater on the dates Doug cannot attend. On the third visit to the theater, Roland finally told Martin.

"The reason you do not see her in the choreography, is simply because she is not in the chorus line. I will have to teach you how to learn body shapes as I have time. It won't be until after next month though, we are swamped at the station."

Martin spent his early evenings working at his desk. He wrote articles for the newspaper, and helped Kent and Jerome improve their skills. They have no lessons tonight, so he worked on a few side columns that run as regulars in the newspaper.

His apartment windows are wide open, the warm night air is fresh after the rain. He heard a noise emanate from the garment mills parking lot and glanced out the window. Their janitor, Olin Wagner, routinely started the hand-cranked cars for those women who drive to work.

The last car he tends every night, is an old 1907 Waltham Orient Runabout; with several ornamental and other parts missing. All the other cars, driven by employees, are newer models. Ella, the head manager, drove the poorest and noisiest car on the lot.

The old car backfired once, as she turned east down Liberty Street. The echo among the factory buildings made it sound like several backfires. She turned north on Pottery Row and as she turned on Klein Avenue, another loud report reverberated, breaking the stillness of the night.

One thing about Ella Thornton, you can set your wristwatch by her comings and goings. Her proper manner of dress is befitting those who dine in the restaurant. Although on her salary, she could never afford to eat there.

Ella worked for her uncle at Platte's Men's Clothing for

over a decade. After her uncle became ill, she took over everything associated with running the store. Following his death, with most men going off to war and sales in a slump, her aunt sold the business.

The owner of the garment mill, Clarence Deckett, received a government contract for Khaki shirts. On hearing the clothing store was closing, he invited Ella to handle all material ordering. Mr. Deckett also operated several factories on the north side of town.

With more contracts pouring in, by underbidding the English and French mills, and buying another mill; he appointed Ella as head manager of the Ash Brooke Garment Mill. A job for which she proved herself experienced and well suited to operate efficiently.

Chapter Nine – Something suspicious about Ella

Martin, a mystery story buff, often solved a case in the book he is reading, before the authors police figure it out. He soon learned the clues in novels are purposely made obvious, so they are not missed by the reader.

Successful in a few attempts at solving real crimes, he considered detective work, his favorite hobby and pastime. More often than not, to hone his sleuthing skills, he created leads to follow, that go nowhere.

Unsure as to why, or what raised his curiosity about Ella Thornton. Throughout the week, he gave the matter considerable thought. The unsuccessful resolution gnawed at him. Finding out became important to him, another new personal case to pursue.

Martin rose early to enjoy a large breakfast before leaving for work. Wednesdays are always hectic, completing the copy for the newspaper. Most often, his duties stretched throughout the lunch hour.

Before heading out the door, he donned a tattered brown hat. As he reached across his desk to grab the stories for this week's paper. A bright reflection on the shade from the morning sun, prompted him to raise it long enough to glance out the window.

He shielded his eyes with the stack of notes held in his hand. It came from a windshield across the street, from a different car parked in Ella's usual spot. He peered over the cars in the parking lot, no sign of Ella's Waltham anywhere.

I wonder if her old car quit again, causing her to be late?

Once outside the building, Martin could hear a few machines running in the garment mill. Curious, he crossed the street to inspect the car. He saw Ella through the window, busy working at her desk.

Not familiar with automobile models, Martin did not recognize the make at first. Olin came from around the corner and paused long enough to fill Martin in on the details.

"Ain't she a real beauty, a 1914 Monroe coupé she is, always garaged too!"

"I'm glad Ella finally bought a newer car."

Olin was half way to the loading dock and did not acknowledge Martin's last comment. Kent passed Martin on his bicycle, then stopped at the corner to wait. He dug a few papers from his pocket and sifted through them.

Kent pushed his bike as he walked with Martin to shove the notes in his hand.

"Mr. Hurston, I've been trying to find out if the factories are returning to their former products or changing what they make."

"Well, most of their contracts ended when the war was over Kent."

"You may want to check out Miller and Crofts yourself. I understand they are keeping their current line and not going back to footwear."

"Didn't they only manufacture military gun belts?"

"Heck no Mr. Hurston, they make all types of holsters, utility belts, rifle straps, gun belts, and several other things."

"With the number of trucks at their place each day, their business doesn't appear to have slowed down."

"I'm surprised the government didn't give them a

contract to make boots, M & C were the best. I can't believe they plan to discontinue them."

"I'll check them out later Kent. Thanks."

Kent swung his leg over the bicycle and disappeared down the road, cutting behind the newspaper. Martin arrived just as a factory whistle blew. John peered over his glasses, then reached for Martin's column articles.

Martin continued to keep his eye on Ella throughout the week. Her strict routine remained unchanged after she got the new car. She always followed the same punctual route.

I wish I could put my finger on why I suspect there is something suspicious about her.

He opened his sleuthing notebook and paged through it to jog his memory. He read aloud a couple of comments Roland made during one of his lessons.

"A gut feeling is usually correct, it never hurts to follow ones own instinct."

Martin had no occasion to find Roland wrong yet. Jerome began ribbing him.

"Who are you talking to Mr. Hurston? Or are you talking to yourself again?"

"Well, at least I'm talking to somebody who knows something! Aren't you supposed to be out working the street?

"No sense in meeting Kent down the road, when we will be coming right back past the paper on our way to Bing's store. Here he comes now, catch ya later."

The following Monday morning, after Martin arrived at the paper, he found J.B. pacing the floor. Every few seconds he would step outside the door.

"I hope nothing has happened to Luella, she is nowhere in sight."

Martin checked his wristwatch, then could not help but tease J.B. with a grin.

"I have not seen the morning bus yet J.B., nor have the factory whistles blew. Do you think something must be up?"

Martin no longer got the words out of his mouth when the bus passed the door and stopped at the corner. The women scurried across the street to the factories. Within the next moment, the factory blew its three short blasts.

J.B. was standing on the threshold with his head sticking out. Luella hurried down the sidewalk. J.B. stepped backwards through the door to keep from being trampled by her.

"You're late."

"I'm not late Mr. Blaine, ten whole minutes early."

He glanced up at the wall clock.

"You are almost an hour late Luella."

"Don't you read your own newspaper Mr. Blaine? Daylight savings time is finally over, we are back on real time now."

Martin smiled and gave Luella a wink.

"I'll reset the clock for you J.B. I noticed a few at the garment mill arriving ahead of schedule this morning, including Miss Thornton."

"Did the mill's manager get herself another car, Martin?"

"Yeah, over two weeks ago now J.B."

Martin handed his articles to J.B., who passed them directly to Luella, without giving them a second glance. J.B. has not changed the order for the galley's in several months. He leaves the headlines and everything exactly the way Martin presents them.

Since Martin's return from the service, the newspaper regained its former glory, and in the layout J.B. has always admired. Circulation increased daily, and the paper, run on clean machines once again, held crisp and ran true.

"I'm running over to Miller and Crofts J.B., then down

to the dress shirt factory. I have a few leads to follow up on. Luella glanced up with a teasing frown.

"Oh please, don't add anything else Martin."

Kent's worst fear became reality. No more M & C boots. During the war, Miller and Crofts failed to land a contract for footwear. They were however, awarded several government contracts for manufactured strip leather goods.

To make the room necessary to manufacture these articles, the old machines were dismantled and placed in storage. New smaller size machines, dedicated to production of the military leather goods, were installed next to one another in long rows.

With these new machines in place, and a growing demand for leather holsters and other strip leather items. They chose to reestablish themselves in a new growing market, by providing several lines of goods geared to law enforcement.

Martin strolled next door to the dress shirt factory. He learned business will continue as usual, just as it did before the war. Since they too installed a few new machines, to make officers dress shirts. They merely changed to business uniform style shirts, primarily for the customer service industry. On display were shirts for mechanics, plumbers, fleet drivers and others.

The little town of Ash Brooke slowly returned to normal after the war. With their military contracts fulfilled, the factories went back to manufacturing consumer products. Those who purchased specialized equipment, altered or changed their original product lines.

Women skilled in operating these machines, retained their present employment positions. To use fully the many machines purchased, companies would trade equipment with one another as they developed or added to their product lines.

For a short time, during the transition to peacetime operations. As their husbands returned home from the service, the women vacated their shared downtown apartments.   This allowed a few living quarters in the industrial area to become available.

Unmarried soldiers, and single women who kept their factory jobs, desiring to stay inside the city limits; made offers for unshared apartments of their own. With most of the service men now home, the population of Ash Brooke doubled overnight.

Chapter Ten – Ella resembles the Chorus Girl

The entertainment district evolved slowly over several generations. Old two and three-story warehouses and stores, unsuited for use as factories, found new life as saloons and dance halls. Vine Avenue split the entertainment area into two distinct sections.

Almost all the owners of buildings to the east, continually renovated and upgraded. They kept pace with the formal enhancements their area now dictated. Many refurbished their upper floors into upscale apartments to accommodate the returning soldiers and their families.

The unemployed and low income families drifted farther west on Liberty Street, to the rough, depressed end of the entertainment district, beyond Vine Avenue. These owners, and a few missions, haphazardly divided their upper floors into small sleeping rooms.

Ash Brooke grew fast, and the need arose for more shops and stores; to provide both products and jobs to the community. Six wealthy servicemen, residents of east town, recognized this unique opportunity and formed a partnership.

Their new corporation purchased two city blocks, three streets north of Liberty Avenue. They razed the abandoned wood structures, and constructed all brick, glass fronted, interconnecting stores. The new shopping center lined both sides of Coventry Road.

City naming conventions rarely make much sense. Along Liberty Street, Vine Avenue is the dividing line between the east and west entertainment area. Simmons

Parkway runs diagonally and the shopping area is divided to the east by Ross Road.

This whole area east of Simmons Parkway is known as Hanley Heights, with Ross Road running right through its center. Locals refer to the Hanley Heights shopping area north of Ross Road as the east side stores; and to the south as the west side stores.

The new shopping center on Coventry Road, is in an area known as West Towne; which is still east of Vine Avenue. Center Bank is in the wedge formed by Coventry Road and Vine Avenue at the Hancock Cut-off, another diagonal road.

This new shopping center extended the posh West Towne shopping district farther east, almost to the west side stores in Hanley Heights. To attract the higher rents this élite area dictated, they established several restrictions.

The type of quality stores allowed were presented in a full page advertisement, placed in the Ash Brooke Citizen newspaper. Construction went fast, and the many new jobs created reduced friction between working women and unemployed veterans.

Many women left their hard, low paying factory jobs, to work in the exquisite boutiques, jewelry and clothing stores. This opened numerous factory jobs for their husbands and other out of work men.

Several other new buildings with employment opportunities sprung up almost overnight. A new movie house opened caddy corner from the Eagle Theater, on the south side of Liberty Street west of Brooks Ferry Road.

A vacant lot one half block west of the Menton Building, sold to a sports company. Martin tried his hand at bowling a few times. He was a little better than most first time players. His duties consumed most of his time, so he declined an invitation to join a league.

Martin continued to enjoy the theater on Friday nights, and always studied the lead singer. The lure of free meals, drew Detective Pease to continue helping Martin further advance his sleuthing hobby. He learned many new procedures and techniques.

Roland continuously pushed Martin to become aware of people's actions. The ability to recognize facial features and describe a persons build, required strict discipline and study. Roland introduced Martin to a sketch artist, so he understood how far off his descriptions were.

After considerable practice using strangers faces, and receiving instructions from the sketch artist. Martin began to recognize the small things he never noticed before. He improved these skills considerably over the next few months.

Martin turned his attention to the person of his longstanding curiosity, Ella Thornton, manager of the garment mill.   Each day he took note of a new and interesting feature he failed to recognize previously. Her features were fast becoming an obsession with him.

He put his new skills to use while attending the theater on Friday nights; and noted the lead singer had a build exactly like Ella.   Martin became intrigued with the similarities and increased his focus on the finer details.

She could almost be her twin.

From his desk by the window, he studied Ella's features even closer than before. Over the course of several months, Martin convinced himself these two women had to be the same person.

Do you know how illogical these thoughts are? She cannot possibly be in two places at the same time.

After a small party at the restaurant, where Martin was asked to speak about the newspaper business to the tenant's guests. They were so pleased with his oratory; as a gift, they refurnished his apartment. For the first time in Martin's life, all his furniture now matched.

He and his friend Doug talked later in Martins apartment, about the success of the little talk.   They discussed how it might become an attraction for the restaurant. Possibly holding such an event on the Friday night the theater does not have a play.

George, the loan officer in apartment number four, persuaded his father to talk about the banking business. Martin ran a full two-page spread in the center of the newspaper, announcing the new 'businessmens night out' feature.

J.B. was not exactly thrilled with giving away the most expensive piece of real estate in his newspaper for free; even if it was only once every few months. However, this gave Martin an idea.

"What do you think about having an entire section devoted strictly to entertainment J.B.? A single page, without removing the articles, one that can be used like a calendar. I'm sure I can find enough advertisers to support a lift out page."

"If you can secure the ads for a slip-sheet in the paper Martin, sure, that can be doable."

Martin spent the next few days designing a sample page, and asked Luella to set it up. After they ran the paper on Thursday, he slipped the galleys in the press and ran his samples. He armed Kent, Jerome, and himself with a few copies, then hit the streets.

A sample presentation page for clients, produced results far greater than Martin imagined. Rather than a single slip-sheet, he needed a full-sheet, representing four pages. With only two days to go, he still had to fill up the rest of page four.

The ads more than covered the cost, and Martin did not have enough time before the presses roll to write a column himself. So he contacted Jessica McRabe, who has been dying to get a permanent column in the newspaper for years. She jumped at the opportunity.

On Friday after work. Martin chose to skip the introductory part of the opening number at the theater. He wanted a closer study of Ella's movements, and double checked his sleuthing notes. He parked himself in a chair on the sidewalk near the east corner of the building.

Before the whistle sounded the day's end, Olin rolled the waste cart out to the loading dock. He left it behind and climbed down the stairs, to go start each of the girl's cars, which required cranking.

As the cars warmed up, he moved around to each in succession, to open the choke and make the needed timing adjustments. The final whistle blew and women poured out of the garment mill as if a dam broke. After they left the lot, Olin closed the gate and disappeared inside.

Martin could see him doing his evening chores; his shadow flickered across the windows as he moved along the near wall. Ella, seated at her desk, closed the ledger book as Olin emptied her trash can.

He rolled a filled cart to the edge of the loading dock, to let sit while he started Ella's car. While it warmed up, he emptied the two carts into the large refuse container. After returning them to the storage shed, he opened the choke and set the timing on Ella's car.

The lights inside the building went out, and Ella emerged at the side door. She turned and bolted the latch, then walked out to her car.

"Thanks Olin."

Olin tipped his hat and promptly walked to the gate. Ella passed through the gate, and Martin checked his wristwatch.

Five-fifty, she never deviates from her schedule.

His eyes followed Ella's car as she drove east on Liberty, turned up Pottery Row and made a right on Klein Avenue. She was headed toward The Boulevard, which takes her home.

Many times Martin found himself at that end of town as she left work. So he knew most of the route she religiously followed each night. Ella took this longer route to avoid passing the old flour mill at Coventry Road.

She always reached The Boulevard at exactly six o'clock sharp. The same time the theater dimmed it lights and the choreographic introduction began.

The only deviation in her nightly routine, of which Martin noted from his apartment window, came on Tuesday nights. Ella would leave her desk long enough to collect the time cards and place them in a pouch.

Martin learned from his conversations with her, she dropped the time cards off at Clarence Deckett's office on her way home. She always took her normal route, which is the long way around to his office; perched at The Boulevard end of Pottery Row Road.

Chapter Eleven – Martin focuses on the Chorus Girl

Avid theater goers, who often arrived early to select their favorite seats; became tired of staring at the maroon velvet curtain. After they started arriving later, close to show time, it created traffic congestion; disturbed early bird patrons, and often delayed the show.

To alleviate the problem, the theater owner decided to hold an amateur comedy contest. The winner is offered a role and allowed to appear in one of the vaudeville routines the following month. They are required to learn the routine, and memorize their lines well to participate.

Some of these performers were horrible. So before the crowd's hisses turned to booing, an usher escorted them off the stage, and another team would take their place. The manner in which they were removed, was often funnier than the skits themselves.

Bored with the pre-show amateur comedy routines, Martin rarely went to the theater before the opening choreographed number. As a regular, and no longer reliant on assigned seating, he was contented to sit in a different area each Friday night.

From these vantage points, he could study the lead singer from distinct new angles. His people recognition skills increased the more features he examined. Martin, now certain that the soloist must be Ella's identical twin sister. Decided to track her movements outside the theater.

In conversations with Martin, Ella stated the fact she was an only child. His sleuthing notes from others substantiated her claim.

"My older brother Earl is a dear, kept my old car going, when no one else could. He owns a grocery store up near the new bridge."

Martin met Earl several times. He often popped in the newspaper to place an ad. Earl wore thick glasses, and smelled like he climbed out of a salt bin. He held a proof copy about one inch from the tip of his nose to check the ad copy.

Earl spoke highly of his mother Adella, and of his sister Ella. He also mentioned an aunt Hattie, who did not drive. She gave Ella her late husbands old runabout. Martin, tried to get Earl to make a slip, while he placed his order for an ad.

"Last week, Ella said your mother was ill, how is she doing?"

"Only a cold, she's over it already and back to her normal self."

"I spotted the car your aunt Hattie gave Ella over by the old flour mill the other day."

"Ella bought a newer car, a Monroe. Neither would she ever go near the flour mill."

"Yes, I've admired the machine. The girl in the car looked just like Ella, perhaps it was her sister?"

"I don't have a sister besides Ella, she was probably Mr. Neal's daughter. She can't drive, so was just sitting in the car, waiting on her dad."

"Must be Earl, I didn't pay close attention. Be careful driving home."

Martin updated the notes in his sleuthing notebook to reflect Earl's comment.

Another dead lead. Earl confirmed Ella's statements again. I wonder why she avoids the flour mill?

Luella came to the front counter, shaking a fistful of papers at Martin.

"Did you approve this copy from that nasty Jessica McRabe?"

Martin glanced over the pages Luella shoved in his face.

"Where did you get these? Of course I never approved them. Wait, here is the column you are supposed to run on page four of the new entertainment lift-out section."

Luella grabbed the single sheet and stormed to the press room. Martin tossed the rest on his desk to review later. He left the building to make his rounds as a reporter; while out, of those he knows attend the theater, he inquired about the lead soloist.

Of all the people he has spoken with throughout the week, not one person in town has seen her outside the theater. He pestered Roland to death for information.

"Without a name, or something tangible to go on, my his hands are tied."

I need a way to meet the singer.

Martin started walking up to the entertainment district to verify ads for next weeks slip-sheet. He paused in front of the closed theater. The marquee listed the upcoming vaudeville acts for the weekend; and one faded side-wall poster depicted the Candy Girls Cabaret.

On his return trip from getting the ads. Martin studied the old notices tacked on the display boards along the Brooks Ferry Road side of the building. He slipped his notepad back in his pocket, finding nothing important to add to his search.

Martin stopped outside the ticket booth, because a changeable sign caught his eye. It gave the evenings opening song and some other information he could not read. He thought about standing in line to make an inquiry at the counter, but holding advance tickets, he strolled inside.

Tonight he followed only the choreographed routine of the star. She moved gracefully to both points of the heart formed by the actresses in the routine. He knows she is the only performer who wears a long gown.

She must keep it pinned up, the boas and fans hide her face and torso.

The bottom of the heart is closest to the audience, and the point the lead singer takes, before the line moves again. The formation expands, moving up the tiered staircase.

A gazebo prop, hidden by a pair of curtains, glides forward as the narrow curtain sections are drawn to the side of the stage. The heart continues to rotate, then tightens, placing the singer at the top point in the heart.

From this point in the routine, she walks through the gazebo, taking her place for the solo. After the performance, she walks straight forward to take her place at the lower point of the heart. The girls follow behind her, filing down from the top point of the heart.

The lower girls in the choreographed pattern form two large moving circles. The lead singer stands motionless in her long gown, as the dancers break to each side, forming a long line across the stage.

After taking a bow, they turn their backs to the audience, bending over to show their bloomers. Then move back together, and hold their fans toward center stage. This hides the soloist as she strolls to the rear and disappears between the now separated tiers.

As the front curtain closed, Martin caught a glimpse of the stage hands moving props into place; and vaudeville actors and actresses finding their assigned stage floor marks. A performer on a bicycle with off-center wheel hubs, wobbled across the stage.

He stopped in the center and announced Act I of the play then moved offstage. The many times Martin attended the theater, he never spied the easel and placard in the corner. The bicycle rider fell against the curtain from behind.

This caused the stagehand switching the sign to snag it on the bulging curtain. It read Candy Girls Cabaret, featuring Rosie. Martin made the notation in his sleuthing notebook and headed toward the front of the theater.

The ticket girl who worked in the box office, just stepped from the booth. Martin stopped her to ask about the sign displaying tonight's songs. After a short conversation, she reached inside, grabbed a program and passed it to Martin.

Martin grazed through the flier and wondered why it did not appear in the newspaper. It contained valuable information about the performers and the shows; including what roles each played that night.

One name blatantly missing from the vaudeville acts was that of the lead singer. The Cabaret soloist was only billed as Rosie. All the other Cabaret performers were listed in the various skits and acts they appeared in.

On the back of the program was a list of all the behind-the-scenes workers, the shows benefactors, and upcoming plays. Martin searched for Wilton Stoddard, owner of the theater, to obtain an ad for the entertainment section of the newspaper.

Before the show closed for the evening, he took his usual place on the Patty Lane bus stop bench behind the theater. He has often stayed on this perch until the theater turned dark and was locked up for the night.

Apparently, Rosie only sings her two solo numbers and leaves, which explains why I've never seen her exit the stage door.

For the next several weekends, Martin arrived at the theater early and dwelt around the back parking lot. He found a secluded spot away from lights. A large row of short posts, provided a place to sit where he would not be spotted.

He watched the performers arrive, and once convinced everyone is there, he walked to the front and entered for the show. Another flawless choreographed routine, and beautiful songs by the soloist.

Immediately after her two solo's, Martin left the theater and hurried to the back parking lot.

If she leaves early, as I suspect she does, I should be able to catch her leave.

Martin sat on the stump, eying the stage door throughout the evening. None of the performers left early, and no sign of the lead singer when the rest filed out of the theater.

More frustrated than ever, Martin arrived at the theater before the doors are unlocked. He wrote in his notebook each car that pulled in, and a short description of each performer. When he heard the show start, he went inside, so he didn't miss Rosie's two solo's.

The following week, Martin was stuck at the newspaper. Jerome needed help with a troubling article for the paper. He arrived at the theater, long after the show started. In the performers parking lot, he discovered a 1916 Saxon Roadster, close to the stage entrance.

He rushed into the theater, and expected to see a new face in at least one skit, the Cabaret, or the play. He stayed for all the performances and everyone was accounted for. No new actors or actresses.

I'm going to solve this elusive puzzle, if it's the last thing I do. Somebody has to know her, or have seen this car about town.

Chapter Twelve – Rosie's Saxon Runabout

Once again, Martin arrived at the theater ahead of everyone else. Tonight he stayed in the shadows until long after the cast and patrons were inside. He chose not to move from his perch until after the show was well underway. Even if he might miss Rosie's first solo. He waited.

The music began to play, and the Candy Girls Cabaret choreographed routine started. Martin moved closer to the theater. His elbows rested on an old barrel, as he stared at the empty parking space next to the stage door.

His hunch was right. The Saxon Roadster pulled into the lot and drove straight up to the door. Rosie jumped from the car and ran inside without turning in Martin's direction. Not wearing a formal gown; she only had precious few seconds to change before her solo began.

Martin rose from his sanctuary, and before he took his first step, Rosie began her first solo number.

I guess it must not be Rosie or her car. Probably belongs to one of the vaudeville performers, and this space is reserved for them. Which one is the star?

Martin made a notation in his notebook before going inside the theater. He still believed in his assumption, no two people can appear so much alike.

Rosie and Ella must be the same person.

He solicited the help of Kent and Jerome to keep an eye on Ella when she left work on Friday night. Jerome is to note her first two turns, and Kent is to report the time she entered the highway. Ella's home is in the opposite direction of the theater.

Martin waited behind the building, closer to the stage door than ever before. He found the perfect spot to catch a clear glimpse of her face as she ran inside.

If she closely resembles Ella, as I suspect, I will say to her, 'Ella, you got a new car.' Just to see her response.

The girl driving the Saxon Roadster looked exactly like Ella. However, she wore gaudy red lipstick and had long hair below her shoulders. This startled Martin so much, he forgot to call Ella's name as she passed.

Could I be so wrong? Ella would never wear lipstick.

Monday morning when Kent and Jerome arrived at the newspaper, they reported Ella's movements on Friday night.

"Same as always Martin, she left exactly at five-fifty."

"She turned on the highway at six sharp, just like usual."

J.B. overheard the conversation and commented on her punctuality. After the boys left the building, Martin confided with J.B., he thinks Rosie the singer and Ella are possibly the same person. J.B. busted out in laughter so hard, he had to grab the edge of his desk as he fell into his chair.

"You sure do have an imagination Martin. Little miss prim and proper would never be caught dead in a dance hall, theater, or any place of such a nature."

"Perhaps you are right J.B., she cannot be in two places at the same time either."

Martin relays his findings to Roland over lunch. He instructed Martin to keep a close eye on Ella, and pay special attention to her hair.

"Her hair might be long, hard to tell the way she wears it up in a bun. She is also always well dressed, probably the best dressed of any factory manager. She never wore any kind of makeup, leastwise not since she started working at the garment mill."

Roland came to the conclusion, Rosie must switch places with a double. Just as the curtain strips separate for the gazebo to move forward. Martin agreed to study his suggestion. The first two girls on each side do pass behind the narrow moving curtains.

Martin paid close attention, looking for a possible swap. To work, Rosie must hide behind the curtain before it opens, and walk with it. She will be moving in the opposite direction as the girl she changes places with.

He studied the maneuver for two more performances, and determined a switch would be too tricky to pull off. To conceal two girls changing position and direction, without disrupting the smooth flow of the choreography, would be noticeable.

The split-second timing to pull an exchange off each week, and without ever making an error. Seemed impossible. The following weekend proved his point. The single large feather fan Rosie held got damaged during the routine.

A broken feather hung down, and stuck forward out-of-place. The feather protruded from the far side of the curtain, before the back of the fan was hidden.

There is no way a switch takes place behind this curtain.

He also discerned the fan did not jiggle, as it would if handed off from one person to another. The fan moved behind the curtain in one continuous smooth motion. Rosie was in complete sight up to the solo, and her later exit between the separated tiers.

Ella no longer met with Martin for access to their storage. If she caught him coming down the sidewalk when she left work. She would find time to wait so they could have a short talk. Any evening except Tuesday or Friday nights.

Martin knew she delivered the employees time cards

to her boss on Tuesday nights. He thought the only reason she avoided him on Friday nights; was because she had to get to the theater. Which is why she would not have a single second to spare.

How did she manage back when she drove that old Waltham Runabout? Which often failed to get her all the way home. If she is the singer, she would surely have missed a performance or two.

For the time being, with other duties pressing, and after talking with Roland several times. Martin finally appeased himself; Rosie and Ella were two different people. But now he was highly suspicious of both women. Sure each were hiding something.

On the days Jerome worked leads in the northwest end of town. Martin asked him to keep an eye out for a 1916 Saxon Roadster moving about the area. He only wanted to know if anyone spotted the magnificent car.

Months go by without the Roadster being seen anywhere, except on Friday nights at the theater. So Martin figured the soloist must drive in from out-of-town to perform. Jerome involved Kent early on in the search for this Roadster.

Doing so finally paid off. Kent rode by on his bicycle, slowed only long enough to shove a note into Martin's hand as he passed. At the time, he thought it just a lead for a story, so did not check the note right away.

Later, while working in the office, Martin read the message. Kent found the dealer who sold a new 1916 Saxon Roadster, two years earlier to a Miss Clara Mae Remmert.

I remember reading her name on the theater program many times.

He rummaged through his desk and checked the old theater programs. Clara is in the chorus line, two skits, and usually the last vaudeville act.

Busy little gal. But wait, the Saxon leaves the theater

while she is still on stage.

Martin now held in his hands, yet another mystery to solve. He made a point to find out which actress is named Clara before Friday nights performance. His efforts were to no avail, the theater is closed until the weekend.

An overcast sky, held smoke from the coal fired furnaces in the factories, down at street level all week. An unexpected late afternoon snow, caught Martin without his heavy overcoat.

At least this snow helped to filter the odor from the air.

Seated at his desk in the warm apartment, through the window he viewed Olin start Ella's car and wipe off her windshield. She appeared to slip getting into her car, apparently no harm done. She left the parking lot right on cue, as always.

Martin leaned closer to the window, to watch her make the turn up Pottery Row. The roads did not appear to be slippery.

I hope she gets home OK.

Chapter Thirteen – Martin meets Janice

Martin studied the notes in his now filled sleuthing notebook. Not one girl's torso in the chorus line resembled Rosie's. He leaned down to pull a new notebook from his bottom drawer, and glanced at his wristwatch.

I better get going if I want to find out Clara's identity.

He grabbed his heaviest overcoat from a hook behind the door. After bundling up, Martin headed off toward the theater. Unsure which chorus girl Clara may be, before the lights dimmed, he studied the program extra close.

The usher offered no help. Being new, he did not know the performers; other than a skit actress named Louise he attended school with. Martin transferred a few notes about body features from his old notebook to the new notepad.

He also made several new notes about the chorus girls features, and failed to detect the routine ran longer than normal. At first glance, he thought the choreography changed. Then as they moved into the heart pattern for the solo, he realized they merely repeated the introduction sequence twice. Martin slapped himself on the forehead.

The snow, of course. Rosie arrived late. I figured it would happen some day.

After she completed her solo, the performers were already on stage behind the curtain, waiting to begin their act. Only men appeared in the first part of the skit. The two girls Martin identified from the program, entered the act later. One would be Clara, the other Janice.

On stage, under the bright lights, discerning their features is hard. Of the two gals in this skit; one is slightly pigeon toed, the other shorter with a wide smile. With so many actresses appearing in the first act of the play, Martin chose to stay for all the shows.

Of these two women, only Janice appeared in the opening vaudeville number, along with three other women. Each wore flowing gowns that reached the floor. The heavy theater makeup made recognition of Janice impossible.

He studied the build of each woman and made a few notes. Two of the girls had wide smiles, which allowed him to eliminate the one with a square jaw. He noted the shape of their noses, figuring one would be Janice.

A comedy skit followed act one, while the stage hands changed the scenery behind the curtain. About one-third into the program, two women entered. Martin checked his notes several times during the show.

One of these girls is Clara. But which one?

Neither girl wore a wide smile, and both of these shorter ladies had pug noses.

Guess I'm not the detective I thought I was.

Clara appeared in the final vaudeville act of the evening, along with six other women. Each of them taller than either Janice or Clara. After they formed a letter V, Martin smiled.

I've found Clara, center front.

To make sure he recognized her again, he jotted down every facial feature he could distinguish. As the theater emptied, the winner of last weeks pre-show amateur contest, provided a short one man comedy skit. His act prompted several folks to stay seated.

This was the first time Martin stayed late at the theater. It surprised him to see so many patrons make their way forward to take a seat closer to the stage. When the skit ended, the curtain opened, and all the play's performers lined up.

They walked forward to the edge of the stage, took a bow, and sat down with their legs dangling off the stage. The patrons lined up to march past, shaking hands, or getting autographs. The parade of patrons moved up the aisle and out of the theater.

Martin waited in line until he spotted Jessica McRabe. To avoid being trapped, he ducked out the west side exit and around the back of the theater. Two male performers and one of the chorus girls turned ahead of him on the sidewalk. He recognized the pigeon toed walk.

"Beautiful show tonight Janice."

He figured, if correct, she would turn to respond. One man turned his eyes back toward Martin.

"Yes, the show was rather grand, and to a packed house on a snowy night."

They all stopped on the sidewalk. The other gentleman spoke.

"Hey, you're that reporter fellow from the newspaper. Care to join us for a drink? Last chance before the new laws go into effect."

"Thanks for the offer, but I'll pass. Been a long day for me."

Martin studied the actress while close up. Her square jaw not as prominent without all the stage makeup.

"I'm pleased to meet you Janice. It is Janice isn't it?"

She cracked her gum while eyeing Martin from head to toe.

"Last time I checked. If you ain't joinin' us. What of it?"

Martin tipped his hat, and they strolled north across the parking lot toward Patty Lane. They passed one building then ducked into an alley.

I'll have to check out what all is up that way during daylight.

He often worked the streets north of the industrial

area, and never found a public drinking establishment. He made a note in his reporters pad to check out the service alley behind the shops.

The cold night air dipped down to freezing. But the day warmed the streets enough the ground heat made the snow slushy; not crunchy underneath. Martin walked home and dropped into bed. In the morning Marie, his neighbor across the hall, brought hot buttered biscuits.

"Wake up sleepyhead."

Martin, up, dressed, and working at his desk since seven, came to the door.

"My, my; you've indeed become a night owl."

"Come on in Marie. Thank you, they smell delicious. Here, take a seat."

"I'm glad I caught you home, I need a favor, and you've been running so much, I hate to pester you."

"You're never a bother Marie. What do you need fixed?"

"Oh, nothing's broken Martin, it's just, well you know, the baby's due soon, and..."

"Don't worry about Mr. Nascent's old rules Marie. He lets me handle..."

"I forgot about the rules, perhaps I shouldn't ask."

"Well, out with it Marie. I won't know what you want if you don't ask."

"I'm sure George mentioned Tyler sold his share of the restaurant back to the company; and is building his own restaurant, up in the new trolley line loop."

"Yes, Doug told me all about the fight with the chef. I thought things simmered down long ago?"

"They did Martin, but Tyler is moving out soon."

"He's not turned in a notice of such intention. What makes you think he is moving?"

"Tyler did not mention moving to any of us either. He did hire our interior designer to look at a place up by the new bridge."

"Now Marie, this is how unfounded gossip gets started. Best you don't say any more, until something happens. He could be having the work done for an entirely different reason."

"Perhaps you are right Martin, but just in case, the favor I wanted to ask. If Tyler does move, can you put us at the top of the list to lease his apartment."

"Don't you like yours anymore?"

"Oh yes, we love our apartment! We would like to have both, for more growing room. Provided we can still stay here after the baby comes."

"That will not be a problem Marie, if none of the other tenants have an objection."

"Great, I'll tell George right away. He was afraid to ask you himself."

"Just tell him, his wife has a way of buttering the manager up, with biscuits."

The entire week passed without Martin hearing anything from Tyler about the possibility of his moving. He managed to side-step Jessica McRabe, so she left her column on his desk at the newspaper. Martin edited her submission and placed the page in Luella's slot.

It warmed up by Friday. Martin left the paper early and hovered around the stage door, hoping to catch Clara arrive. Several performers came early, parked and went inside. She was not among them.

He heard a car and turned. The Saxon entered the lot. Martin checked his wristwatch, six-eleven. Rosie pulled in her reserved parking spot. She squeaked in a high-pitched voice, as she ran past to go inside.

"Nice evening."

She flew by so fast, Martin did not have time to tip his hat. She looked straight at him, close up, then squinted her eyes when she spoke.

I've never seen Ella squint, nor does she speak in that octave range. Yet I can recognize Ella anywhere. Definitely her face.

He rushed inside to catch Rosie's solo, and remained for the first skit. Martin promised J.B. he would listen to a new band. He left the theater and rushed down to the entertainment district. J.B. wanted verification of Jessica's rave review.

Martin did not prefer the type of music played. They did play more mellow than most, so he enjoyed the tunes. Even found himself tapping his foot during the last two numbers. Made a memo to tell J.B., they are better than Jessica stated in her column.

The newspaper had grown, and J.B. hired a sports journalist and two columnists. The entertainment section grew as well. J.B. continually felt Jessica overemphasized each musicians abilities. Many were pushing him for a mention in the new music column as well.

Chapter Fourteen – Martin introduced to Clara

His task for J.B. completed, Martin returned to the theater as the show ended. He walked down the west side of the building to the performers parking lot. He found a utility pole to lean against, while viewing the exit.

The third person out the stage door was Janice. She lit a cigarette the minute her foot was off the last step. She spotted Martin and hurried over to him.

"What'cha waitin' 'round here for? Gotta girl in the show?"

"Hi Janice, no girl, merely hoping to talk to Clara about business is all."

"What kinda biz-ness? Did she do somethin' you wanna put in the paper?"

"No, nothing like that Janice. I only want to ask her about a car she bought."

Janice stomped her cigarette out on the sidewalk. Opened a stick of gum, and after folding, shoved it in her mouth.

"Where are your two bodyguards?"

"They're still clean-in the stage. Didn't ya catch the last act?"

"Sorry, I missed the end, I worked down in the entertain..."

"Hey, there's Clara! Clara, Clara, come on over here, I want ya to meet a friend of mine."

"Hello Mr. Hurston, I am pleased to meet you."

"Just call him Martin, eh-ryone elsa does. Ain't that right Martin?"

Janice stuck her gum against the utility pole as two men came out the stage door.

"I hafta run, neva turn down a free drink is my motto."

Janice scampered away. Clara's eyes followed her until she caught up with the two gents. She turned back toward Martin.

"She's a wild one, Mr. Hurston!"

"Appears that way. You can call me Martin - 'Eh-ryone elsa does.'"

Martin added, mimicking Janice.

"I'm glad we finally met. I wanted to thank you for getting our program back in the newspaper."

"Mr. Blaine dropped a lot of articles during the war. With subscriptions increasing, he is allowing many to return."

"My father was a reporter for the Greenwood Herald. He taught me how to sniff out newsworthy stories, and where to get the really juicy stuff too."

"Ever considered working for a newspaper Clara?"

"Father said I would never be a writer. I love the theater, and now work for them under contract."

"I truly enjoy the shows. How do you remember all those steps and lines, with the play changing each week?"

"Simple, the routines are broken down into sets. But if I tell you too much, you will no longer enjoy the opening Cabaret."

"Can you offer some backstage tidbits for our readers? I'll be glad to pass them on to our new entertainment columnist."

"I talked with her already, all she is interested in is theater stuff. She is pleasant, not as pushy as that crabby, stuck-up, Jessica McRabe."

"Don't tell anyone, but I avoid her as much as possible myself."

"Martin, I can pass other leads to you. It would not bother me if you cannot use most of them. Learned that from dad too. Oh my, it's getting late. Mother will be frantic. I should have been home by now."

"I won't keep you Clara, have a safe drive home."

"I've spotted you in the audience many times, and am glad we finally met."

They walked over to Clara's car, the only one left in the parking lot. He pulled the door open for her to get in. Martin remembered his question.

"I did have something I wanted to ask you, but will wait until next week."

"I'll catch you then, ta-ta."

She replied as the car started. Martin walked in the same direction, up the sidewalk toward home. Clara took Liberty Street all the way to The Boulevard.

In his apartment, someone slid an unmarked envelope under the door. It is Tyler's moving out notification.

"Dear Mr. Hurston; I hate to leave the best manager from whom I have ever leased. I opened a new restaurant on the north side, at the loop, and found a large apartment up on Oak Road, by the bridge. Nowhere near like the deal you gave, but I can walk to work from there. I am giving you an extra two-weeks notification, so you may find a new tenant before I leave. I will give you ad copy for the restaurant before Wednesday. Please, come up and visit me here sometime. Same courtesy as before. Tyler."

Martin kept an eye out for Tyler all week, so he could speak with him in person. He learned from Jerome, Tyler supervised the stocking of the restaurant, and similar renovations as he did in apartment number three. Martin understood these are time intensive projects.

In his ventures down the side alleys he checked on several taverns being converted to stores. He also found some late night specialized eateries, catering to the after theater crowd.

Doug was waiting on the sidewalk for Martin to get off work, he preferred they sit together for the shows. Doug is the tenant that ensures Martin is never without theater tickets or a meal in the restaurant.

"You missed a super show last week Martin. Funniest one yet!"

"Sorry about that Doug. J.B. put me on a special night assignment."

"Stopped by the paper the other day to let you know Tyler is moving. I did not recognize anyone, only a bunch of new faces milling about."

"J.B. hired several journalists and a couple of reporters from up north. Yes, Tyler turned in his request last weekend. He will be around for at least another month."

"He's moving none to soon for me Martin. He can't seem to get along with any chef we ever hired. I think his problem is he doesn't like good food."

"I know he doesn't want anything on his meat, nor his foods touching one another."

"We had a new steak dish, simply wonderful. He wouldn't touch a single bite. Sulked around in the kitchen for over an hour. Found him sitting on a stool, eating cold cuts."

Martin sat with Doug throughout all the shows. While Doug enjoyed the performances, Martin was busy paying close attention to Janice and Clara's movements on stage. To him, each routine appeared unique, fresh and different.

When the final act closed, Martin bid Doug a good evening, and slipped out the side door; to wait behind the building for Clara. He stepped back in the shadows when Janice came out and lit her cigarette. But she was too quick for him.

She started to head in Martin's direction. Stopped as her two drinking buddies came out. She waved at Martin, then turned to catch up with them. It appeared all the performers were out of the theater. Martin wondered if he somehow missed Clara, or did she use another door.

After Janice was out of sight, Martin moved to the west corner; where he could check both doors the performers may use. After seeing where Janice stuck her gum, he thought best not to use the utility pole to lean on anymore.

He heard someone pull on the side door, and the security bar being dropped into place on the inside. The light over the side door and along the row of poster indents went out. Martin walked back over near the stage door, but stayed in the shadows.

Chapter Fifteen – Martin and Clara at Curt's Under Corner

The lights in the backstage area went dark, and the stage door burst open. Clara backed out, holding the door with open with her rump, digging in her purse. Finding the keys, she turned and locked the door; then glanced around, hoping Martin waited for her.

"I'm so glad you waited, I so looked forward to continuing our conversation. Oh, here are some leads for you too."

While Clara was digging around in her overstuffed, over-cluttered purse to find them, Martin offered her an invitation.

"I discovered this little late night pie shop up the street..."

"Curt's Under Corner, I love his place."

Clara began marching briskly in Curt's direction. Martin gulped.

What am I getting myself into?

"Here are the leads I promised, I'll tell you about them inside where it's warm."

Curt's was packed when they arrived. However, the crowd thinned fast, and by the time they were seated, only a few were still talking. An older lady, wearing a checkered apron, approached the table. She rattled off a list of pies and desserts from memory.

"We do not allow drinking in here. So if you brought a bottle, take it down the street."

Martin was startled by her tone. Clara glanced up at her.

"Patricia, don't you ever get tired of saying that? Sounds like you're trying to run the customers off."

"Only when I spot a new face, sorry, didn't recognize your friend here. What'll you have?"

"I'll take an apple pie with a slice of cheese on top, heated please."

"Sound delicious Clara. I'll order the same."

Patricia hurried to the kitchen to get the desserts. Two customers from the theater stood, being obnoxious about going down the block to whet their whistles. One patted his pockets to make sure he was well supplied for the night.

"Sorry I was so late getting out tonight. I work for the theater, and one of my jobs is to lock up the back every other Friday."

"Where is the caretaker? Doesn't he usually handle such things."

"He does, but his wife is ill. If he is not the last out of the building, after he locks up the front and side, we do not detain him."

"Sorry she is not well. I hope she soon recovers from her illness."

"She's not likely to Martin. The doctors did not expect her to live this long. Here, take a gander at these leads, I have a couple I need to make clear before Curt closes."

Martin pulled the notes from his jacket pocket and handed them back to Clara. She shuffled through each, and as she began to explain the first one, Curt brought the pies to their table.

"Did Pat forget your drinks?"

"You know Patricia, no drinking or get out."

"I'm so glad you decided to visit my fine establishment Mr. Hurston. It gets a little crazy in here right after the show. Saw you come in. Glad Pat didn't run you off.

Enjoy your pies."

Clara dug right in, stopped when the pie touched her tongue, and began blowing on the bite on her fork. She glanced over at Martin with a grin.

"For some reason, they always bake them way too hot."

"Never met a baker who could cook in a cold oven Clara."

She took the now cool bite, set her fork down, and picked up her notes. Martin's eyebrow raised as she explained them to him.

"You weren't kidding when you said you had some juicy stuff. Don't think J.B. will go for publishing this."

"Oh, you can word it any way you want Martin. Helps to know the whole story; dad would always say."

"Before I forget again, I'm curious about a particular car, the Saxon Roadster."

"Long story behind that deal Martin. Rosie won the amateur show, brought the house to their feet she did. A fifteen minute standing ovation."

"So she won a prize?"

"Oh. What? No, not a prize, the car came later. After winning the contest, and returning for several guest appearances, the theater hired her to sing. She only did so after the skits, right before the play starts."

"About the car?"

"Right, coming up. After Mr. Stoddard bought the theater, he added the Candy Girls Cabaret as the opening number. A small dance troupe, consisting of a few female performers from the vaudeville routines. We were a disaster."

"The show is splendid, most impressive Clara."

"It is now, but wasn't always. Wilton changed the routine to a simple chorus line, which helped. After he started the amateur show, winning females were asked to join the chorus line."

"Ahem, about the Saxon."

"I'm getting to the car. Some of the girls were really good, and added more interesting choreography to the routine. This began drawing customers to the theater earlier. Wilton hired a professional to work with us and develop the routines you are familiar with."

"The car Clara, the car. I want to learn about the Saxon Rosie drives."

"OK, OK, the car. Wilton wanted to add Rosie to the chorus line, but she would not have anything at all to do with such vulgarity; as she put it. Wilton finally convinced her she didn't need to appear in the chorus line itself."

"Wait, are you saying Rosie is not in the chorus line? Not a part of the routine?"

"That's right, she just sings her solo on the center platform, mid-point during the choreographed routine. She cannot arrive at the theater early enough, because she works a real job, part of the war effort."

"Most interesting Clara, we will talk more about this later. Are you getting to the car yet?"

"Yes. About the car. Mr. Stoddard offered Rosie a new car, so she could get here faster. She was still too late for an earlier number, so he set her first solo to near the end of the opening number. Right where she sings every Friday night now."

Curt turned off half the lights and announced from behind the counter.

"Hey you two, it's long past closing time."

"Sorry Curt, we're on our way."

Clara hopped right up, reached back and grabbed the last bite of her pie. She mumbled something with her mouth full as we left the shop.

She never stopped talking about her notes on the short walk with Martin back to her car. After she handed the notes back to him, he folded and slipped them in his pocket. The way Clara fumbled around in her purse for keys, always amused him.

Tonight she pulled out of the parking lot on Klein Avenue and took it to The Boulevard. Martin lived in Ash Brooke his entire life, and never heard the highway referred to by any other name. Truckers referenced the state road by a number.

Martin was home getting ready for bed, when he realized he still did not learn why Clara bought the car. Although he finally learned why Rosie was the driver.

What did Clara say about Rosie having a real job. One that made it hard for her to arrive at the theater in time for a mid-chorus line solo? I'll have to sleep on that new bit of info.

Chapter Sixteen – Friday nights with Clara

Martin sat at his desk on Saturday morning to peruse his sleuthing notebooks. Tired of flipping the pages back and forth. He placed a sheet of paper in his typewriter, and typed each entry he made about Rosie and Ella.

He reached in the slot for his long scissors, to cut the paper into strips, then remembered he lent them to Marie. Martin walked across the hall and tapped on her door. George answered in his robe and slippers.

"Sorry George, did I wake you? I thought you were at work."

"Marie didn't sleep well last night, and with the baby so close, I decided to stay home with her. Just in case."

"I lent my long scissors to Marie. I can wait until later."

"Your scissors is right here on the counter, just a sec. - Here you go, thanks for letting her borrow it."

"Oh George, one other thing. Tyler is moving out as Marie thought. Please let..."

"That's wonderful news Martin! Did Marie mention we would like the apartment next door?"

"Yes, and I will hold it for you, Marie, and your new baby."

Martin returned to his apartment and finished the project he started. The more he studied his notes, now cut in several strips he can move around. The more he figured they cannot be the same person; yet at the same time, the stronger his gut instinct told him otherwise.

His week is consumed following up on all the leads Clara presented to him. Each were excellent, and produced valuable content for the newspaper.

Clara learned her father's lessons well. That girl has a nose for news, even if we cannot print some of them.

Jerome was a little put off by one column Martin included in the paper. Jerome started the article strong, but hit a dead lead and never finished. He confronted Martin, holding the last issue up to his face.

"I should have told you about this project I'm working on before now."

Martin gave Jerome several unused notes to add to his own.

"Here Jerome, take these, and with what you have, build an impressive follow up for the next issue."

"Wow, these are perfect, so much information to work with here. Thanks boss!"

The notes appeased Jerome. A long day now over, Martin stopped to talk with Ella on his way home. In conversation with her, the topic of her ailing mother, Adella, arose. Tonight, Ella mentioned the ladies from their church coming often to visit.

Martin, familiar with the strict tenets Grace Miracle Church held, and the way Ella dressed; placed her a world apart from the theater performers. Still certain his assumption is correct, he continued to keep an eye on her.

He cannot get the similarity between these two girls out of his head. Roland had an appointment at Miller and Crofts to be fitted for a shoulder holster. Martin retyped his notes in the order he aligned the cut strips, and went to meet Roland as he came out.

"Listen to me Martin. For Ella to even mention their name in public, or come close to that type of theater; man oh man, what a stir that would create with her family."

"I realize the thought of her being on stage is ludicrous."

"Yes it is Martin. They cannot possibly be the same person. Get it through your thick head, Ella is not Rosie. You have stated so yourself. She cannot be in two places at the same time."

To Martin, whatever J.B. or Roland said did not matter. By his way of understanding, he is certain he is correct. The thought gnawed at him continuously, and his clues were slowly coming together.

Martin was also concerned about Clara showing a greater than intended interest in him. Even though she provided him with excellent leads after the theater, and they would chat for a bit. He chose to decline further invitations to Curt's.

Tracking Ella and Rosie threw Martin behind on his work. Combined with the extra duties J.B. added to his workload as the newspaper grew; his excuses were honest. Even though he might find the time needed to get his work done.

After they left the theater, the pouring rain forced Martin and Clara to run to Curt's for shelter. The previous afternoon, Curt stopped at the newspaper to place an ad. He added a salad to his nightly offerings.

Curt wanted everyone to know. But he was a day too late, the paper already went to typesetting. So no one outside Curt's employees and Martin learned about the new addition to the menu. After they were seated, Martin asked Clara.

"Do you like salads? I think I can get Curt to toss one for you."

"I love a good salad, but I hope it's not too big. I want to leave room for pie. Hey, are you trying to be funny? Curt don't serve salads."

Pat came to take their order, being her usual nasty self, she barked.

"What'll it be, you know the menu."

"We will each have a salad."

Pat rattled off, without missing a beat.

"French, Italian or Thousand Island?"

"French for me. On the side please." Clara said.

"I'll try your Thousand Island."

"Comin' right up."

Pat shuffled her way to the kitchen. Clara just sat and stared at Martin, her lower jaw hung down in awe.

"Guess it pays to be in the newspaper business Martin. You learn things before everyone else."

Amid his conversation with Clara, she inadvertently divulged she exchanged places with Rosie. This peaked Martin's interest, because he studied for a swap, and could not see any possible way. Leastwise, not at the point he presumed the switch took place.

The idea Rosie might be behind the fans, before they were held behind the gazebo, never became apparent to him. This meant she did not take or hold the fan with the broken feather at all. Even though such an exchange appeared that way when his was seated in the audience.

With the topic back on the theater once again, Martin redirected to get his previous questions answered.

"Clara, you said the theater bought Rosie the car. How was it presented to her? Or did she select one at the dealer herself?"

"She told Mr. Stoddard what kind of car she wanted, and he searched until he found a dealer with the exact model. Wilton drove me over to pick the car up for her."

"I have to admit, I learned you are the person who paid for the car. Can I ask why?"

"I figured as much, reporters catch every little thing; don't we."

"Not everything, and not always."

"Wilton looked over the car, then climbed in and handed me the money. I went inside to pay, while he drove it around the block a couple of times. After I came out, he tossed me his keys and asked me to follow behind him, back to the theater."

The rain finally slowed to a drizzle. Clara pulled a wad of papers from her purse. As they walked back to the theater, she glanced through her notes, then poked them into Martin's coat pocket. Martin stood under an awning until her car warmed up. She left by the rear entrance.

Now that Martin understood where to watch for the switch; the following Friday he studied the choreography extra close. He never took his eyes off Clara as she passed behind the curtain and came out the other side.

He kept his eye on her hands as she lowered the fans and continued down to the upper point of the heart. However, Rosie stood at the point, not Clara.

How did I miss her exchange again?

Martin waited until after the show to go out in the cold to wait for Clara.

"No time for pie tonight Clara. J.B. asked me to rework a column for the paper."

"You have all week to do that Martin. I think you are trying to avoid me, unless you want something."

Martin blushed.

"I get the feeling you already have a girl."

"Maybe, maybe not. Come on, let's go get that pie."

Chapter Seventeen – Clara explains her switch with Rosie

Curt's Under Corner was packed solid. Word of the new salad offering got around fast. The after theater crowd also dissipated later than usual. After a long wait, Curt himself seated them in a back corner, close to the rear kitchen service door.

"What do you two think about my adding soup to the menu? Not right away. The salad is successful now, but I'm sure sales will taper off soon."

"I love your pies. The salad's a delightful change of pace, but I've only ordered it once."

"Probably a little late to say this now Curt, but I would have preferred soup, to warm up from the cold. A crisp cold salad might be better as a summer treat."

"I thought of that too Martin, after I placed a standing order for salad ingredients. I have considered ice cream as a summer treat. I only thought of the soup today."

Pat brought our desserts, and the place quieted down to a dull roar.

"I never took my eyes off you the entire routine, you never switched with Rosie."

"You misunderstood Martin. I never said I switched with her. I said I exchanged places with her."

Martin points to Clara's hand.

"Impossible, you are wearing this sapphire ring, I never took my eyes off it for a second."

"That my dear Martin, is exactly why you didn't catch Rosie take the point. She simply stepped ahead of me, and I followed her left arm."

"Well Clara, you have stumped this reporter."

Clara dug in her purse for her notepad and pencil.

"Oh, here are some more notes Martin, they are self-explanatory."

"Thanks, I appreciate them. You provide some fantastic leads and stories."

Clara is busy sketching the stage, and mumbles.

"Don't mention it, all in a days work."

She got up and moved around to Martin's side of the table.

"Here, try to follow these steps."

She drew several circles and a few stars on the page, forming the finished heart. After she blackened in the upper point circle, she said.

"This is where Rosie performs her solo."

Clara went on to draw two lines for the narrow curtains; a box for the gazebo, and another black dot behind the curtain to represent Rosie's starting point.

"If Rosie is not standing here when we begin to form the heart; we turn out, away from the gazebo, to form two circles, like this."

"Yes, I caught that last month, the night we had the heavy snow."

"Did you detect we were also missing three other girls that night?"

"No, can't say that I did, the show was fabulous as usual."

"Now you understand why we learn the routines in sets. So you can't tell something is different, or someone is missing. Now, study this very close Martin."

Clara moved her pencil around on the paper, to signify her steps.

"I am following these stars, I stop here and don't step forward into Rosie's circle. Her foot would land right on top of mine if I tried."

Martin was told these moves previously, but they went over his head. He finally realized his serious mistake, Rosie is not in the choreograph routine.

"How did Rosie get in position, without being in the moving chorus line?"

"I'll show you how that works now. The sequence is simple. The curtains open first, and the gazebo slides forward. We hide Rosie from the audience with our fans, as the curtains move open. She begins right here on this dot, which I already showed you a minute ago."

"Wait, before you continue. What happened to the fans Rosie held?"

"Rosie won't touch a fan, she is most adamant about that too. Neither will she take a place in the chorus line."

"But I see her with a fan."

"No, Julia and I each hold a fan, our hands almost touch Rosie's. Our other fan is partly hiding our hands, and Rosie is completely hidden. I thought detective work was your hobby Martin?"

"Looks like I may have to give up being a sleuth after seeing this."

Clara removed a page from her notebook and tore a piece in the shape of the gazebo. She continued tearing the page, until she made strips representing the curtains, and a corner from the paper became Rosie. She tore two more corners off to be used as Julia and herself.

"We are all constantly moving, so give me a second to adjust the pieces, I'll move them one step at a time."

Clara stopped to tear some more slivers of paper.

"These are our feather fans. Oops, forgot, I should show the leading pair of curtains, the ones we pass behind as the gazebo moves forward."

She tears two more strips of paper, and places them on the notepad drawing. Clara moves the pieces of paper, showing each half-step of the choreography. Then shifts the position of the curtains slightly, and moves the papers representing the fans.

"Rosie is behind the gazebo, hid by these two curtains."

Clara moves the fans in unison, then slides the center curtain open, the fans and gazebo hide Rosie.

"With all the movement up and down the tiers, the fans waving, and the front curtains opening. Unless one pays close attention to the rear set of curtains; they would never catch them move along with the front pair of narrow curtains."

"What about these curtains in front of the gazebo prop?"

"They open before the platform begins to move forward. These are the ones that move to either side of the stage. The chorus line is moving toward the gazebo as the curtains are moving away. Only the first two girls on each side pass behind these curtains before they are outside the formation."

Martin understood how they are behind these curtains for only a split-second. Clara begins moving the paper shreds used as the fans.

"We reach the gazebo, as it moves past this point, and lower our fans behind it. This is when the second set of curtains move to follow the first set we passed behind."

Clara moved all the pieces of paper, showing how the chorus line moved into the heart shape. The line kept pace with the gazebo's forward movement. She moved Rosie in step right behind the gazebo.

The girls next in line lower their fans, as Clara and Julia raise theirs, so Rosie is still hidden from view. Clara and Julia, still moving forward in the choreography, lower their fans in front of the gazebo; then lift them again, in one continuous motion.

"Now pay attention to this Martin. The gazebo stops, but Rosie is still stepping forward, in rhythm with the chorus line, on to the gazebo. The fans swing away, and peel off, one girl behind the other, to form the feather heart."

"Is this the point where the girls in the chorus line are hiding themselves behind the fans?"

"Yes, and in some routines; this is where I remove my long gown and toss it in a box on the back of the gazebo; or reach to put it back on. All the fans are held motionless while Rosie does her solo."

Martin knows from his observations. When Rosie finishes her solo, the choreography starts again, from the bottom of the heart. The girls form a circle on each side of the stage, which tightens closer to the gazebo.

As the circle rotates, the fans are once again used to hide the gazebo. The gazebo moves up and back while hidden. The curtains move back in front of the gazebo. The tiers separate leaving a narrow aisle between them.

"Clara, where is Rosie? She must be off the gazebo before it moved back up. To be able to walk between the risers to backstage."

"You are correct Martin. In both routines, she steps off the gazebo and on the right tier. Hidden by fans, she steps down to stage level."

"I've seen her at the low point of the heart, then walk back between the tiers."

"Only in one routine Martin. Rosie will never be a part of the chorus line. The times you think she walked to the low point of the heart, either Julia or I, took her place, usually me."

"I have watched her step off the gazebo and walk forward to the low point."

"No, that was me in her gown, standing at the top point, and then walking forward. Rosie is already backstage when the fans lift from in front of the gazebo. Remember, the fans hide the gazebo, and Rosie, before moving back up."

"Her gown is exposed under the fans, right on the point."

"Believe me, Rosie is already off the gazebo when I step forward to take the point position."

"I guess with all the fans waving and the chorus line moving, I just missed the swap."

Martin took a while to comprehend this. He studied Clara's diagram closer. The low point girls turn out, and form a line across the stage. They turn their rears to the audience to show their bloomers. Then form the rotating circles to file out between the open tiers in a double column.

"Rosie has changed clothes Martin, and is often out the back door. Before the first skit following the opening number has started."

At the next performance, Martin paid close attention to everything Clara taught him. From the audience, before Rosie appears, the fans make it impossible to catch that Clara does not take the last additional step.

The feet I see taking the point position are Rosie's. The fans raise, hiding all the girls, as the spotlight narrows on Rosie. At the end of the performance, who's eyes are not squinting to ogle at the girls flashing their bloomers? No wonder I always miss it!

Chapter Eighteen – A surprise at Luella's wedding

"Good morning J.B., I didn't expect to see you here this early."

"Figured you might need some help in the back."

"Douglas Dentmar came by yesterday, right after you left. He said the Clepstein's had their baby."

"Yes, a girl, six pounds, eleven ounces, around 3:36am Tuesday."

John and Martin moved to the press room, and lined up their copy sheets.

"Been awhile since you set type Martin, why don't you sit over on this side and pull the headlines first."

"I'm not swift like Luella, but should be a snap with these new chases. How long will Luella be gone?"

"She only asked for one week off. I ran her out of here Thursday after the press run. I do not expect her back until next Wednesday, in time to set type."

"I didn't recognize half of the people who attended her wedding."

"Nor did I Martin, most looked like Clopton Hills uplanders."

"Figured as much, the way they were all decked out. When Luella gets back from her honeymoon, I will ask her how she met Rosie."

"Who did you say Martin?"

"Rosie, the soloist who sang up in the choir loft."

"Her name is not Rosie. Hattie sang in the choir, and her niece sang the processional. I do not remember which choir member sang the next number."

"The singer was Rosie, J.B. I recognized her voice, and her car was parked behind the church."

"The only solo sung from the choir loft was by Hattie's niece."

"Do you know her name J.B.?"

"She goes to Grace Miracle Church, and only sings at our church on special occasions. Seems like her name is something like Stella. I can ask Mrs. Platte for you on Sunday."

"I would appreciate it J.B. Since you are back here, would you mind 'blocking' for me?"

"Just like old times, eh Martin?"

"I remember. Except you were working the cases and I was 'blocking,' the old hard way too, with 'quoins.'"

"Yes, the times are changing Martin. I feel they are becoming too fast for me."

"You have ink for blood J.B., I look forward to working with you for years to come."

"Glad you said so Martin. I have a proposition for you."

"How about if you save it until after the presses roll. Hard to set type and talk at the same time."

"That's what I want to talk to you about, but can wait. We do not want to miss deadline."

J.B. wielded the 'sticks' like the master he is. A little noisy leveling the type, beating the 'planer-block' with a decades old leather mallet he made when he opened the paper. Kent and Jerome came flying through the door, as Martin set the last galley on the print rack.

"Cut it pretty close Martin."

"I would have finished earlier, if you didn't talk my ears off J.B."

Kent prepared the paper rolls while Jerome loaded the plate and brayer feed with ink. J.B. walked to the power box and threw the switch, announcing.

"Let's make music boys."

A faint smell of ozone filled the air as the capacitor start motors came alive. Kent and Jerome, now proficient in running the presses, kept them in perfect tune. This gave Martin a chance to take a short break. He glanced at J.B.

"I forgot how sore my hands and fingers get, they will probably ache clear through next Thursday."

J.B. chuckled.

"Don't understand how they got sore, as slow as you are."

"I beat deadline didn't I."

He slapped Martin on the back, pushing him in the direction of the carts.

"Let's get these loaded Martin, do not need a pile up."

The presses sang until the job completed. J.B. powered them down and doused the lights.

"I want you boys back here at six am sharp."

Kent and Jerome, now accomplished reporters, still handled getting the newspapers distributed to the team of newsboys. They did most of the dirty jobs Martin used to do. Clean the presses, wash the galleys, and help Luella put away the type.

Martin oversaw the journalists and columnists, and edited everything which went in the paper. The newspaper grew steadily after the war. The current issue is twice as large as any ever produced before the war, and takes a whole day longer to prepare.

Business in the factories grew. So they could start earlier, the bus lines added two early buses, to bring workers to the industrial area. Factory owners arrived ahead of their employees, and desired to receive their morning paper early.   Expecting the paper on their doorstep when they arrived.

Their advertising supported the newspaper. So J.B. established a new timetable, to ensure the paper was in their hands before they unlocked the doors to their buildings. Martin arrived earlier than normal, in case the boys needed some extra help.

When the last cart returned, and all staff members hit the street, the newspaper office fell quiet. The only sounds, came from J.B. shuffling paperwork on his desk; and the old clock beside the doorway, next to the type cases ticking away.

"Martin, you still in back?"

"Yes sir, refilling the upper tank. Give me a second."

"I'm hoping you do not need to do that much longer."

"You don't have to yell, I can hear you just fine. Hiring more help J.B.?"

"That all depends on you Martin. Sit down, let's talk. Not up on the stool, pull your chair beside my desk."

J.B. had something serious to talk about, wanting Martin down to face him at eye level. Worry caused beads of perspiration to appear on his forehead. Martin pulled his chair over and sat down.

"How long do you intend to keep working here at the paper Martin?"

"What an odd question J.B. I'll be here as long as you'll have me."

"Exactly what I wanted you to say Martin. About time we made some major changes around here. No way around them, if we want the paper to grow any larger."

"We could use some more room, but I don't think a larger building is available anywhere close to here. Were you thinking of constructing a new building?"

"You are getting ahead of me again Martin. No, I was not thinking about moving, although having more room to work in would be wonderful. To keep up with how fast the paper is growing, we need to get one of those Linotype machines."

"Mighty expensive they are J.B."

"I checked around. The war put several papers and a small book publisher out of business. The Moberleigh Times ordered a new machine as the war started. They closed before the machine was delivered."

"Without a new building, the presses could be moved closer to the front. The type cases will fit on the dock and we can enclose around them. We may have to miss one or two issues."

"I do not expect to miss any issues Martin. The bank offered the machine to the Ash Brooke Citizen Newspaper, under fair and lenient terms."

"I'm sure you considered this quite well, and will take them up on that offer J.B."

"They didn't offer the Linotype to me Martin, they offered the machine to the newspaper."

"Isn't that the same thing?"

"Not exactly Martin, and this is what I want to talk to you about."

Chapter Nineteen – J.B. gives Martin the Citizen

Martin had not noticed J.B. cut down the amount of work he did each day. Some jobs were delegated to other employees as the business grew. But J.B. always handled everything important and worked right along beside him.

"I'm getting up in years Martin, and for the last two, I have considered turning the Ash Brooke Citizen over to you. This is the reason I stayed in the sidelines, out of your way. I wanted to make sure ink truly flowed in your veins."

"Wow Mr. Blaine, I appreciate the offer. But this business is you, it's your life."

"Martin, my dearest friend and fellow pressman, will you hire this old man and let him take a seat behind his old desk; and continue to do what he has done these past many years?"

"You're talking crazy J.B. No one can take your place, and no one can touch your desk, or sit in your chair."

J.B. slowly opened his right desk drawer and withdrew a large envelope. He held it up for Martin to take, but kept his grip firm.

"I figured you would think that way Martin. My conditions are simple. Our working relation must remain the same, I do what I've always done, only now you run the show."

Mr. Blaine released his grip on the envelope. Martin took it, but slowly set it back down on J.B.'s desk.

"You should put this in the safe, here is the combination. I've already transferred the business, land, building, and all contents over to you. All outstanding bills are paid in full, and the bank was informed you are taking over."

The two men just sat facing each other, silently collecting their thoughts. A full half-hour passed before J.B. spoke.

"I am too old to get a long term loan. This ledger shows the company assets and our monthly receipts. The newspaper can well afford the terms of the contract."

Martin looked over the ledger book and contract papers from the bank.

"You will not find a better deal Martin. Stop by the bank and sign for the new Linotype machine. I would myself if I were younger."

"I don't know what to say J.B. I understand the situation and will do as you ask. However, as far as I'm concerned, nothing is changed. You are still the boss and call all the shots."

"Everyone will learn soon enough Martin. You will be signing the checks from now on. Now get over to the bank before they change their mind. I would hate for you to lose this deal."

"Yes Sir, on my way."

Nothing much changed at the newspaper. Martin took care of the things he usually handled, and J.B. went about his normal routine. Only now Martin had to do all the book work, payroll, pay the bills, and order supplies.

Luella mastered using an early style used Linotype long before her parents closed their business. Several weeks would elapse before the installation of the new machine. Martin spent most of the week, sitting behind his desk. He studied well past closing time every night.

Whew, I never thought so much paperwork was involved in running a company.

Roland waited outside Martin's apartment for over an hour before driving up to the paper to check on him. Finding the lights still on, he went inside. Martin glanced up at the wall clock.

"Oh, I'm so sorry Roland, I forgot about our studies tonight."

"I brought a special case to use as a tutorial. The captain pulled from his files, the perfect mystery for you to study."

"I need a break from all this paperwork. Care to join me for dinner? We can go over your folder between each dinner course."

"How could I ever pass up a fancy meal in your tenants restaurant?"

On Monday morning, Martin made a special effort to

beat J.B. to work. He followed the customary routine, and entered through the rear entrance; turned on the lights, then went to the front windows and opened the shades.

He found a surprise when he raised the shade on the door, his name painted on the glass.

Martin Thomas Hurston, Editor in Chief.

He felt embarrassed, and had hoped J.B. would keep the change quiet. He turned to go to his desk, it was gone. The office side of the room was changed. J.B.'s desk was moved forward and turned around. A new larger roll top desk sat over J.B.'s original spot.

The lid was up, and everything concerning the business from J.B.'s desk was placed in the right hand drawers or in the pigeon-holes. All the things from Martin's old desk was neatly placed on top of the new desk; right where he had left them on his desk.

The contents of his drawers were boxed and stacked on the two pull-out shelves, rather than placed inside the left hand drawers. The drawer and lid keys were in an envelope behind a new pen set. The front read, Congratulations Mellow Martin Hurston.

Mr. Blaine entered by the front door wearing his best Sunday suit. J.B. always wore an old suit jacket outside the office, to hide his wide green suspenders. No one inside the office, could recall ever seeing him with the coat on. He tipped his hat.

"Good morning Mr. Hurston. Pleasant day. I am ready to dig right in."

Martin decided to play his little game.

"You may call me Martin."

"Yes sir, I mean Martin sir. Yes, I think I will like working with you Thomas."

"Are you looking to get fired your first day on the job? I don't ever want to hear you call me that again."

That comment prompted both to burst forth in uncontrollable laughter. They were still holding their aching sides as other employees arrived.

"Martin, I got the scoop you asked about last week."

After everything that happened, whatever he requested, slipped Martin's mind.

"And what scoop did I ask about J.B.?"

"The singer's name at Luella's wedding."

Chapter Twenty – Martin learns Ella is a singer

Martin pulled a chair next to the edge of J.B.'s desk; a side which has not seen daylight in over four decades. He could not help but admire how beautiful the desk once was.

"Hattie Platte from my church, sang the first three songs with the choir, leading up to the processional. The soloist you inquired about, the one who sang the processional hymn from the choir loft. She is from Grace Miracle Church as I thought."

"Yes, she's the one. Did you get her name?"

"I did. However, I am concerned about your interest in her."

"Only curiosity J.B. Her name please."

"I must warn you, she belongs to a very strict church."

"OK, I understand J.B., you've made it quite clear."

"Her name is Ella Thornton."

"Aha, my suspicions were correct."

"Who is this Rosie you mentioned last week?"

"Oh, nobody J.B."

"Must be somebody Martin, you recognized what kind of car she drives."

"I can't tell you until I am absolutely certain. Been doing a bit of amateur detective work, and a coincidence caught my eye. The circumstances make it impossible. They could be detrimental to the individual or individuals if I made a wrong assumption."

"You need not say anything more Martin, I understand. Remember, I have a nose for news too, and can see right through you."

"You think so J.B.?"

"You told me all I need to know. You believe this singer called Rosie, and Ella are the same person. Based on a parked car and the sound of her voice."

"There is more to it than that. Things which make no sense, and impossible timetables."

"You are wise to keep the information to yourself Martin. Many people are hurt by wrong assumptions. What you presume as correct, often turns out to be something entirely different. You of all people should understand those principles by now."

"Oh, I understand J.B., which is why I don't want to say any more at this time."

"That is good, keep the information to yourself Martin, even after you believe you figured it out. Give it plenty of time to prove itself, and even then, best not to say anything."

"I agree J.B."

"Well boss, I am going to hit the streets and try to turn up a few leads for a story."

"I would appreciate your not calling me boss. You are still my boss J.B."

"Fair enough Martin."

Martin often spoke with Ella when she unlocked the side storage area, and waited for materials to be stored or retrieved. From his apartment window, he spied Ella crossing the street and ran downstairs to meet her.

"This side doors appear to be working out remarkably well for you Ella."

"Yes they are. Don't tell me the restaurant needs the room back, a big shipment is coming in tomorrow."

"Their rear storage room is more than enough space,

no worries there."

"You looked a little nervous, like you had something you wanted to say, and couldn't figure out the best way."

"Well, I realize this is a long shot Ella, but I would like to ask you something."

"Whatever it is, the answer is, en oh, No. I am not married. I'm not seeing anyone, and I am not interested in dating."

"Wait Ella, nothing like that. You come from a large family, so this could only be a coincidence."

"Are you asking as a reporter Martin? I've never seen you so nervous before."

"No, not for the paper, I want to ask you about Luella's wedding."

"Her wedding was beautiful, wonderful service, and a most lovely ceremony."

"Yes it was, so I guess you answered my question, without my asking."

"Ask about what Martin?"

"You are blessed with a beautiful voice, I love your singing."

"Why thank you Martin. Aunt Hattie hounds me to death to sing at her church when some special event is going on."

"Sometimes I don't understand you at all Martin. You used to come up with a million things to say. After the restaurant opened, you rarely stop to talk anymore, unless we are here at the storage room door."

"Had a lot on my mind, helping J.B. get the newspaper back to normal."

"Oh by the way, congratulations. I understand J.B. made you the new editor."

"You heard already?"

"Mr. Blaine is telling everyone in town, bragging like a new father about your promotion."

Ella locked the storage room door and returned to her desk across the street. Martin continued to study her daily movements. Especially on Friday nights, trying to put the pieces of the puzzle together.

Each time he thinks he is getting close, a new discovery drops a brick wall in front of him. Martin had never seen her wear makeup, not even to cover the rash on her face last summer. She drove that old runabout until the wheels were ready to fall off; and the used coupé she currently drives to work is showing signs of wear.

When he spied the Saxon Roadster at Luella's wedding, he failed to check further, to note if Ella's coupé was in the lot. A serious mistake a reputable detective would never make.

Though Ella dressed in a fine woman's business suit. She never wore anything costly, nor did she wear jewelry. In comparison, Rosie wore too much makeup, tons of jewelry, and worked in a place Ella would never step foot inside. Rosie also drove an expensive car.

Even so, I know I'm right.

Because Clara is no longer enamored with Martin, it became customary for them to meet after the theater for a pie or salad at Curt's. She had a new boyfriend, and never failed to talk about him and his father.

Dale's father owns a large furniture store in the more affluent area of Clopton Hills. His family lived a little further south, still on the hill. Clara's home is only two blocks east, closer to the old shopping district.

After meeting Dale, the number of leads she passed to Martin dwindled. Yet they were all hot items and always usable. How Clara dug up some of these leads, is a secret she never shared with Martin.

Dale showed a little jealousy about his gal spending time with Martin. Later he came to appreciate the fact martin stayed with her after work, until he arrived to pick her up. Friday's were always busy at the furniture store, so Curt never ran Martin and Clara out.

"I enjoy having you two around to talk to, and keep me company while I clean up for the night. Clara's beau is here, time to lock up. Be safe walking home Martin."

The hallway to his apartment was lined with some of Marie and Georges old furniture. Obviously their renovations were complete. In the morning, Marie popped over to Martins to show off her new baby.

"Sorry about the furniture in the way. We did the baby's room in the new apartment first, and were only going light with the new furniture. But George found a bargain, and you remember how he is when a big sale comes along."

Martin was holding the baby when Marie's phone began to ring. When she ran to answer, the baby instantly began to cry. She stopped when Martin touched her cheek. Marie was back in a flash.

"George will move the furniture sometime tomorrow morning. She needs changing."

Marie slipped out the door, before Martin learned what they named their new baby.

Curt's Under Corner had standing room only when Martin and Clara arrived from the theater. He never missed Rosie's solo, so she or her songs became the topic of conversation many evenings.

"Out of curiosity Clara, does Rosie use a last name?"

"Rosie is her stage name. Yes, the name on her dressing room door, under the gold star, says Rose Thorn."

"Rose Thorn is likely her professional pseudonym."

"No, must be her real name. I've seen it on her paycheck envelope."

"Well, it's sorta obvious Clara. Rose and Thorn together as a name, can't be real."

"Does sound a little strange Martin. I'll see what I can find out for you."

"Thanks, much appreciated. – Hi Pat, make mine a

slice of apple tonight."

"Me too Pat. – Rosie is a strange one, might be hard for me to get a chance to talk to her. I'm on stage when she arrives, and after her number, she's gone, poof, just like that."

"She always does two solo's. Could you catch her between them?"

"I'm in the skit following her solo, so am changing and taking my place on stage. The only time we can talk, is if the show changes and we need to learn the new routine."

"I've been hoping to meet her in person for a long time now."

"You men are all alike, always wanting to meet the star. But you're different, you don't imagine her as an idol, do you?"

"Not at all Clara. I thought I would be cordial and let her know how much I enjoy hearing her sing. Nothing more."

Two months pass before the show changed, giving Clara a chance to talk with Rosie in private. She took advantage of a long break between rehearsals, to sit down with Rosie for a chat.

"You know Rosie, you have an admirer in the audience who never missed one of your performances. A real charming guy too, not one of those star struck nuts. He would like to meet you, only for the purpose of paying you a compliment."

"Have you found out his name?"

"Yes, its Martin Hurston, editor of the Ash Brooke Citizen."

Rosie clenched her teeth and sprung from the stool.

"I do not do interviews for anyone, especially newspapers."

Clara followed Rosie as she paced back and forth backstage, trying to talk to her.

"It is not for the paper, he only wants to meet you."

"Impossible Clara."

"Just give him one minute of your time. It won't hurt you to say hi to a fan of yours."

Rosie stopped complaining long enough to stare at Clara's expression for a short time.

"You don't understand Clara."

"Well, I know Martin extremely well. We meet after every show at Curt's. He truly likes your singing, and wants to pay his compliments is all Rosie."

"Has he said anything else about me?"

"He talks about you, actually your voice, every time we are together."

"What about the other singers or actresses?"

"He's never mentioned anyone else."

"Tell him no Clara. You cannot trust a reporter."

Throughout the rest of the rehearsal, Rosie thought about her comments to Clara.

Avoiding Martin will make him more suspicious. I'm sure he doesn't suspect anything.

During a break in the new routine, Rosie pulls Clara behind the curtain.

"You tell this Martin fellow, I will give him one minute. Not this coming weekend, but after next weeks' performance."

"At the stage door?"

"No, tell him to wait on the curb at the front exit. He can speak his peace from there, when I stop to turn out of the parking lot."

"OK, I'll tell him to be at the gate. He will be so pleased to hear the news."

Clara had many thoughts, before she met with Martin after the next show.

Should I question him more, or just tell him the good

news? Is she really that afraid of reporters? I wonder why? Is she hiding some scandalous secret?

By the time the weekend rolled around, Clara forgot all about her questions. Roland spent the weekend with Martin, going over what he learned from working the case he used for training. Marie invited Martin to join them for lunch. He held baby Alyssa while the table was set.

Chapter Twenty-one – Jealous Ella

Not having the opportunity to speak with Martin for over two months, Ella felt shunned. But she still kept an eye out for him. With his added duties at the newspaper, they rarely crossed each others paths anymore.

She enjoyed their talks when she unlocked the storage room door, and chatted with him while her employees moved materials in or out. Martin often spotted her from his apartment desk, and came down to meet her. Now he is always at the paper working.

Ella thought back to the last time they talked casually, and her harsh comments.

The only eligible bachelor that's ever shown an interest in me. Have I scared him away. I need to make up with him. It can't wait, I must do it tonight.

Unsure of what to say, or how he felt, Ella made an attempt to learn his thoughts. She broke her longstanding tradition, and waited by her car. When Martin came down the street, she crossed over to meet him. On seeing her, Martin checked his wristwatch.

Ella should be long home by now.

"Hi Ella. Car problems?"

"My car is fine Martin. I hung around after work to apologize to you."

"Whatever do you mean? You've never done anything that you must apologize to me for Ella."

"I was a little harsh the last time we spoke, and said things I should not..."

"Think nothing of it Ella, we all suffer from stressful days. No harm done."

"You appeared overly nervous and I thought the worst. I reacted to that emotion, before I learned what you wished to ask."

"Oh worry, worry. You worry way too much about things Ella."

"Well, I only wanted to say I am sorry. I must get going, my mother will be furious."

"Yes, go tend to your mom, and be careful along the way."

Martin took to heart he had not stopped to talk with Ella much lately. He was familiar with the exact time she stopped work each day to eat lunch. Ella usually brought a sandwich and ate at her desk.

He left the paper early, and as soon as Ella opened the drawer to take out her sack, Martin tapped on the window. He did not startle her. She spied him coming down the street, and it was impossible to miss his smiling face peering through the glass.

Martin held up his brown bag and motioned for her to come outside. She came to the side door, carrying her lunch sack.

"You can't stay cooped up inside all day, join me for lunch."

"Just because I apologized for being harsh, don't mean I changed my mind about what I said Martin."

"I'm hungry. It's a beautiful day, and no one is at the picnic table. You can join me if you like."

Martin walked behind the building and sat down to eat. Ella remained on the stoop until he was seated. She smiled at his cute dimples and joined him.

"Highly irregular Martin, eating away from my desk."

"Well, I didn't want you to think I was avoiding you on purpose."

"I know you Martin. You are up to something under those sleeves, and whatever it is, you can count me out."

Martin pulls his shirt sleeves up past his elbow, grinning from ear to ear.

"Nope, behold, nothing up my sleeves."

"You are downright crazy Martin."

"So they say! How's your mom doing Ella?"

"She enjoys her good days and suffers on bad days. Holding her own better than last year, but shows no recent improvement."

A whistle from a nearby factory blew, and employees came out of nowhere, to head inside.

"I must get back to my desk Martin. We are not supposed to allow workers inside if I'm not in there with them."

"J.B. is probably wondering why I'm not back yet as well."

The following day, Ella stared out the window before opening her lunch. She wished Martin could join her again, and also hoped he would not. Then realized it was Thursday, the day they ran the presses. She remembered he was always swamped on Fridays as well.

What is the matter with you Ella Rose? You are too busy for such nonsense.

Ella's desk held a considerable amount of work to finish before the weekend. Plus an important meeting with a new supplies vendor. Whom she hoped does not detain her too far into the late afternoon.

Martin was late getting out of the paper on Friday night. Doug ate dinner and went on ahead to the theater without him. Before the show, Clara watched for Martin, to remind him of the good news.

She had to finish getting ready for her performance, so was not able to wait any longer. This was not a problem, as she would meet him after the show. They had not missed going to Curt's together for well over six months.

During the performance break, Clara only had a chance to say to Rosie.

"Don't forget next Friday."

Rosie nodded back, she remembered. After her solo, Rosie left in a flash, as usual. The show ended and Clara met Martin at the stage door and they walked down to Curt's together.

"Martin, I bear wonderful news tonight. Rosie said she would meet with you."

"Thanks Clara, I can't wait to meet her in person."

"She said for you to stand on the curb near the front exit. You can speak to her in her car when she stops. I think she is terrified of reporters."

"Why? Do you think she is hiding something?"

"As many years as we all worked together, nobody knows anything about her. She shows up, ducks in her dressing room, appears on stage, sings her solos, changes back into her street clothes and leaves. Before they changed the show, she used to take time to talk with us. We are sure she thoroughly hates doing the early number."

When they arrived at Curt's, they found the door locked. Martin look in through the glass, but the curtains prevent him from seeing inside. Clara waited in front while Martin went around back to check if he is cleaning up or simply not there.

The back door is locked also, and no lights can be seen inside. He returned to the front to tell Clara. Clara commented about the usual theater crowds absence; but pointed out their cars are present in the lot across the street.

"I'll run upstairs and ask them what's up."

On his way back down the hill, he met Clara halfway. She learned everyone is upstairs, and went to meet Martin.

"Curt now owns the whole building, he is serving on

the first floor."

"Some reporter you turned out to be. They made the announcement at the theater, before the final act."

Martin slapped himself on the forehead.

"Of course. I forgot. Curt changed the name to Curt's Over the Under Corner Deli, and ran an ad in the entertainment section to tell everyone."

Martin ate lunch at the picnic table with Ella on Monday and Wednesday this week. After their usual idle conversation during the latter day.

"I'm seriously considering changing to aunt Hattie's church permanently."

"Is it closer to where you live?"

"No, it's two blocks farther away. More to do with mother and her pastor coming to visit so often."

"They are the same faith, so what's the difference?"

"Mother is concerned I do not dress appropriately. She and her church members think wearing a suit jacket over a skirt is most improper. Her pastor would not approve."

"You've worn a suit ever since I met you."

"Mother's ailments are also causing her to be a little more grouchy. Aunt Hattie's church, although the same faith, is nowhere near as strict."

"I realize it is hard on you Ella, perhaps the move is a good idea."

The whistle blew, saving Ella from making a further comment. Martin met J.B. pacing the floor when he returned to the paper.

"I have two appointments Martin, and I'm late for one already. I could not leave with new people here until you returned."

"Sorry J.B., I was late leaving for lunch."

"Missed you at the diner, but noted you've been bringing your own lunch lately."

"Only so I could talk with someone J.B."

"Yeah, and I know who too. You need to get that crazy idea of yours out of your head."

"Well J.B., I will have more details after the weekend. I'm meeting Rosie in person."

"Don't jump to any conclusions Martin. Whatever resolution you come up with, or details you think you solved. I hope you realize they are impossible. People simply cannot be in two places at the same time."

Chapter Twenty-two – Martin meets Rosie

Martin's anticipation of meeting Rosie, made the entire week drag on forever. Friday night finally came, and Rosie's solo performance was excellent. She sang one of Martin's favorite songs.

He sat near the back to make a fast exit and be at the curb when she pulled out. As promised, Rosie stopped her car at the gate. Martin played it cool.

"I'm pleased to meet you Rosie. I enjoy your singing, and tonight was fabulous as always. Thank you for stopping."

Rosie's speaking voice was nothing like Ella's. Her heavy east side slang and nasal tone came as a shock.

"Clara says y'all catch my every show."

"I wouldn't miss your solos for the world. Your beautiful songs are the highlight of my week."

"I'm on a tight schedule, and must appear at another important engagement this evening. Thank you for coming to the show."

"The pleasure is all mine Rosie, drive safe."

Rosie waved a white gloved hand through the window as she pulled out of the parking lot. Martin stood for the longest time, to make a mental picture of Rosie's face.

He noted a mole on her cheek, highlighted with black. Long curled eyelashes, and her hair reached almost to her elbows.

Despite the heavy makeup and lipstick, her facial

features closely resembled Ella's. Martin paid close
attention to her voice.

Did she disguise it to throw me off?

The more he thought about her words. Her east side
twang is not something even an actress could master
without years of practice. He thought back to his many
conversations with Ella. Not once did he recall her ever
using any type of slang; and she definitely does not possess
a trace of east side in her voice.

Martin's gut still told him, they look too much alike to
be two different people. He strolled toward the hub of the
entertainment district to kill an hour before Clara got off
work. He spotted Janice at an outdoor table, sitting by
herself. Martin checked his wristwatch.

"Out early?"

She looked up, in the direction of the voice.

"Oh, it's you'a Martin. You neva come uppa this way.
What'cha doin'?"

"Just went for a walk. Why aren't you in the show?"

"Didn't Clara tell ya? I got myself fired, three weeks
ago now."

"No, she never said a word. What happened?"

"Well, a, I drink a lot, an' b'tween shows too. I guess I,
well, ya know."

"That's a shame Janice."

"No biggie. I work uppa heya now. Make mo long
green too!"

A drummer poked his head out the door to tell Janice
she was up next. As Martin walked back toward the
theater, he mumbled to himself.

*I'm sure they are the same person. Why else would
Ella suddenly spend more time with me. Chattering away
right after Rosie agreed to talk to me. She probably
wanted to make certain I paid attention to her voice and
mannerisms.*

Martin arrived back at the theater and stood by the stage door to wait for Clara.

Rosie not only overdid her makeup, but over enunciated her nasal tone. I'm going to ask Clara whether she is aware of Rosie removing her makeup before leaving the theater.

Martin's wait was short. He sat down on the back stoop to take a rock from his shoe when the door burst open. He and Clara walked down to Curt's Over the Under Corner Deli.

"You never mentioned anything about Janice getting fired."

"Is that what she told you?

"Yes, she said she was drinking between shows and got caught."

"I wonder why she would lie to you? Trying to get your sympathy no doubt. She landed another job and just up and quit. Put the whole show in a bind. She does drink too much, but she was not fired."

"One other thing Clara. You speak with Rosie during rehearsals. How would you describe her voice?"

"Like anyone else, normal, nothing odd, if that's what you mean."

"Does she sound nasal to you, or present any hint of slang."

"Oh, sometimes she is whiny sounding, normal for her."

"Do you have an idea where she might live?"

"She must live on the east side, she sounds like an uplander."

One thing a detective learns is to draw information from those to whom he is speaking. This was no exception. Clara went from saying she sounded normal, to mentioning she sounds like she is from the east side. Not the answers he hoped to receive about Rosie.

Once again I failed as a detective. I forgot to ask if her nasal tone and accent are more pronounced now than last month.

When they reached Curt's, Dale was already waiting for her.

I overheard him say, he came to get her to help out at the store. A big sale going on and not enough help.

Martin jotted down the questions he wanted to ask Clara, and will get to them next weekend. The next time Martin talked with Ella, he paid more attention to her hair and eyebrows.

Can such long tresses be hidden by the bun she wears?

Martin is careful never to mention he goes to the theater in front of Ella. He did hope to discuss her singing when he got the chance. He lucked out. When he joined her at the picnic table for lunch, she started the topic herself.

"Sure were a lot of people at Luella's wedding. I didn't recognize most of them."

"Interesting you should bring up the wedding. It was on my mind also Ella."

"I was surprised when auntie said she recognized almost everyone."

"Several were Luella's neighbors. The Crolloff family lives in the Clopton Hills area."

"A lot of busybodies live in that area Martin."

"Luella mentioned it was one reason she moved further south."

"Yes, she lives down the street from my brother Earl. He often bumps into her shopping at his grocery store."

Lunch seemed always to pass by fast, before Martin has a chance to ask his questions. He did study her face, paying close attention to the shape of her eyebrows. Rosie's mole and eyebrows are obviously enhanced with a makeup pencil.

Martin watched Ella walk back to her desk. He paid special attention to the bun in her hair. Much larger than the one his mother wore. He wondered, was it because Rosie had such long hair.

While having lunch with Ella on Wednesday, she appeared more relaxed. Yet at the same time, she seemed withdrawn and sad. She ate most of her lunch before speaking. For the first time, she reached across the table to grasp Martin's hand.

"Earl made arrangements to put mom in the Royce Care Facility. They picked her up yesterday afternoon, while I was here at work.

"Perhaps a new home will be better for her, and you too Ella. Royce is one of the best."

"Yes they are most comfortable. But it is like Earl is shoving mom aside."

"Do you remember mentioning to me last month, the many problems you were having with the home nurses?"

"They let her fall twice, and do not keep her clean or fed properly."

"You inferred they were not taking well enough care of her while you are at work."

"Blasted whistle, I must go inside now."

Martin sensed Ella did not want to let go of his hand. She held tight as she stood, then let go when her arm became outstretched. He hurried back to the paper, J.B. scheduled several appointments for after lunch.

His desk was piled with articles to proof. J.B. no longer handled editing or proofing, and none of his stories ever needed double checked. J.B.'s work was always perfect. Kent often helped Martin with the edits, but took this week off to move to his new home.

Thursday night after leaving work, Ella came over to the apartment building to visit Alyssa and talk for a bit with Marie. Martin only spotted Ella after she returned to her side of the street, and Marie never let on they had talked about him.

Chapter Twenty-three – A new chorus routine

As Martin neared the theater, Dale sped away after dropping Clara off. She ran along the side of the building to the stage door at the rear. Martin checked his wristwatch.

I wonder why Clara is running so late?

Martin took his seat next to Doug. Two actors entered the stage in front of the curtain and started a little skit. Martin glanced over at the easel. The man who changes the cards kept looking at the stage. While flipping through the cards and scratching his head.

"Appears they changed the routine again Martin."

"On my way here, I witnessed a chorus girl arrive late."

The impromptu skit ended, the lights dimmed, and the main curtain opened. The choreographed routine did change. The women entered from both sides of the stage, and moved down front where they usually form their closing chorus line.

"They have added something new Doug."

The girls put their arms around each others waists and danced a high-kick number. Afterward they moved backwards forming two large moving circles. The tiers were not pushed together, and in place of the gazebo, sat a long descending staircase.

Rather than one large heart, two smaller heart shapes formed on each side of the staircase. The spotlight narrowed on a curtain at the top. It opened and all eyes turned to Rosie. She descended the upper part of the staircase.

She stopped on a wide platform, like a landing midway down the staircase, adorned with gold newels, topped by a red velvet rails. Rosie added several minor dance steps to her solo, which shocked Martin.

Rosie always stood in the same spot, motionless except for her arms. Both feet firmly planted as she graced the audience with her solo. Tonight she sang two solo's back to back. The second was a fast-paced number, which was rather out of style for Rosie.

Her performance solicited a greater round of applause, and the patrons rose for a standing ovation. She did a shallow curtsy and the audience sat down as she descended the rest of the staircase to the main stage floor.

The spotlight widened as she walked forward, almost to the front of the stage. She left enough room between her and the edge for the chorus line to engulf her. Hidden by the fans the girls held, the staircase moved rearward. Rosie followed and the curtains closed behind her.

An excellent choreographic performance hid Rosie's departure from the audience. Martin ducked out of the theater, to wait at the exit when she pulled out. He hoped she would stop, but as she backed her car up, she spotted him.

Rosie had removed her makeup, which is why she chose to leave by the rear parking lot exit. Martin returned to enjoy the rest of the show. Clara performed well in both skits and the final act. After the show, Martin met her on the stoop. She shook from exhaustion.

"I loved your new routine. Was the show hard tonight?"

"No more than usual. I am tired from helping out at the store all day."

"The furniture store?"

"Yes. Today was their annual home from Houston sale. One of Dale's customers almost caused me to be late for tonight's show."

Nothing more was said while they walked. Curt was outside changing a light bulb, so held the door open as they went inside. Martin did not resist the temptation to tease him, and dropped a penny in his outstretched hand.

"Is that all I'm worth? I have a new pie for you to try tonight, I was going to make it on-the-house. But for such a heavy tipper, I'm apt to charge you."

"Now Curt, you know it's bad manners to tip the owner. A new pie sound wonderful."

"Who ever said tipping the hardest worker in this place was bad manners? I'll take every dime, 'or penny' I can get. I've reserved your table in the back corner. Keeps you out of my hair when I'm cleaning."

Clara pulled Martin through the crowd to the back table, and plopped down.

"Speaking of hair. I have a question for you Clara."

"I doubt I can answer your question, not with my wild rats nest."

"Your curly hair is saucy and fixed cute. How much hair can a woman roll into a bun?"

"A considerable amount Martin. Depends on the size of the doughnut, or if she made a coil and rolled with a twist."

"Do you think Rosie has too much hair to roll into a bun?"

"Oh, not at all. In fact, Rosie's fine blond hair is almost too short for a bun."

"Here's a special pie for the beautiful lady, and another for my heavy tipper."

Curt did not leave the table right away. He turned his back, and held his hand out behind him, moving it slightly up and down in front of Martin. Then laughed as he walked away.

"Mighty good pie. What do you think Clara?"

"I wonder what Curt calls his creation? I've never had peaches and cherries in the same pie before."

"That cream really tops it off, but I would prefer a double dollop."

"Same here Martin. Hey Curt, Curt, what do you call this?

"Twin Jubilee. Now pipe down, you'll scare my last new customer away."

"Were you invited to Luella's wedding Clara?"

"No, she did tell us about it yet. When is the event?"

"The wedding was the week before last."

"You are crazy as a loon Martin, Louella's not married."

"Sure is. I was at her wedding."

"You must mean a different Louella?"

"The one who works at the newspaper."

"I don't know anyone who works with you. I thought you were talking about our Louella, Lulu Guynes, on the program. Hey wait, did you say two weeks ago?"

"Yes, the wedding at Blessed Hope Baptist Church."

"I'm pretty sure that's the wedding Wilton brought some of our sound equipment to. Would you like me to ask him?"

"If you don't mind."

"The funniest thing happened that afternoon Martin. After Wilton loaded the equipment in his car, he backed over that low post by the stage door, and hit the corner of the stoop. His car was stuck fast on the post."

"What did he do then Clara?"

"The only thing he could do. He commandeered Rosie's car, and dropped her off after practice at her house. Then went to set up for the wedding."

"You answered my question, so no need to ask Mr. Stoddard."

Dale pulled up outside and blew his horn an extended blast. Clara ran out to meet him. Martin stayed at the table, and pulled a notepad from his pocket. Martin is beside himself. Clara confirmed Ella was not driving Rosie's car.

But she did prove a correlation between the theater and the church. This may mean there is some connection between Ella and Mr. Stoddard.

Curt turned off the dining area lights, so Martin rushed to beat him to the front door. He did not want to pseudo tip Curt a second time in one day. Curt held the door ajar and stuck his flat hand outside, waving it up and down to taunt Martin. Then locked the door behind him.

Chapter Twenty-four – An invitation from Ella

Martin spent the remainder of the weekend going over his notes. He shared some more information with his friend Roland. Who by now, listened to so many of Martins new personal cases, he cannot keep them straight.

He hoped Roland might catch some missing clue. Martin no longer mentioned names, and is careful never to bring up Rosie; or Roland would only shun him away again. So Martin cleverly disguised each round of questions.

"Whatever mystery you are working on this week Martin. Like all the rest, the details do not mesh together. I need more to go on than what scant information you provided."

Monday morning rolled around, and Martin is busy working at his desk. J.B. finished what he was working on and pulled his chair over by Martin's desk.

"How about an update on that theory you worked on for so long Martin?"

"The details still seem impossible. But I know I'm right about this."

"From what you told me so far, it appears you clearly proved yourself wrong."

"It sure comes out that way on paper J.B. With so many unanswered questions, I cannot give up until they are resolved."

"You should quit wasting your time Martin. Perhaps no solution exists for those questions. Besides, more important things need worked on."

"I only mess with such things when all my other work is caught up J.B."

"Will you drop this ad copy over at Miller and Crofts when you go to lunch?"

"Sure thing J.B."

"They are considering a four page spread as an insert, with extra copies for mailing to their clients. Luella put a lot of effort in this new sample page."

"Don't know how you do it J.B."

"Experience my boy, experience."

Martin ran all the way to the mill from Miller and Crofts. Ella was waiting patiently when he arrived. Martin sat down panting, hardly able to speak.

"I was beginning to think you forgot about me."

"Boy am I out of shape. Had to run an errand for J.B., glad you waited. How's your mom?"

"For someone so sick, she's having the time of her life. She loves soaking in all the attention they are giving her."

"So, are you still mad at Earl then?"

"How can I be? With Royce only two blocks east of his store, he visits her more now than ever before. Hey that rhymes, store, before. Oh, my crazy mind."

"Cute. I noticed your boss coming and going frequently last week. The fellow with him last Thursday appeared to be taking several measurements. He's not selling the place is he?"

"Heck no, he ordered some new automated cutting machines. I guess you missed the four men from that company the day before."

"They must be working inside. The guys I mentioned were taking measurements outside."

"The inside men were constantly in the way. The men you spotted outside, turned in an estimate to remodel the buildings exterior."

A Secret in Ash Brooke

"That old building sure could use a facelift."

"Those were the exact words Mr. Deckett used."

"Don't be late Wednesday, I'm taking an extra fifteen minutes for lunch."

Ella was in a light, playful mood when he next arrived for lunch. A little more cocky than usual, and wore a bright, wide glowing smile.

"I brought something special for you today Martin."

She pulled two steaming foil packages from a large bag.

"Aunt Hattie bakes the best Shepherds pie I ever tasted."

"Looks like I'll have to save room for dessert."

"It's our meal you silly goose."

"Pie for lunch?"

Ella tore a dish open and passed it across the table to Martin, then opened hers.

"Better eat before it gets cold Martin."

"This is wonderful Ella. I've never eaten anything like this before. Give my compliments to your aunt."

"Will do. Hey, before I forget, I wish to invite you to aunt Hattie's church. I'm singing two hymns on Sunday."

"I wouldn't miss you sing for anything in the world Ella. Another special occasion?"

"Nothing special. I'm attending Blessed Hope with my aunt now."

"I'll bet they are elated you chose to sing for them."

"Don't expect it to be like at the wedding, they do not own a sound system. But the acoustics in that small church are wonderful, even without a microphone."

Martin failed to mention he does not own a car. He rode with J.B. to Luella's wedding. He pondered this situation as he crossed the street to his apartment.

Perhaps I can borrow Kent's bicycle. I wonder if I

still know how to ride one?

Not paying attention to where he is walking, he almost bumped into Mr. Nascent leaving the restaurant.

"Hey Tom, I'm glad you stopped by. The tenants requested permission to do some more remodeling work to the staircase and hallway. They will cover the costs like always."

"I didn't think they can improve any further on what they already did. How you ever come up with such amazing neighbors is a wonder. George and Marie's baby is adorable! Whatever you choose to allow done to the building is perfectly fine with me."

"Odd to catch you over this way during the day Tom."

"I was checking the cost for them to cater a small gathering I put together. Much higher than I can afford."

"Who did you talk to Tom? Did you let them know you own the building?"

"A new fellow I did not recognize."

"Sounds like one of the hired staff. Wait here, while I go get an owner."

Martin ran upstairs and knocked on George's door. Marie said he was working at the bank. He tried Dan's door, got no answer; so went to apartment number one. He lucked out, and caught Jim home working.

"Hi Jim, Tom, our landlord, is putting together a little party he needs catered. He doesn't have enough money to cover the cost. As a favor to me, will your group cover the expense?"

"Tell him we've got him covered for whatever he wants. No charge."

"He'll be glad to hear that Jim, thanks a million."

Martin came running back down the stairs with a huge smile on his face. Calling Tom to follow him back inside the restaurant. Martin talked to the catering attendant.

"May I check the details you worked up for Tom's

order?"

"Yes, sorry Martin, let me pull the ticket from the trash can."

Martin glanced over the order, and noted many basic line items scratched out.

"This order is painfully sparse. What can we do to make a memorable feast?"

"Mr. Hurston, sir, the gentleman's budget. How do I say this? It is lacking. I cut some of the essentials, and the cost is still more than he can afford."

"May I see the order placed by Mr. Crofts. Not the business order, the one for his mother's birthday party."

The caterer left to fetch the Crofts order from his office, Martin asked Tom a few pertinent questions about his party. Number of guests and type of event.

"Here we are Mr. Hurston."

Martin took the Crofts order and after looking over the menu; made a few pencil changes, and handed the paper to Tom to study.

"Would something like this be more like what you intended Tom?"

"Yes, this would be perfect. But look at the cost Martin, I could never come up with this amount of money."

Martin only smiled at Tom, and showed the order to the attendant, pointing out the pencil notations.

"Duplicate this order for Tom, and make the necessary adjustments to fit the type of gathering and number of guests. Do not discuss costs, they are fully covered."

"Yes Sir Mr. Hurston."

"Martin, you can't afford this either."

"Don't worry Tom, a gift from your tenants to their favorite landlord."

Chapter Twenty-five – Rosie smitten with Martin

The newspaper continued to grow fast. J.B. spent his days out visiting new clients, drumming up more stories and advertisers. Martin's first slip-sheet started a new trend among area businesses.

Rather than competing, they pooled resources to reach specific market areas. The new lift-out way of advertising, brought several like-kind stores together. Each store offered different items on sale each week. This combined effort, brought more customers to each store.

Items buyers need, are found on sale at only one store each week. Ella's brother Earl was skeptical at first, to place an ad on the same page with his competitors. Until he learned, items he offered on sale during the week; no other stores offered in the same week.

Martin hired another full-time person, to handle these combined lift-out type ads. They made sure no two stores accidentally offered the same sales. Over time, certain items became customary, and customers learned the weekly rotation.

Martin always looked forward to locking up on Friday's, and get out of the office to attend the theater. Tonight he stepped out into the pouring rain. Afterward, he joined Clara at Curt's Over the Under Corner Deli.

"I'm sure glad this rain decided to let up Clara, before I grow a set of gills."

"Rain is good Martin, it kept you inside for the whole

show. You didn't duck out once."

"I thought you couldn't see the audience from the stage?"

"Before they dim the lights, we can identify everyone with ease. Only when the spotlights are burning us to a crisp, can we not recognize much of anything."

"Interesting Clara."

"Once we spot where someone is seated, we can make them out from the wings. Oh, I've been keeping my eye on Rosie. Curious about why she seemed so afraid to meet you. I figure she might be trying to hide something."

"Well, what did an ace reporter like yourself find out about her Clara?"

"It's not what I found out so far, but what I haven't yet. She changed a little."

"I listen to her sing every Friday, ever since returning from the service. Beautiful voice, nothing changed in her voice or manner."

"You wouldn't unless you were backstage. She now studies the audience looking for you?"

"I didn't realize she even knew I existed."

"Oh, she is aware alright, and long before you asked to speak to her."

"Honestly?"

"Yes, and after meeting you, she changed the most."

"What do you mean by changed Clara?"

"I sensed she was nervous the first time she spotted you in the audience. Everyone knows you are a reporter, and she loathes reporters with a passion."

"We're not so bad Clara."

"To her, you are, by the impressions she gives. She ran back to her dressing room to put on more makeup, which caused us to run a double routine the first night. She was so upset, about seeing you. I thought she was hiding from someone."

"You say it happened the first time she spotted me in the audience?"

"Yes. The second or third week after you moved into your apartment."

"Were you spying on me Clara?"

"No, but I did sorta keep my eye on you for a while, before I met Dale."

"I remember. You did leave a somewhat strong impression."

"Yeah, well anyway, back to what I was saying. Rosie didn't seem so nervous, once she learned you were a regular. She often gazed around the curtain to find where you were sitting. She also mentioned you did not always stay for the whole show."

"How did you learn she caught me slipping out?"

"She made a few comments. Even said once, on your salary perhaps you could only stay for the solo. I overheard Wilton tell her you bought the most costly, center loge seat tickets. Which is why I became interested in you."

"I'm glad Dale rescued me. Dare I ask what other types of comments she made?"

"Oh, only idle backstage talk. She did get to bragging about how 'she' had an edge-of-the-seat admirer, whom often only stayed long enough for 'her' solos, then leaves."

"Well, she is right, I often do come, for the sole purpose of listening to her sing."

"Gee whiz, thanks a lot Martin. You really know how to hurt a girl."

"I didn't mean it that way Clara."

"Oh Martin, just razz-in ya. Hey, when I first mentioned you wanted to meet her, she nearly freaked out big time. Ranting and raving about how reporters do this, that and the other thing."

"Now this I've gotta hear."

"Later, midway through the show. She comes up to

me and tells me to ask you meet her at the exit, right after her week after next's solo. On the night you met, she did the strangest thing Martin."

"What did she do?"

"She came out of her dressing room with all her makeup still on, and even added more touch-ups."

"So, she usually removes her makeup?"

"Yes, we all try to get this theater grease off our faces as soon as possible. It is awful on our complexion."

"You said she changed after meeting me."

"Yes, and noticeable too. Well, not immediately, but over the next couple of weeks. Rather than being nervous, she looked forward to seeing you in the audience. One other thing too. She started facing you when she sang. Unless you were too far off to the side."

"Only a coincidence Clara."

"I don't think so Martin, she sings with a smile on her face. A bit more than only being happy you came. Like she is trying to impress you as well."

"Now you are kidding with me, of course."

"No I'm not Martin. I caught something I don't understand at all. If you are not in your seat when she leaves her dressing room. She becomes a big jumble of nerves. Almost like she is afraid to leave the theater."

"Makes no sense to me. Does it to you?"

"Maybe. Last week, she opened the stage door to leave, turned around and ran back to her dressing room. She came out wearing some fresh light makeup, and drove out the rear exit. I'm sure she is hiding something."

"She certainly is paranoid about reporters?"

A horn honked by the door.

"Dale's here, thanks for waiting with me."

Clara ran out the door before Martin could respond. Curt was still in the back cleaning up. So Martin stayed in his seat thinking about the information Clara shared with him about Rosie.

Clara is not privy to Ella and I eating lunch together, or about her showing a greater interest in me. Did I play my cards right? Ella no longer thinks I associate her to Rosie. If they are not the same person, does Ella even know Rosie? They must be the same person, that's all there is to it. I need to get to the bottom of this.

Chapter Twenty-six – Ella smitten with Martin

Kent left his bicycle on the newspaper's loading dock. Before walking home on Friday night after work, he gave Martin the key to the lock. Sunday morning brought heavy rain, and Martin truly desired to hear Ella sing again. A car kept honking in front of the restaurant.

The restaurant is closed, what does that idiot want anyway.

Jim tapped on Martin's door, then knocked harder.

"Your ride is here Martin."

"Thanks Jim."

Martin grabbed his coat, wondering who it is. He got downstairs where Kent is waiting.

"I didn't know you had a car Kent."

"Keep it between you and me Martin. J.B. thinks he pays me too much as it is."

"Your secret is safe with me."

"I realized when I got up this morning, you wouldn't be able to use my bike; and wherever you wanted to go, seemed mighty important to you."

"I have an invitation to attend a church, this side of Clopton Hills."

"Which church? I hope not the one with a preacher who sounds like a tobacco auctioneer. You can hear him scream six blocks away."

"I hope not myself Kent. Blessed Hope is where I need to go."

"That's where Luella got married. Best church in town, I'll get you there in a jiffy."

"You are welcome to come in Kent."

"Can't, not allowed by my church."

"Though you just said it was the best church in town."

"I did, because it is. I could go to Luella's wedding, but I cannot attend their services. I'll explain on Monday. If I'm late getting to my church, they make us go a second time. Bye."

Martin could not help but chuckle to himself as Kent sped down the street. Before going inside, he glanced around at the parked cars. Ella's coupé was near the back of the church, and no sign of Rosie's roadster; which he did not expect to see.

The church is crowded, extra folding chairs were placed under the choir loft. More chairs were added behind the side aisles to catch the overflow. Martin took a seat under the leading edge of the choir loft.

He cocked his head to one side, and kept his eyes turned up, hoping to catch Ella if she leaned over the rail. At this angle, he could never tell if she peered over it anyway. The stair to the loft squeaked, and he turned toward the sound.

Ella was standing on a step, searching the back pews, checking each person. Her head turned side to side as she followed each row. She stepped off the stairs to view the those seated under the loft. When she spotted Martin, she smiled and ran up the stairs as if floating on wings.

Is Ella so interested in me, she went out of her way to check if I was here?

A bent feather in a lady's hat several pew's up caught Martin's eye. The angle reminded him of the theater. He visualized the broken fan which closed another theory he once held. His focus shifted to the many things Clara mentioned about Rosie's recent behavioral changes.

Martin stifled a grin, as the choir began to sing slightly

off key for the first few notes. When they finished, a pitch pipe above him, sounded a note. Martin leaned back in his seat and closed his eyes. Ella's voice filled the church.

No one in the congregation moved a muscle as she sang. No sound, other than her beautiful voice, the tones of which Martin recognized all too well. He closed his eyes again, a slight trill gave her away. An image of Rosie in her flowing gown filled his mind.

How long shall I hide the fact I am now certain? No two people can sing exactly alike.

The preacher gave a wonderful, authoritatively pious, yet reserved sermon. Informative and memorable, without the theatrics so commonly displayed in other area churches. Another short song by the choir faded into the background as Ella joined in.

This blended chorus enhanced the quality of the music. The bass singers kept a steady beat, a rhythmic tempo, which rose and fell with Ella's inflections.

She sings better here in church, purer and more lovely than at the theater.

The choir sang their final psalm of the day, and as they lowered their voices; the preacher made the usual closing invitational, prevalent in this denomination. After a prayer, he announced everyone should move to the ancillary building for dinner.

I didn't wonder about finding where, by myself, as Ella rushed to my side.

"We serve a little bite to eat out back, would you like to join me?"

"Thought you would never ask. I would love to join you."

Ella introduced Martin to the pastor first, then to a few parishioners who served as greeters at the door. Once inside, she pulled him over to meet her aunt Hattie, who was tending the refreshments counter.

For each introduction, especially when she introduced

Martin to her aunt Hattie, Ella did so in a most formal manner.

"Auntie, this is Mr. Hurston, Editor in Chief, of the Ash Brooke Citizen newspaper."

Ella and Martin made their way through the serving line and selected a seat. Martin gasped, almost choked on his food, when he spotted Wilton Stoddard seated at the far end of the next table over.

I know Ella perceived where I was looking, and how seeing him startled me.

Martin paid attention throughout his meal, of how the people moved around and talked with one another. As Ella and Martin milled around the room, he could tell Mr. Stoddard kept as far a distance as possible from Ella. Each time they moved, he moved.

Wilton reached the point of obviously avoiding being near Ella and I. Martin, quit thinking nonsense, Roland would tell you, it's all in your head.

Martin stopped to speak with one man from the choir, while Ella helped her aunt clear the tables. Another man carried one of the trash containers outside. Two men walked across the room and stood right behind Martin. He overheard their conversation.

"Who is that robust fellow speaking with the pastor's wife?

"Don't know his name Ed, only seen him here a couple of times, for special shindigs."

"That's right, he's the fellow who brought the sound equipment. Never visited on a Sunday. Have you met him?"

Another coincidence, or did they stage this to throw me off?

"I'm not to fond of overly crowded rooms Martin, I need some fresh air."

As they walked toward the door, several members stopped Ella to thank her for joining their church. Each complimenting her with higher accolades than the one before.

"Looks like you are a big hit Ella!"

"Aunt Hattie made sure everyone learned I joined her church, which is why so many crowded in today. Including several from Grace Miracle. They looked bored to death during the sermon."

"I'm sure they only came to enjoy your singing."

"Or report back to my mother's pastor I defected. I'm bound to get some flack over leaving them."

"I wouldn't let them worry you Ella. I can tell you feel more comfortable here."

"Auntie sure is proud I agreed to join."

"Her glowing face shows how thrilled she is with you."

Most of the folks were gone. Hattie is still inside, making sure the room is cleaned up properly. Ella looked around at the remaining cars.

"How far away did you park Martin?"

"Due to the rain, Kent Horn dropped me off at the door."

"Open tops are dreadful in the rain."

"So are bicycles. I made arrangements to use Kent's to get here today. He surprised me by stopping at the apartment to offer me a ride this morning. Wait, Kent's car isn't an open top. It's a runabout, like your Waltham, only older."

"Then he must own more than one car. He passes by the mill on his bicycle every night. From the back window I can view his parked bike inside the gate at the wire works. He hops in a little open top two-seater, and drives up Simmons Parkway."

"Well I'll be. I wondered how he was able to get so many north side stories and ads."

"He is a most thoughtful and conscientious boy. Delivers the paper right to my desk every Friday morning.

He even sharpens my pencils while waiting for Jerome to bring another cart of papers, for the west subscribers."

Hattie locked the door and marched over to Ella and Martin.

"We best be going Ella, I have patients to visit, and I'm late."

"Just a second auntie. How are you getting home Martin?"

"No sign of rain, I can use the exercise of a pleasant walk.

"Nonsense, you can ride with us."

Hattie let out a loud sound of disapproval. Ella leaned over to whisper in Martins ear.

"I must run to drop auntie off at the hospital. If you don't mind waiting for ten minutes, I'll be right back. You can view their tower from here."

Ella went to get her car. Aunt Hattie gave Martin a sharp-eyed good looking over.

"Well, I guess you can stand on the running board."

"That won't be necessary Mrs. Platte. I only live a few blocks away, and you are going in the opposite direction. It was a pleasure meeting you."

Martin began walking toward home, knowing he would not get far in only ten minutes. Ella tooted her horn lightly as she pulled next to aunt Hattie, who was watching Martin cross the street.

"You must be careful around those reporter fellows Ella, can't trust a single one of them."

"He's the Editor in Chief of the newspaper auntie, nothing to worry about."

"No matter Ella, he's still a reporter, and that can be mighty dangerous."

"Here we are auntie, I'll pick you up at three sharp."

"Don't be late, I need to prepare dinner."

Ella found Martin only two blocks from the church,

and began teasing him.

"If you keep walking that slow, you'll never get home. Need a ride stranger?"

"Howdy ma'am, yes ma'am, appreciate the lift ma'am."

"You nut, get in before I change my mind."

"I enjoyed a wonderful service, met a distinguished pastor; listened to an excellent choir, and the best soloist ever who graced the church with her beautiful voice. Think she'll be back anytime soon?"

"She might, never can tell. Thanks for coming Martin."

"I would walk the whole way in the rain, to listen to you sing Ella."

"You are sweet Martin. Well, here we are. Tomorrow it's back to the same old routine."

"I dread the thought. I'll meet you for lunch on Monday."

Martin sat in the car staring into Ella's eyes. He felt she may be leaning toward him, coming closer, closer. Her voice shattered the moment.

"I can't wait here all day. Are you getting out?"

"Sorry, I thought you were getting ready to, uh, say something."

Martin got out and stepped up on the curb.

"Thanks for the ride Ella."

"You are most welcome. Oh, if it's raining tomorrow, we recently placed another lunch table on the covered west dock."

Chapter Twenty-seven – Martin abandons his theory

Martin climbed the stairs to his apartment, and plopped down in the new overstuffed chair. He leaned back and stared at the ceiling, thinking. His mind is in a whirl, confused, yet certain. Questions roll through his mind.

Who started our lunches together, Ella or I? Why did she invite me to hear her sing today? Rosie is aware I never missed a performance. If Rosie and Ella are the same person, surely she would realize I could recognize her by her voice. Would she take such a chance, if she didn't want to be discovered? What happened in the car?

Martin moved over to his desk and sifted through a folder. Rosie, Ella, Rosie, Ella, he read each note before crushing the paper between his hands. After a tight squeeze, he let the crumpled ball drop into the waste can.

Martin, you are a fool, you know that, a downright fool.

He grabbed the waste can and marched down the back stairs. He dumped the contents into the ash pit and struck a match. As a flaming ball unfurled, he caught a two year old date. Martin sat down on a crate, and stared into the pit. His thoughts race as he picked up a stick to turn the last few scraps.

What if I'm wrong? I'm sure I am not, but what if I am? It could ruin everything.

Martin continued to sit and stare into the pit. With

the tip of his stick, he flicked the cold dead ashes over and over. Suddenly the serious expression on his face faded, and he generated a smile.

I enjoyed my time with Ella today, and I think she did too.

He picked up the waste can and bounded up the stairs, two steps at a time. The empty folder on his desk, representing two wasted years, glared back, mocking him. He ripped the folder to shreds, as if inflicting the death sentence.

The pieces fell atop his desk. He retrieved each piece and tore them over and over, until nothing but confetti remained. With a final sweep of his hand, he brushed them away. The trash can devour every last speck of his madness.

A ray of sunshine from the setting sun reflected from a glass pyramid paperweight. Past dinnertime, and almost bedtime. Martin checked the refrigerator for some cold cuts.

Where has the day gone?

After bathing, he climbed into bed. He tossed and turned, sat up, stared out the window, then fell backwards on his pillow. The ceiling seemed to laugh at him. He turned over and buried his face in the pillow, now the clock taunts him, tick, tick, tick.

A distant factory horn warned him to skip breakfast or be late. Martin cannot concentrate at work. The clock dragged on ever so slowly and appeared not to move. He heard the first factory lunch whistle. A lifetime passed before the next whistle blew.

Martin grabbed his lunch bag and shot out the door. He checked his wristwatch every fifteen seconds while seated at the picnic table. Another eternity passed before Ella came out the door.

"Appears they are making way for the new machines."

"Yes they are, and what a dusty mess they made

inside."

Ella had not taken her eyes off his, since they started eating. Martin tried to focus on his sandwich, only catching short glimpses, long enough to note she remained transfixed. When he finally peered into her eyes, she turned her head down long enough to take one bite.

For the rest of the lunch period, they stared into each others eyes, finishing their sandwiches without checking each bite. Ella giggled first. The contagion was overcoming, and Martin soon followed.

Other than an occasional giggle, not another word was spoken. A whistle blew, Martin reached to crumple his empty bag. Ella reached to do the same, her hand landed on top of his. They both pulled back as if shocked. Ella giggled as she stood, then hurried inside.

Martin remained seated until Ella sat down at her desk. She glanced outside at Martin still sitting, watching her through the window. She made a motion with her hand to shoo him away. He smiled as he stood and turned to return to the newspaper.

Luella understood that look all too well, and while alone in the building, she teased Martin mercilessly. When another employee entered the front office, Luella warned.

"Better go wash the smirk off your face before J.B. gets back."

She offered the perfect escape line, so he moved far away from Luella as ordered. Martin ducked into the washroom to study his face in the mirror.

Looks like the same old face to me.

He washed up anyway, then returned to his desk. By the time J.B. came in the door, Martin was hard at work. He dropped a stack of notes on Martin's desk as he whisked by. After hanging up his coat, J.B. snapped his wide green suspenders and returned to Martins desk.

"Need you to check these out Martin, I'm getting conflicting stories. I believe you are familiar with two of the witnesses."

Martin flipped through the notes.

"I'm acquainted with one of them, I'll get right to work J.B."

He grabbed his hat and coat and slipped out the door. When he turned to push it shut, Luella made a seductive face and gesture at him from the back room.

The next evening, Roland stopped at the newspaper.

"Hey Martin, you ready to go?"

The men crossed each others' path on Liberty Street last week, and Roland invited Martin to his home for a Tuesday night dinner.

"Give me one second Roland, I don't want to keep your better half waiting too long."

They conversed on their drive from the newspaper over to Roland's house.

"I picked up a little information you may be interested in. A case I'm working on took me up to the north side Friday evening, around the dinner hour."

"Still working on the robbery at the Trolley Depot?"

"Heck no, we nailed the suspect over a week ago. I'm on a new case. The police found an abandoned, hollowed out lumber truck, filled with empty whiskey kegs."

"The one with a canvas top and green painted stakes on the side?"

Roland's ears captured the comment and he questioned Martin.

"Why, yes. What can you tell me about this vehicle?"

"The truck passed under my apartment window a few times. I was curious why they loaded the cargo the same way each trip. Most unusual."

"Which way was he headed?"

"Toward the entertainment district. But always crossed the hill without stopping."

"Ever see him going in the opposite direction?"

"Can't say that I have Roland. What's up?"

"An officer found the left wheels tight against a curb, headed east, past Miller and Crofts, with the motor running. No sign of the driver. The police suspect foul play and dumped the case into my lap."

"Wrong side of the road. Sounds interesting, can I join you while you work?"

"Not this time Martin. After they brought the truck to the impound yard, they discovered the rear stack of planks opened like a door."

"Sounds like a whiskey runner for sure. Tell me how the story turns out."

Roland turned to back up his driveway. They went in and enjoyed a wonderful dinner.

"Mighty fine meal Mrs. Pease, mighty fine."

"Thank you Martin. Now you two scoot on in to the den while I clean up."

"The department must be paying you way too much Roland, all this new furniture."

"None is new Martin, I'm just never home long enough to sit. We've had it ever since before Platte's closed. Wonderful couple, shame Hattie had to close the clothing store after Oscar died."

"I rarely get up to the north side Roland."

"Hattie's niece works right across the street from your apartment."

"Yes, at the garment mill. Ella introduced me to her aunt a few times."

"Ella is who I learned some details about."

"I gave up on that nonsense, confused my brain for too long. You even said it was impossible."

"You never told me who you were following Martin. But I put two and two together and figured it must be Ella. She's the only gal in town one can set their clocks by."

"She's never deviated from her route yet."

"Only because you do not live up this way Martin."

"What do you mean? I have kept an eye on her, and she follows the exact same route home every single night."

"Every night except Friday nights, the night you were most interested in Martin."

"She tends to her mom."

"True, but on Tuesdays and Fridays she arrives home from the opposite direction. Tuesdays she is fifteen minutes later than usual, and Fridays she is over an hour later, than during the rest of the week."

"I can explain the reason Roland. On Tuesdays she drops the time cards off at Mr. Deckett's north office, she has told me this much herself."

"What about Fridays Martin?"

"Well, she never told me this, but Kent and Jerome pay attention to her route. She visits her aunt Hattie on Fridays. Hattie fixes a meal for them and one to take home to her mom. She is normally there for over an hour before she heads home."

"I'm glad you explained that lost hour on Friday nights Martin."

"Maybe not Roland. From what you said, she is still an hour late getting home."

"That she is Martin. Her Friday night routine has not varied one iota."

"Her mom is in the Royce Care Center now. Maybe she stops to visit on the way home?"

"Not possible Martin, she arrives coming from the southwest. Royce is in the northwest."

"I've talked to the Rosie in person myself, and although they closely resemble each other, almost a perfect double, they don't talk or act alike."

"You remember what I told you about hunches Martin. A gut feeling is usually correct. No matter how impossible it seems."

"Yes, you have said so many times before Roland, but many of my hunches never panned out. Ella sure is a mystery though. If you don't mind, let's drive past her aunt Hattie's on the way home. I want to make sure I picked the right house."

Roland took the long way around heading toward Martin's apartment.

"Coming up on the right Roland, second house in the next block."

"I didn't realize her house was so close to their old clothing store."

"Ella mentioned the store was only two blocks away."

"Well Martin, this explains why she comes home traveling east."

"Thanks for dinner and the ride Roland."

"We can dine together again Tuesday after next."

Chapter Twenty-eight – Double jeopardy

Martin sat at a news desk studying a map of the area, and thought about the things Roland told him. None of the information he supplied is something Martin was not already aware of. Except for Ella arriving home from the west on Fridays.

I'll bet she still stops by her aunt Hattie's on the way home from work. Perhaps she eats dinner with her like always. I wonder when she goes to visit her mom?

Jerome popped in the front door and stopped at Martin's desk.

"Here, Roland said to give this to you. Where is Mr. Blaine?"

"J.B. is up the street, he is meeting Mr. Burrow's. They should be outside, on the sidewalk in front of the Air Chute Company's building."

Jerome ducked out the back door. A second later he came around the building, passing the front windows on his way east to find Mr. Blaine. Martin read the note from Roland.

"We found the driver, he is alive, but in no condition to speak. Will fill you in later."

The first distant lunch whistle blew. Martin pulled his coat from the rack and tossed it over his arm. Dan, one tenant in his building, was turning the door handle one way, while Martin turned the other. Dan stepped back in a huff, to let Martin come out.

"Big trouble Martin, Mr. Nascent sold our building."

"Simmer down Dan. I talked to him yesterday, he did not mention putting it up for sale. In fact, he assured me he would not be selling the building at all."

"A huge sold sign is plastered across the front, between the two right columns."

Both men trotted down the sidewalk toward the restaurant. From a block away, the edge of the large sign was visible, and bowing out in the breeze. Martin stepped to the center of the street as they reached the front of the building. Big red letters with one word 'Sold.'

"I'll find out what I can Dan, I'm sure someone made a mistake."

Dan went upstairs to his apartment, and Martin crossed the street to meet Ella for lunch. Due to the seriousness of what was on his mind, Martin was not the slight bit giddy when he first sat down to eat.

After he and Ella sat for a bit, hurrying through their late meal, they looked like two star struck teenagers. Martin took the last bite of his sandwich before speaking.

"How's your mom Ella?"

"She is doing better. Loves living at Royce, and made many new friends. Thank you for asking about her."

"Do you get to visit her often?"

"I visit her every night, and on Saturday's right after dinner. In the afternoon on Sundays."

"Sounds wonderful. Must be hard on you though. When do you ever find time to rest?"

"They are not allowed visitors during dinner hour; so I go home, change clothes, prepare dinner, eat, and drive over afterward."

"Aren't visiting hours over soon after dinner?"

"Not until eight. Mom would never play cards or bingo, so I visit her in the lounge during those activities. They do run past visiting hours, but they are fairly lenient. I always head straight toward the door when they flash the hall lights, so they don't say anything."

"I hear their service and care is wonderful."

A whistle on another factory blew. Ella jumped to run inside.

"I'll pick you up for church on Sunday Martin."

"What about your aunt Hattie?"

"She likes to arrive early. After I drop her off, I will come to get you."

"I hate for you to go out of your way Ella."

"I like having my best fan listening."

Oh my, did I say that?

"I consider you more than a fan Martin. I must get inside now."

Ella reached for Martin's hand as her factory whistle shrieked. Martin took to heart the words she spoke. He arrived at the newspaper to find Luella crawling around on the floor collecting type.

"It's a good thing we are getting the Linotype soon. These old cabinets are falling apart."

Martin slipped the front rail back in its slot, using a strip of paper to wedge the bar tight. He helped Luella sort the type back to their proper slots in the drawer.

"They will start the installation in two more weeks Luella."

"Yeah right, they promised to deliver in two weeks for over three months now."

"This time it's for real, and the installers are on their way."

"What, we haven't made enough room yet."

"Don't need to. I rented the back of Mike's new diner extension. They will cut a door right here, and we get half of his loading dock too."

"Wonderful, we definitely needed more space in here."

"The new machine is huge, larger than I expected. The

components that go with it fill several crates. There, I'm done, would you like me to help you set type?"

"I'm almost finished, but if you could block the chases, it would be a big help."

Martin could perform the task in his sleep, and drifted into intense thought. Luella finished, put her coat on, and left to catch her bus. Martin did not realize she had gone until J.B. barked at him.

"What's the matter with you Martin? You've been pacing the floor for the past hour. Time to go home."

"Oh nothing J.B., only something about Friday nights and leaving the paper for the weekend."

"Well, ducking out of here never bothered you before. Let's go."

J.B. slipped out the front door. Martin locked up behind him and pulled down the shades. J.B. paused on the sidewalk long enough to see Martin douse the lights. When he heard the back door close, he got in and started his car.

Don't know what's with that boy lately. He's been acting mighty peculiar these past few weeks. Like a kid in love for the first time. I'm sure he's not seeing or dating anyone. Or is he?

He pulled the car far enough forward to make certain Martin was walking home. Satisfied, J.B. pulled out to get himself home. Martin reached his apartment, he had not seen Mr. Nascent to ask about the big sold sign on the building.

I hope I don't have to face any of the tenants, until I find out what's up.

Martin climbed the stairs to his apartment. He dropped down in his easy chair, unsure of himself about going to the theater tonight.

If I don't go, this will be the first time I will miss Rosie's solo. What if she is looking for me? If I do go, and Rosie is Ella, how they feel about me will be evident.

Maybe I can stay in the back and not be seen.

It was after dark when Martin arrived at the theater. He waited in the lobby until the lights dimmed. Sensing it safe, he crept inside the door, and found a seat in the upper loge. Rosie's performance was flawless as usual. Obvious to Martin, she over enunciated her tell tale trill, more so than ever before.

Did she emphasize on purpose? Is she trying to let me know? Only one way to find out.

Martin left the theater and stood at the exit Rosie normally uses. He made sure he was under the street light, and in clear view of her car. Rosie changed her gown, but did not remove her makeup.

Rosie backed from her parking space, and drove to the decision area of the drive; where she could choose to leave by the front gate or the rear exit. She sat for the longest time before turning her wheels in his direction. She pulled up to the gate and stopped.

"So, my favorite fan awaits once again."

Her east side twang was more than strong tonight. Martin leaned down, the top of her car shaded her eyes.

"Your voice is the best and most beautiful Rosie."

"I almost didn't find you. Why were you way up in the balcony tonight?"

"Well, I was running late, and didn't want to disturb anyone."

"I must run now, catch you next Friday."

Rosie reached up and set her hand on Martin's, resting on the door. She gave a gentle pat, exactly the way Ella does. A surge of energy drained from his legs. His heart lodged in his throat. He tried to call out Ella's name. His mouth opened, but emitted no sound.

After she pulled out of the parking lot, Rosie only drove to the end of the block. She stopped and turned her head. Looking at Martin through the back window of her car, she backed up about five feet and stopped.

Whatever her thoughts, she changed her mind, put the car in forward gear and proceeded on down the street. She turned up Pottery Row rather than going straight to the highway. The same way Ella goes home.

Was she going to come clean and admit she is Ella? Is that why she turned where she did?

Martin returned to the theater for the remainder of the nights show. Not seeing Clara, he skipped the last part of the closing number. When he reached the back stoop, she was patiently waiting, seated on the steps at the stage door.

"My, you are out early tonight."

"I was not in the last act. Wilton gave my spot to one of the contest winners. The poor girl is an excellent performer and needed a break with a better part."

"Good for her, bad for you, eh."

"I'm OK with what he does from time to time. I'm still paid regardless. Let's hurry and get down to Curt's, I need to talk to you."

"What's up Clara? Curt's will be packed as usual."

"He still uses the Under Corner for private parties."

After they arrived at Curt's, Clara stopped a waitress Curt hired when he moved upstairs.

"Martin and I will be downstairs in the corner. I would like a pecan pie tonight."

Clara nods at Martin.

"I think the Russian salad for me tonight Nora."

Clara led Martin down the side stairs and they take a table by the window.

"You must have something mighty serious to say tonight Clara."

"I have a few things, but first, here is a blazing hot scoop for you."

"Whoa Clara, is this accurate? You should alert the police."

"Already did Martin, they will follow up tomorrow

morning. You should be at the scene."

"Thanks, I will be."

"Oh, and here is more about the abandoned truck."

"How do you come up with this stuff Clara?"

"Well Martin, street words get around fast."

Nora delivered the pie and salad, pulled Martin's hat off his head and set it on a table behind her. No sooner than she scooted back up the stairs, Clara scowls and lays into Martin.

"What on earth is going on between you and Rosie?"

Martin choked on his bite, and grabbed the glass of water. A leaf of lettuce stuck to the roof of his mouth. Once freed with his fork, he took another drink.

"What do you mean Clara? Absolutely nothing is going on. We've been all through this before. Rosie did stop at the exit tonight, but only for a moment."

"You know exactly what I mean Martin."

"Honest Clara, I have no idea about what you are talking about."

"You can't be serious Martin, plain as the nose on your face. I hope you never try to play poker, you can't hide anything."

"Let's start over Clara. Fill me in on what you think and we can go from there."

Clara glares at Martin for the longest time, devouring two whole bites of pie and took a drink before saying another word. Studying Martin's bewildered face the whole time.

"You honestly don't know, do you?"

"Haven't the foggiest Clara."

"You are aware Rosie looks for you in the audience every week."

"Yes, I realize she does. You mentioned so several times."

"She didn't locate you tonight, and I couldn't tell for sure if she was upset, or if her sigh meant relief or something else."

"I was there."

"I know you were. Everyone backstage keeps and eye out to tell Rosie where you are seated."

"So now I'm a marked patron, eh."

"No, but after Linda told Rosie you were up in the balcony, she ran to the side curtain. After she spotted you, it was like she melted. Her entire face lit up like a school girl."

"Well, I am her favorite fan."

"It's much deeper Martin. Are you two seeing each other in secret, away from the theater?"

"Clara, I've only spoken to Rosie three times now, the third time was tonight. Each time was at the parking lot exit."

"I don't believe you Martin, you both wear that look."

"That look eh. Well Clara, I can explain. Luella teased me about it the other day. I am seeing someone, sorta, but neither of us have admitted to it ourselves yet."

Clara changes chairs, so her back is to the window, and she can be closer to Martin's ear.

"Tell me more Martin, and don't leave out the juicy stuff either."

"Nothing to tell. We only had a few short lunches together. But recently we've had the giggles when we are together."

"That's what I mean Martin, Rosie is acting the same way."

Curt yelled down the stairs.

"Clara, Dale's outside blasting that confounded loud horn of his."

"Coming Curt. Better go before Curt rings his neck."

Martin, overwhelmed by the scolding from Clara, and

intrigued by her accusations; stayed in his chair to let her words sink in.

Rosie's voice had Ella's distinctive trill. She stopped to talk, then stopped again. Now Clara thinks we have something going on. Says Rosie is giddy now too. Could my suspicions be right? Or just another coincidence?

Ella enjoys picking me up for Sunday services, and I think she is feeling the same things I am. Rosie's touch reminded me of Ella's. Can it only be my wild imagination playing tricks on me? What if they are two different people, and I'm sensing the same attraction to both. If so, man am I in trouble now!

"Closing up Martin."

"On my way Curt."

"Looks like you generated some girl problems Martin."

"Why is everyone telling me it's written all over my face?"

"Well, if I were you Martin, I would avoid considering Clara."

"Clara, Clara, she's just a friend Curt, nothing more, I assure you."

"Your face tells a different story Martin."

"It's not Clara, Curt. I might have a girl, not sure yet, and not Clara."

"The question is, does this girl feel the same about you Martin? Now get outta here."

Chapter Twenty-nine – A stroll in the park with Ella

From his apartment window, Martin kept vigil for Ella to come driving down the street. As she turned on Liberty, he hurried downstairs to meet her.

"Good Morning, what a beautiful day."

"Yes, and if not for aunt Hattie, the top would be down."

"I appreciate you going out of your way."

Martin's hands are resting on his legs. Ella reached over and set her hand on his.

"We've been seeing a lot of each other lately. I enjoy having lunch with you."

"I sense a 'but' coming on."

"Oh no, nothing like that Martin."

Ella squeezed the back of his hand. A girlish smile hinted at hiding a giggle.

"It's, well, you know so little about me, and told me almost everything about you."

Ella put her hand around Martin's neck and pulled him closer. She leaned and gave him a quick peck on the cheek. Sat upright and reached down to put the car in gear.

"So, you are feeling the same things I am, aren't you Ella."

She smiled back at him without saying a word. After they turned in the church parking lot, Ella responded to his question.

"Yes Martin, I have for a long time now, but wasn't sure about how you felt, until recently."

Martin ran around the car to get Ella's door. When he reached to take her hand to help her out, she pulled back.

"Not here, not yet."

Ella winked at Martin, which gave him pause for a second. He also thought about her last comment. He followed behind her in to the church. Hattie came running to the door.

"Martin, I'm glad you are here early. Would you be a dear and be so kind as to pull another cart of chairs over, and help set them up."

"Glad to help Mrs. Platte."

"We're expecting a larger crowd than last week."

"I'm sure Ella is the reason."

The church filled to capacity. Even though they had more chairs available, not a spot remained large enough to open another. Martin stood by the staircase leading to the choir loft, leaning against the large wooden column.

Hattie came down the aisle between the pews and the chairs, and pulled on Martin's jacket to follow her. The third pew from the front was reserved for church workers. She motioned for Martin to take a seat, then she sat down beside him, on the end.

She was up and down a few times, switched a vase of flowers with two ferns at the podium. Martin caught her glancing up toward the choir loft, so he turned and looked up as well.

I did not realize the choir had so many members.

He did not find Ella among them. A small bell rang and he turned back toward the front. Hattie opened the hymn book and held it centered between Martin and herself. He reached over to help support the weight.

A placard on the wall, opposite the podium, displayed

the page numbers for today's hymns. Hattie turned to a
hymn Martin can sing well. Martin never studied music, so
was unfamiliar with the notes or key. His tenor voice
blended perfectly with Hattie's alto, enough so, Hattie was
more than pleased. She put her right hand on his arm and
gave a squeeze.

*For somebody who hates reporters, she sure
appeared to change her mind mighty fast.*

The choir sang the next beautiful hymn, and when Ella
began to sing, the choir quieted and slowly fell to a soft
background accompaniment.

From the corner of my eye, I caught the smile on
Hattie's face every time Ella sang. She was proud of her
niece and it showed.

Hattie removed a compact from her purse, and
discreetly positioned the mirror in her palm. She focused
on the reflection of Ella in the choir. After the sermon, the
choir sang again. Ella's pronounced trill was more evident
during her last solo.

Then, as a surprise to Martin, and apparently, even a
bigger surprise to Hattie. Ella used a closing crescendo.
Obviously Rosie's trademark. Hattie made a sharp turn
and glared toward the choir. When she turned back, she
was not smiling.

Could Hattie possibly know Ella is Rosie? What
ridiculous thoughts you have Martin. Or are they? I
perceived Hattie's intent stare, as if trying to read my face.

Hattie had things to attend to up front after the
services. She started down the aisle, and Martin stopped
her.

"Would you like me to stow the chairs Mrs. Platte?"

"Thought you would never ask, yes please."

"Your niece sure has a beautiful voice."

She did not comment, but forced a smile before
scurrying off to perform other chores. With the help of
several church members; the chairs were returned to the

carts, and the carts moved behind a divider in the front part of the church.

Martin did not recognize a single soul in church this week, except Hattie, Ella, and perhaps a person who resembled Mr. Morgan. Ella descended the stairs, and Hattie rushed over to her. Martin could not hear what was said, but it appeared to be a mild scolding.

Why would Hattie do that? Unless she is fully aware Ella is Rosie. Nonsense Martin.

The last two men shuffled outside, Ella and Hattie walked over to Martin. Ella was talking to Hattie.

"What a crowd, several from mom's church visited again today."

"They didn't come for the services, they only came to hear you sing."

"I'll go get the car auntie."

Hattie locked the church, and as Ella pulled up, Martin walked a few steps across the parking lot, headed toward the street. Hattie called after him.

"Wait up Martin."

Martin returned to the car. Hattie scooted herself so tight against Ella, she could push her right through the door. Hattie patted the seat beside her. Martin sat down and snuggled up tight against the passenger door; to leave space between Hattie and himself.

Hattie inched her way closer to Martin, to give Ella room to shift gears.

"Ella tells me you are not one of those reporter types."

"Oh auntie, don't go drilling Martin."

"It's OK Ella. I never was much of a reporter Mrs. Platte. I ran the presses until I joined the service."

"He now runs the paper auntie, Editor in Chief."

Ella gave her aunt a big smile.

"Here we are auntie."

Martin got out to let Hattie out.

"You be back here at three sharp Ella."

"Yes auntie, I won't forget. You have to fix dinner."

Martin did not get back in the car until Hattie was inside the hospital.

Should I mention to Ella I did not miss the addition of a crescendo? Better not.

"Help me put the top down Martin, too beautiful of a day to leave it up."

Ella only drove one block, then turned away from the route to Martin's apartment. She turned on Ninth Street, before they reached the highway. This road led to the older residential area. A sharp left turn on Elm soon brought them to a little wooded city park.

She stopped the car, took a long slow inhale through her nose and smiled. Martin turned to open his door. Ella hopped out of the car and trotted to the edge of the woods. She turned and laughed.

"C'mon slow poke."

Martin ran to catch up with her. Together they hiked down a short narrow walking path, which led to a heavily wooded section. After reaching a wider main trail, Ella took Martin's hand and they strolled side by side.

She led him down another narrow path, through the thickest part of the forest. The overgrown path led up to an abandoned service shed. Against the shed was a small park bench, partially hidden from the main trail by bushes.

Ella sat down and patted the seat. Martin took the cue and sat down beside her. She glanced around a few times before their eyes met.

"Beautiful here, isn't it Martin?"

"Yes, very!"

"I simply adore all the dainty flowers, the fresh clean smell of the air, and..."

Ella leaned toward Martin while speaking. Her comment cut short when their lips touched. Martin slid his arm around her waist, then partly opened one eye, to see Ella's were still closed. After a long kiss, she finally opened her eyes.

"Shame, shame, you opened yours first Martin."

They both erupted in giggles, and sat hand in hand, staring at each other for the longest time. As they stood to leave after cuddling, Martin made a mental note of the area. Centered under the bench, an unusual twinned pipe caught his eye.

Ella pulled Martin around and gave him a big hug and another kiss, followed by a peck on his cheek. With hands clasped, arms swinging together, they slowly walked back toward the car. Ella talked about the flowers, and Martin pointed out the occasional small critter.

Martin opened the car door and waited for Ella to be comfortably seated before closing it. Ella playfully pulled forward, as Martin walked around the back of the car.

On the trip home, Ella focused on diving, while Martin kept his eyes on her. She stopped in front of his apartment and hopped out of the car.

"Help me get the top back up, Hattie won't ride with it down."

Martin thought they were far from his apartment. He was so busy watching Ella, arriving home so fast surprised him.

"Home already? Thank you for a wonderful day Ella."

"Don't bring lunch tomorrow. I'm sure auntie will have a whole meal packed."

Martin walked around the car, hoping for one last kiss, and checked his wristwatch on the way.

"Five till three, you better run. Be careful."

Ella waved as she pulled away, and continued waving until she reached her turn. Martin stood vigilant on the sidewalk as she crossed over the hill on Pottery Row. Jim pulled into the parking lot, so Martin ducked behind the building to avoid speaking with him. He still had not learned anything about the sold sign.

Chapter Thirty – Martin buys the Menton Building

Two building contractors who work with the Linotype installers; were waiting in their truck when Martin arrived at the newspaper Monday morning. They made several measurements, and removed part of the wall; to check for wiring or pipes where they would cut the doorway.

Luella was furious about the workmen getting plaster chips in the type cases. Lunchtime drew close, so Martin slipped out the door to meet Ella. She appeared at the factory door, wearing oven mitts and holding a large pan.

"Let's eat on the other side. No windows face the back dock."

Martin attempted to take the heavy pan from her, but she pulled back. He followed her around to the back picnic table where she set their meal down.

"I'll be back in a sec with the dinnerware. No, sit on the other side facing me. I can't admire you when you are sitting next to me."

Ella returned, seated herself across from Martin, passed him a napkin, plate and utensils.

"I thoroughly enjoyed walking with you in the park yesterday Ella."

"Me too, and I loved sitting on the bench with you better."

Ella blew Martin a kiss, and they both giggled with each other as they ate.

"Wow, your aunt Hattie outdid herself. This is

exceptional."

"You like?"

"Better than like, I love it!"

"I confess, auntie didn't bake our lunch, I did!"

"You are a better cook than your aunt."

Ella frowned.

"So. You didn't like last Mondays lunch?"

"It was perfect Ella. I was giving you a compliment. Your aunt is a fantastic cook as well."

"You didn't like last weeks?"

"I didn't say that Ella. The meal was truly super good. Heck, we cleaned the dish and I think I ate the most."

"I'll let you off the hook this time Martin."

"There goes the whistle."

"I would like to strangle it. Help me clean up Martin."

"Yes dear."

They both continued their giggles while cleaning up after lunch.

"You go on in to work. I'll wipe down the table before going back to the paper."

Martin chuckled when he caught sight of a few mill workers making goo-goo eyes at Ella, as they clocked in. They were not as teasing as Luella was with him.

Martin was busy editing a new journalist's column when Mr. Nascent stopped in.

"Thomas, I've been hunting for you everywhere. All the tenants are curious about the big sold sign on the building."

"Didn't you get my message? I handed a note to John, two days before the sign went up."

"No I didn't. John's not passed anything to me recently."

"I put the sign up to stop the west side buyers from pestering me."

"So the building is not sold then?"

"No it's not, and it is not for sale either. Remember my promise?"

"Well, your tenants will be glad to learn they are still safe."

"Martin, this is the only building I own down in this area. You handle almost everything for me, ever since the renovations were completed."

"It was the least I could do for you Tom. You gave me a fantastic break."

"I have a better deal for you now. How would you like to buy this building from me?"

"Oh my, I could never afford the payments Tom, you're knowledgeable of my salary."

"Since you collect the rents, you are aware of the bank deposits."

"True, but I must consider what the expenses are."

"There are only a few expenses Martin, because the tenants you selected pay for everything themselves. How you managed to find these types of tenants is beyond me. They must be crazy wanting to remodel things they don't own. Most tear a place to pieces."

"They are model residents for sure, and even bought the two lots next to the building."

"Which is why I think you should own the building, before they decide to make an offer."

"I don't think I can Tom. Working at the paper takes most of my time."

"Nothing will change from what you are doing now, and will save me the trips down here."

"How much are you asking Tom?

"That's not important. What I'm asking, and what I will sell the building to you for, is considerably different. We can also avoid using additional bank loans."

"What do you mean Tom?"

"Even though I paid cash for the building. I got a loan to buy two other buildings. The mortgage is small, and the rent from the two smallest apartments will cover the payment."

"That's not much, and you can't be selling your building for such a tiny amount."

"No, but here is the deal I'm willing to offer Martin. You take over the payments to the bank on the mortgage, and I will agree to accept a monthly payment; equivalent to what the restaurant pays in rent, as the monthly payment to buy the building.

"Taxes, insurance and utilities will take about half of the highest tenants rent. Which leaves a fair amount left over for you to keep."

"Sounds like a most generous offer. But why would you turn down the income?"

"Let's just say I have my reasons, and leave it at that Martin. However, since you are always honest with me, like the son I never had. I'll explain. I made a few bad deals I must make full restitution, or lose everything.

I do not want this building to become a part of my loss, and would hate to see what you accomplished here go to waste."

"You, a bad deal? Sure don't sound like you Tom."

"Well, things happen Martin. I speculated on some prime far west property, back when a large aircraft manufacturer was looking in this area. Now the government is considering a hydroelectric dam, which will put the land under water. They only pay farmland prices, which is far less than my mortgage."

"Maybe not Tom. Everyone is opposed to the dam, and the final location is not yet determined. If they locate the dam at Tyler's Pass, your land will be more valuable, near the edge of the lake."

"That would be wonderful, but I cannot get another extension. Consider what I am offering, you must decide by next Tuesday. I will stop in again then."

Mr. Nascent slipped out the door as J.B. entered the newspaper.

"Heard anything more about the dam J.B.?"

"Not much, other than they are looking farther north. Why do you ask?"

"Oh, no reason in-particular J.B., it just came up in a conversation is all."

"With Thomas? He owns land which may get flooded."

"Yes, and he doesn't want the dam either."

"Nobody around here does Martin. I must run up the street to talk with a womens' group on their lunch break."

"You'll have fun J.B., you always do at their meetings."

J.B. snorted at Martin's comment and stormed out the door. Luella poked Martin in the ribcage and told him to scoot, making a kissy face at him.

Chapter Thirty-one – Martin joins the choir

Martin grabbed the lunch sack from his desk and met Ella at the back picnic table.

"I didn't get to mention how much I enjoyed your solos last Sunday."

"Singing at aunties church is more enjoyable than at mom's church. Since I moved over to her church, several from mothers are now filling our pews."

"Hattie gave me the forms to fill out to become a member. She said I fit like a glove."

"You impressed her with the first hymn. She did say you could use some improvement on the others. But don't you dare tell her I told you."

"My lips are sealed."

"What's the matter with your sandwich Martin?"

"Not especially hungry."

"That's not like you. Is something bothering you?"

"Several things going on all at the same time. Getting an expensive new huge machine at the newspaper. Tom offered to sell me the building I'm living in."

"Sell you the building? What's up with the big sold sign?"

"Oh nothing. Mr. Nascent got tired of being pestered to sell the building. He moved the sign here from one of his other buildings. Sure upset and scared the tenants."

"It is a good solid building, in the perfect place too, and fully renovated. You should consider accepting his offer Martin."

"He gave me one week to study the proposition."

"Something else is on your mind besides work and the building. Shows in your eyes."

"I'm beginning to believe my face is transparent as glass. Luella even ribbed me a week before I thought sure of myself."

Ella burst forth with a contagious giggle, and Martin followed in suit. After he regained his composure enough to speak clearly.

"The new movie house opens Saturday, and they gave the newspaper several tickets. J.B. took the matinée and Luella the evening tickets. I took the afternoon tickets, and was sorta thinking it was time I asked you out on a casual date."

"Yes."

"They are in the entertainment district, and I realize how you avoid that area."

"That's fine."

"So it's OK if you don't want to go, I understand."

"I said yes Martin."

"Oh, you said yes. For real? I though you were only agreeing to what I was saying."

"I will love to go to the movies with you Saturday. Is that plain enough?"

"Wow, I never thought you would say yes Ella."

Martin abruptly turned his face toward the ground.

"Sorry, I didn't mean to put you in shock Martin. What's the problem?"

"I don't have a car, or any way to pick you up."

"Not a problem Martin. I'll meet you here at two Saturday, and we can go around by way of the River Road."

"You don't mind?"

"Not at all. I thought you would never ask, and figured

it was because you didn't own a car. Don't feel alone, I would'a never got one if auntie didn't give me her husbands old car. I hated using the bus."

"I don't like the bus either, besides, they never go where I need to."

"Boy, that's the truth."

The first distant whistle blew.

"You are a lucky man Martin. Had you asked about any other time except Saturday afternoon, I would be forced to turn you down. And I really didn't want to be in such a position when you did ask me out on our first real date. I have several obligations besides work, which consume a lot of my time."

"I know you visit your mother and Hattie."

The second whistle blew. Ella jumped to her feet, and finished the conversation as she ran toward the door.

"I also help Mr. Deckett with his other factories, practice with the choir, take auntie shopping and to the hospital. I'm busy most of the..."

The mill's side door closed, cutting off her last words. Martin took his time walking back to the paper. Several thoughts raced through his mind.

Of all the tracking and note taking I've done over the past couple of years, I never learned what Ella did on Wednesday evenings. She probably goes straight home.

His curiosity got the better of him. After closing the paper, he returned to the garment mill and waited for Ella to come out. He did not want her to discover he was waiting for her. So he walked around the building to appear as if casually passing by, from the opposite direction.

"Hey Martin, I'm glad you are up this way tonight. Auntie would love for you to come for choir practice."

Martin did not want to be part of any choir, however, for a chance to be with Ella.

"I would love to join you!"

Ella drove straight to aunt Hattie's home. She was waiting on the porch until she spotted the car coming, then hurried down to the gate. Martin got out to let her in, and took his seat tight against the door.

The scene struck Martin a little funny when he walked in. Most of the choir members were dressed in casual or work clothes. Some were in uniforms, not their Sunday best. Hattie introduced Martin to those already present, and the few who arrived after Martin.

Almost everyone identified Martin from where he worked. However, he only recognized Hattie and a teller from the bank. An older fellow in a suit came through the door, and all conversation came to a halt.

Everyone took their normal place, as they would if they were standing in the choir. Except they lined up taking the fourth through eighth pew, facing the front.

"Hattie and I stood in the ninth pew, near the end."

The man rapped his baton on the podium and Hattie blew a note on the pitch pipe. Everyone went through a few practice scales.

"Hattie nudged me, and motioned I should do the same."

The conductor motioned for two of the men and one woman to take the front.

"Hattie elbowed me to step out in the aisle, and kept a knuckle in my back, forcing me to walk to the front."

The conductor pointed to the left of the two men and nodded for me to stand next to them. He lifted his baton and the woman sang a single note. Another wave of his baton and the first man sang a slightly lower note.

He moved his baton again, and the next man sang a little lower, he pointed his baton at Martin. Martin was a little off, but corrected his pitch. The conductor swung his wand, and up to this point, he had not said a single word since entering the church.

"Hello Martin, I am Horace. I teach 'a cappella' at the high school. Hattie informed me you executed hymn 463 perfectly."

"A pleasure to meet you. I remembered the one hymn, so joined in."

The conductor turned to the others in the front.

"Let's try this again."

Pointing his baton at the woman. This time Martin was both on cue and on key. The conductor smiled and walked back to the podium. Those in the front, including Martin, returned to their seats. Horace announced to the choir.

"Please turn to hymn 463, I wish to hear perfect myself."

Martin cringed, because he understood the conductor made reference to what Hattie told him. Horace glance across the choir members.

"Martin, will you please move to the third row, one voice left of center."

This disrupted half the pew. They had to sit to let Martin by, then stand back up again.

"Fine, fine, now let's get started."

Horace raised his baton and Hattie blew a note on the pitch pipe. The conductor kept pointing his baton at Martin, lifting and jiggling it around. He wanted Martin to do something, although Martin had no idea what.

The conductor rapped on the podium, and vigorously swished his baton back and forth. Everyone stopped singing.

"Appears we need a short lesson here, for those new to the choir."

He didn't say, because of Martin, however, Martin turned red as a beet. The lesson was fast, simple and easily learned. Martin did well during the rehearsal of the hymn. The next three were like a nightmare.

Horace asked one man and one younger lady, to come up front and sing each of them, one at a time. They were reasonably simple, so Martin picked them up with ease. They did not have time to sing the last song as a choir, rehearsal time was over.

The conductor walked down the aisle and out the door, before anyone dare move from their pews. Martin searched around the room and up toward the choir loft. No sign of Ella. Hattie came over to Martin.

"You did fine Martin. Horace rarely smiles, he was pleased with you tonight."

Most of the folks left right away. A few stood around talking near the door. Some of the older women stopped to thank Martin for joining. Hattie rescued Martin, by sending him to turn off the lights, as she urged the folks to head on home.

Martin made his way down the dark aisle to the front door, where Hattie is waiting. They step outside on the stoop and Hattie locked the door. Martin glanced around, no sign of Ella's car. He checked his wristwatch.

"My niece will be along shortly Martin. I usually wait for her over there, unless it's raining."

Hattie started down the stairs. Martin thought she pointed toward a seat at the bus stop, near the road. He began to walk in that direction; until he noticed Hattie turned left down the sidewalk, next to the church.

Between the sidewalk and the side parking area are two small benches, inside an arched trellis. After Hattie took a seat, Martin sat down on the bench across from her.

"I didn't see Ella in church."

Before Martin could say anything else, Hattie butted in.

"Ella has a reher..., uh, practice, I mean she takes voice lessons. Not every week, she'll be here for sure next week."

Martin caught Hattie's slight slips of the tongue, but kept them to himself.

"Is she always this late?"

"Not often, she usually pulls in before I get this far. Here she comes now."

Hattie rose and quickly moved to the parking lot. As Ella stopped, she said.

"How were your voice lessons Ella?"

Hattie over enunciated the word 'voice' which made Ella frown.

"Sorry I'm late auntie, we are learning something new again."

Ella dropped Hattie off at her house, and we waited until she was safely inside and her door bolted.

"I'm sorry I was running late Martin. I hope auntie didn't talk your ears off."

"I thought you came in the door with me, afterward I didn't see you in the church anywhere."

"I did come in with you. Almost forgot my prac..., lesson, no time to tell you I would be back. Besides, auntie already had you under her thumb."

"She does seem to take control."

"That's my auntie!"

Chapter Thirty-two – A new theater routine

Ella turned into the alley behind the garment mill, and pulled up to a darkened area. The building blocked both street lights and the ambient lighting from the entertainment district. She shut the engine off. Martin glanced around, no residential windows visible from that spot.

"You are not afraid of the dark, are you Martin?"

Ella giggled as she reached to pull Martin's arm behind her.

"Do you need instructions?"

She teased as she leaned over for a long kiss. Ella smelled fresh, with no hint of cologne to mask her crisp natural cleanliness. A car sped past on Brooks Ferry Road. They both sat upright, staring at each other, and giggled like two young teenagers.

Martin freed his left hand and reached up to touch her cheek with the back of his fingers. His hand unfurled as it passed in front of her ear, to allow his fingers to stroke her soft blond hair. He teasingly outlined the back of her ear with his fingertip.

As they embrace in another kiss, Martin's hand caresses her neck. His hand slid down her back, intending to move his arm down back around her waist again. He jerked away as his fingers felt the back of her undergarment through the blouse.

Martin's face turned beet red. Ella pulled him in for another kiss. She felt he would think she did not notice.

His embarrassment broke the special moment. A faint bell in the distance pealed. Martin leaned back upright against the seat and checked his wristwatch.

"We have to work tomorrow Ella."

"Yes, and you have to run the presses all day too."

Ella started the car and pulled around the mill to drop Martin off in front of his apartment. Once stopped, she leaned over for one last kiss. Ella stared deeply into Martin's eyes, until he stifled a giggle and got out of the car.

"Don't forget our date Saturday Ella."

"I wouldn't miss it for anything in the world. Ta-ta."

Martin watched her taillights flicker between pairs of buildings as she drove up Pottery Row. He spotted them once again on The Boulevard as she crossed the overpass. Martin thought about their wonderful evening together until he dozed off.

He forgot to set his alarm, and was late getting to the newspaper. Luella ribbed him about the possibility he may have stayed out too long the night before. Martin knew she didn't know anything about his being with Ella.

"I had trouble getting all the gals out of my apartment this morning."

"Yeah, I bet. You only wish Martin, you only wish."

Martin found it difficult, trying to decide whether to go to the theater on Friday night.

Clara thinks something is going on between me and Rosie. Curt thinks the same about Clara and I, and despite the similarities between Ella and Rosie; too many things just don't add up. I know Hattie almost said rehearsal, then cued Ella about voice lessons.

He finished working on another column for the newspaper, then allowed his mind to wander again.

Surely Hattie cued Ella about where she told me Ella was, and why she was late. If I go to the theater, will

Rosie stop again? Will she come clean? Is it worth the risk, or can it mess up everything between Ella and I?

The rest of the week was hectic, which kept Martin's mind off his worries. Friday finally rolled around, and Doug was waiting for him, tickets in hand. The theater was not as crowded as usual. Martin, aware the new movie house did not officially open until tomorrow, asked.

"Where do you think everyone is Doug?"

"Probably at the fair Martin, it started today. Remember last year the fourth fell on a Friday, so the theater was vacant. This year the fireworks are on Sunday night, and many of the factories will be closed on Monday."

"I wish we were, but the paper never rests. This is new!"

The theater lights dimmed while Martin finished his comment to Doug. The spotlights swept around the audience before returning to the stage as the curtains parted. The theater shuffled the choreography routines around again, to give the show a fresh appearance.

Martin did not recognize any part of the routines they were performing. Everything was different, and totally unlike any segment he had seen before. The staircase that took the place of the gazebo was not present.

Another curtain opened, a new wide platform now spanned the third tier. Martin glanced at his wristwatch. The routine ran longer than usual.

Is Rosie late?

The girls formed two double-layered circles at each side of the platform. They held their fans in a unique way, forming inner and outer bands with a gap between the rings in each. A single chorus girl moved through the gap in the opposite direction of the rings movement.

The lone girls reached the top of their respective circles and all movement stopped. The spotlights narrowed, and focused on the curtain behind the platform. Martin realized the heart formation is no longer a part of the routine.

Martin spotted Clara on a point of the arc closest to the audience. He glanced over at the other circle and Deborah was in a like position. A drum roll played as the curtains above the new platform opened, sound effects added a clip-clopping of hooves.

A country trail scene emerged as the setting. A paper horse and surrey moved across the platform, stopped in the center for a moment. As it moved off stage, Rosie stood there wearing a flowing gown, large lace hat, and carried a parasol.

She walked forward to the center of the platform, pretending to pick flowers along the way. After smelling them, she tossed real flower petals off each side of the platform, down to the girls below.

The circles closed together as colored spotlights illuminated their rising fans, simulating flower blooms opening. The audience loved this unique illusion. The lower spotlights faded and the main spotlight pinpointed Rosie on the platform.

With the theater goers used to her slow smooth ballad type of songs, the popular hot number she sang; about keeping folks on the farm after visiting Paris, came as a shock. She also danced around the platform, making gestures befitting the song.

The music slowly faded as Rosie ended her solo and she curled down on the platform. The large parasol completely covered her. The spotlight dimmed slightly, then changed to a pink glow. Other spotlights caught large soap bubbles blowing toward center stage.

More spotlights came on, and followed the bubbles until they popped. At that instant, each spotlight went out, then came back on again, focused on the parasol, which had changed to a large multicolored umbrella.

Rosie sang about blowing bubbles forever. At the end, she stepped farther back, allowing a large paper bubble to cross the stage and pass in front of her. The spotlights dimmed and she slipped backstage.

The chorus girls were moving simultaneously from the circle, to a line across the front of the stage. After Rosie's spotlight dimmed, the front stage lights went to full brightness. The girls did a new number, the Charleston, afterward the audience stood calling for an encore.

"We want Rosie, we want Rosie, we want Rosie."

Performers scheduled to do the next skit, casually came on stage carrying chairs. They sat down with their backs to the audience, and stared up at the platform, joining in the chant. Everyone could tell this was not part of their planned routine.

A stage hand ran across the stage to the orchestra pit. It got quiet in the theater and everyone sat down, as a drum roll announced a new number. The spotlights lit the curtains above the new platform.

From the side curtain, at stage floor level, Rosie appeared, wrapped in a blanket to hide her street clothes. The spotlights swung down to her position. She cleverly used this blanket as a prop during her specially selected song.

"You made me love you."

She approached each of the seated skit performers, pulling the blanket over their shoulders or back. Rosie made several enticing gestures as she sang to each one individually. Her teasing encore brought the house down. A twenty minute standing ovation followed.

Rosie sauntered off stage, and the vaudeville performers, including Clara and Deborah, swarmed the stage. The skit actors dashed out of their way, no time now for their routine tonight. Prop men worked as fast as possible, not hidden by the curtains.

With the tiers rolled forward in their way, the curtains remained open as scene segments were pulled on stage. Everything was out of sync and way behind schedule. When able to close the curtains, a good part of the audience was still standing and applauding.

The orchestra began the opening musical number for the play. The stage lights were raised, and the curtain separated. Martin ducked outside and ran to the exit gate. He was sure Rosie would probably be long gone by now.

She did get out of the theater before Martin, and was waiting in her car to see if he came out. The second she spotted Martin, she pulled up near the exit, without blocking the exit lane. Martin could not believe his eyes.

Rosie is in street clothes, no theatrical makeup, and she looks exactly like Ella. But of course she does, she is Ella. Isn't she?

Chapter Thirty-three – A hard decision about Rosie

Martin hurried over to where Rosie stopped. Rosie dropped her east side twang, and used a heavy southern Georgia drawl.

"Hey there, big boy, how did y'all like the show tonight?"

Martin is too shocked to speak at first. He is also studying her face. Black eyelashes, not the big fake ones; lipstick, and her faint mole is hard to detect.

"You were wonderful as usual Rosie. Amazing, super fantastic show tonight, plenty of action."

Martin squatted down a little to make better eye contact. He shifted a step toward the front of the car, to allow a street light to highlight Rosie's facial features.

Rosie dropped the southern drawl, leaving a hint of east side twang present in her voice.

"The crowd seemed pleased with my changes."

Martin placed his hand on the door for support. Rosie rested her hand on the back of his while making her comments. He stared into her eyes while saying.

"You bet they were. I thought they would tear the theater apart, had you not performed the last number. You brought the house down tonight Ella."

Martin's ploy failed to work, he did not get the response he had hoped for.

"I have a few minutes to spare tonight Martin. Your name is Martin, isn't it?"

"Now you're teasing me, you know my name Ella."

"Why are you calling me Ella? I think we need to talk.
Clara says there's a pie shop open at night around here
somewhere."

"Yes, Curt's Over Under, right around the corner."

"Hop in, I'll swing on over."

"It would be better if you left your car here. They're
closer than their own parking lot."

Martin noticed how Rosie exited the car, not the way
Ella gets out. Rosie also walked straight and more upright,
shorter steps than Ella's normal stride. She talked about
the changes to the show, her east side twang evident as
always.

"I'm sure you take voice lessons Rosie. Who's the best
to study under?"

"I couldn't recommend anyone in this area Martin.
Why do you ask?"

"The aunt of a friend invited me to join their church
choir."

They neared the door. Rosie stopped dead in her
tracks and turned to Martin.

"Do you know anyone at this pie place?"

"Why yes, of course I do. The owner and most of the
staff. Clara and I stop in every Friday night for dessert."

"I don't think we should be seen together Martin."

"Nonsense Rosie. It is an honor to be seen with you."

"You don't understand Martin. You own a business,
are a church goer, and I'm a show girl. Being seen with me,
well, you should consider your reputation first."

Rosie turned and started walking at a brisk pace, back
toward the theater. Her stride is almost, but not identical
to Ella's.

When they reached the corner and turned toward
Rosie's car, her heel caught a crack in the sidewalk. Martin
caught her arm, preventing a fall. She held his hand while

slipping her shoe back on. She did not let go as they walked to her car.

The touch of her hand, the way she is holding mine, is identical to Ella's clasp. The way she rubs her thumb on the back of my hand, is exactly what Ella always does.

"What is it you wanted to talk to me about Rosie?"

"Hop in the car so we have some privacy."

Martin went around the front of the car and climbed in the passenger seat.

"I have a couple of problems Martin, and things I wish to share with you."

Martin kept quiet while thinking to himself.

Perfect, she's finally going to come clean.

"I love singing at the theater. Tonight is the first time I've ever interacted with the chorus performers, although only in a small way."

"The little show you did for an encore is what brought the house down."

"I shouldn't admit this Martin, but if the audience demanded an encore, they are planned ahead of time. Not the part with the skit actors in their chairs. I did not expect one, and pulled my gown off. I could not hear the audience in my dressing room, until I came out to leave."

"For being done impromptu, and without a rehearsal, you performed beautifully."

"Of course my favorite fan would think so. Which is what I want to talk to you about. I'm not going to say I've not become attracted to you. But I live a whole other life outside the theater."

Wow, she's finally going to admit she is indeed Ella.

"A life that must remain completely separate from this job. I have additional responsibilities which require more money than I can make at my weekday job."

"I understand Ella."

"Please do not refer to me as Ella. Do you not grasp

what I am trying to say? Clara talked me into stopping to say hello to you. I didn't want to, but I sorta felt something. Your eyes proved it was more than a naïve crush on a star.

"When I stopped the second time, and our hands touched. I shouldn't, but I sensed the same spark as you. I can't help it, I'm falling in love with you too."

Martin sat without speaking for the longest time. Both staring intently at each other.

"I don't know what to say Rosie."

Rosie did not get the emotional response she expected from Martin.

"I thought as much. The way you first viewed me changed somehow. You love my singing, however, you always seem to study me. Like I'm a puzzle to solve."

Martin opened the car door, and turned to stare Rosie straight in the eye.

"You are correct Rosie. I thought you were someone I am madly in love with. Since you claim not to be her, I am dishonoring both of you by continuing this charade. I'm going to ask you point blank to be honest with me."

"Please do not ask me something you may regret asking Martin."

"I truly enjoy your singing, and can recognize your unique trill anywhere. The way you trail off a crescendo would be an impossible coincidence to duplicate. So I will ask in this manner. Are you Ella, playing the part of Rosie?"

"Martin, I asked you not to call me Ella, and I'm not some puzzle to be solved. Now good night."

Martin stood up and held the door from falling shut.

"I'm sorry if I offended you Rosie. I think it best, if I no longer attend the theater."

"Don't say that Martin, I so look forward to singing for you. Have I lost my favorite fan?"

"Ella is your identical twin Rosie. If you are not she, then I would be two timing, and that is something I cannot do."

Martin closed the door and walked toward the back of the theater. She remained parked in her Saxon until patrons began leaving the theater.

Chapter Thirty-four – Martin solves the time factor

Rosie started her car. She waited for some theater goers to cross the drive, before she pulled through the front exit gate. Clara came out the stage door, and from the stoop noticed Rosie driving east down Liberty Street.

"I knew it, you lied to me Martin."

"You are so wrong Clara. Rosie and I have nothing to do with each other, nothing at all."

"Do you realize how hard she worked, how hard we all worked, to put together tonight's show? What she went through to make it special; all for you."

"She didn't do so for me Clara."

"You think not? She does talk to me sometimes. She's aware we meet after ever show. The week before last, she asked if I was your gal. I told her no, and she confided in me she likes you a lot, more than just a lot. She expected to tell you tonight."

"She did!"

"Well?"

"I told her I am madly in love with someone else. Also, I will not be coming to the theater anymore."

"Wow Martin, a true lady of class, and you hit her with a double whammy like that."

"It's for the best Clara. Admittedly for the both of us."

"You are impossible Martin. Please leave. I'll wait for Dale right here."

"I'm disinterested in dessert myself. Will you be OK waiting by yourself?"

"Dale will be here in a minute. They closed early, everyone is at the fair anyway. Now get out of my face."

Martin started walking toward home. On his way, he turned back to check Clara a few times. Dale approached from The Boulevard, Martin motioned for him to stop."

"Clara is at the stage door. We didn't go to Curt's tonight."

"I recognize her silhouette, thanks."

Martin sat on his bed, staring out the window at the darkened theater.

How can I be so wrong? Everything about Rosie is identical to Ella. I figured Rosie faked her voice, she must be, and is good at doing so too. No two people can sing exactly alike, touch alike, use the same words to describe things.

If they are not the same person, they must be identical twins. I wonder. If they are the same, Ella knows exactly what happened all along. Is she testing me like I tested Rosie?

Martin woke up, his neck stiff, arm and hand asleep. He is still dressed, and an imprint of the window frame formed a crease in his face. His heart ached, like he lost his best friend. Martin walked over to his desk, shook his head while looking down.

What a jumbled mess. Unfinished book work, columns to edit.

Martin slammed his fist down hard on the desk. Kicked his chair hard against the wall. It bounced at an angle, slamming into the file cabinet. He jerked the chair back toward his desk, and dropped down into the seat while the chair is still rolling.

He stared out the window toward the garment mill, unable to bring the building into focus. His thoughts from the night before made it impossible to concentrate on the work he needed to get done today. His mind wandered aimlessly.

If Rosie really is Ella, I feel she would not be so upset. My thinking they are the same person, gave a false impression of my feelings for her. Now I have deeply hurt her.

Martin sat down at his messy desk, and shuffled through his notes, stacking them in piles.   An advertisement in the newspaper's entertainment section caught his eye. 'Only a three minute drive from Liberty and Vine to Paulson's Diner.'

This can't be right. Paulson's is two blocks past the turn off to Ella's aunt's house. Takes a good seven minutes to get to Hattie's from here. I'm sure Luella missed setting the number one in front of the time required to traverse the route.

Dan dropped a restaurant pan in the hallway. Martin jumped to his feet and swung his door open. Dan often tries to carry more than he can handle.

"Need some help Dan?"

Martin asked as he retrieved the pan from the floor, and took a couple of others from Dan's overloaded arms.

"Thanks for the help Martin."

"Something wrong in the kitchen?"

"No, I decided to polish these up a bit before the new chef arrives."

"Is Rene leaving?"

"Not on your life Martin. We landed a few new clients with special tastes, who hold a lot of catered affairs."

"In other words, you snagged the Holland Towers account."

"Does anything happen that you don't learn about before everyone else Martin?"

"Probably a lot Don. Like the work being done up the street, I don't know why yet."

"Should increase traffic to the restaurant, and help reduce congestion on Liberty."

"Those new stores certainly draw many folks to the entertainment district."

"They are hurting the older clubs Martin, more than helping."

"How's that Dan? They appear packed every night from here."

"A whole different world in the lower district since Prohibition began. Folks bring their own, and doctors write prescriptions so they can drink their fill."

"I'm sure nothing good can follow such nonsense Dan."

"I believe you are right Martin."

"Where do you want me to set the rest of these pans down Dan."

"Oh, I guess put them on the living room couch."

"You own a car, may I ask a question?"

"I don't understand much about mechanics, but go ahead, shoot."

"Only a question about driving. How long does it take to drive from the center of the entertainment district, to lets say; up around where the old bakery used to stand?"

"That depends on which route you take Martin. From here, under six minutes if you make all the correct turns. Most folks take the slow easy route, about ten to twelve minutes."

"What about from Liberty and Vine to Paulson's?"

"Driving up Vine Avenue to Cook Street, about five or six minutes. However, you can get to Paulson's in less than three minutes by taking the Hancock Cut-off."

"Are you sure Dan?"

"I sure am. We get our meat from Lackey's, only half block from Paulson's, and our beverages from Ross Brother's Supply, right behind Jimmy's. I drive the route often."

"Thanks for your time Dan. I'm loaded with work to get done myself today."

Martin is excellent in mathematics and journalism, but possesses no sense of direction. He would get lost in a grocery store if the aisles were not perfectly straight. He got twisted around in the furniture store more than once. Martin returned to his apartment to make some calculations.

Now let's see here. Ella could leave the mill and drive to her aunt's house in time to switch cars. Then drive to the theater, change clothes, and still have ten minutes to spare.

Martin looked out the window, trying to visualize Hattie's house. A scaffold in front of the garment mill distracted his thoughts for a few seconds.

I've been to Hattie's, no place to hide a second car. Or is there? Just forget your foolishness, Ella is not Rosie. She made that perfectly clear last night.

A few hunger pangs strike. Martin checked his wristwatch, then fixed a sandwich for a late lunch. After editing another two columns for the newspaper; he got cleaned up for his first real date with Ella.

Chapter Thirty-five – A date with Ella

Martin shuffled through the meager collection of better clothes in his closet, and selected the perfect suit for this occasion. He remembered a new hat, only worn once, tucked in the back of the living room coat closet.

While in the coat closet, he removed his overcoats individually, holding his hat next to each. Satisfied with his selection, he sat down to polish his shoes again, for the third time. Ironed his shirt and got dressed.

The afternoon is warm, so Martin would not normally wear an overcoat, but rains threaten. He moved a kitchen chair near the door and placed his coat and hat over the back. He patted each of his pockets and placed the movie tickets in his jacket's inside pocket.

He was afraid if he left them on his desk, he will forget and go out the door without them. He counted the money in his billfold, twice, it did not grow. Martin paced the floor, sat at the desk, stood and paced some more. He sat down again to watch up the street, and fidgeted with everything on his desk. Until he spotted Ella's car turn at the intersection.

OK Martin, remember, act like a gentleman, and don't be so nervous.

Martin sailed down the stairs, skipping every other step, and reached the lower landing as Ella came to a stop. He cannot believe his eyes. For a split second, she looked like Rosie. Ella is wearing lipstick, and a hint of light makeup. The sun glistened from her long flowing hair.

"Wow, you look gorgeous tonight Ella."

"You don't look half bad yourself Martin, for a newspaperman that is."

No sooner than Martin sat down in the car, Ella leaned over and gave him a kiss on the cheek. She giggled at the lipstick mark she left, and decided not to say anything until later. She turned around in the restaurant parking area, but not fast enough to prevent a whistle from inside.

"Pay the crude fellow no mind Ella."

"I don't think Irwin recognized me Martin."

"He knows your car."

"I don't think he noticed the car Martin. Do you?"

Ella glanced down at herself while making her last comment. Martin blushed.

Ella exposed almost as much upper torso as Rosie.

"Been practicing your scales Martin?"

"Not had much time to, but some."

As they drove down Liberty, Ella sang a simple étude, then asked Martin to copy her. He did, and they sang another.

"That is perfect Martin, Hattie will be so proud of you."

Ella turned south on Brooks Ferry Road, and drove to the River Road. At the river, she turned east away from the falls.

"Mmm, so beautiful down here, I love the bluffs, and how they glisten this time of day."

She continued about a mile, to where another road leads back toward town; but turned on a small gravel road that led down to the river. Ella pulled down a second small drive, barely graveled; which brought them south to the river, and a clearing filled with picnic tables.

"Looks like you've been here before Ella."

"During the war, before Clarence bought another store, and loaded me down with work. I came down here with some of the girls during lunch. We had a full hour for lunch, and Mary Ellen drove a large car. I could never trust my old Runabout on these gravel roads."

Ella took Martins hand and pulled him closer.

"What do you do to keep from getting bored?"

"Work at the paper keeps me more than busy."

"I mean after work. Not much to do since you avoid the entertainment district."

"I don't shun this area entirely Ella. Tried my hand at bowling a few times, and while the baseball toss was open, I threw several games."

"I'm sure you do other things Martin."

Ella ran her thumb on the back of Martin's hand, making him nervous.

"Well, I did meet this gal, and we eat lunch together a couple of times a week."

"Don't be silly Martin, what about weekends? Everyone must do something that's fun."

Martin tried to avoid answering the question, but Ella persisted.

"Tell me what you do on Friday nights Martin."

"I don't want you to think any lesser of me Ella. About the only thing to do around here is attend the vaudeville show. I can only afford to go when the tenants give me tickets. I usually don't stay long, some of those skits get pretty rough."

"I hear they do just that Martin."

Ella pulled Martin closer yet, and stared deeply into his eyes.

"Eyes are the windows to the soul."

She said as she closed hers and leaned in to a kiss, moving her hands up and around his neck. When she opened her eyes, Martin stared back into hers, their noses almost touching. Ella's eyes sparkled like diamonds floating in a deep pool.

"I am in love with you Ella."

"Me too you."

She whispered as their lips touched again. Their moment was broken when they heard an angler in the distance go 'whoop fish.' Martin checked his wristwatch.

"The movie starts in fifteen minutes."

Ella started the car, and handed Martin a couple of tissues. She turned the mirror so he could check his face. They both giggled. Ella freshened her lipstick, put the used tissues in a pouch on her door, and they drove off.

She found a lone parking space in the second row.

"Our lucky day."

"I didn't think they would be this packed Ella."

They walked past the long line standing at the ticket booth. A sign in the lobby directed advance ticket holders to the left. An usher checked the tickets and directed them to a raised center loge.

"This is perfect Martin, we couldn't ask for better seats."

Front row in this tier of seats, is two-thirds back from the screen. Far enough forward, those in the upper balcony could not drop popcorn down their necks.

"Would you like a soda or some popcorn?"

"I would love some Martin."

Martin stood to go to the refreshment stand, and an usher swiftly moved toward him.

"Can I help you sir?"

"Going to get some refreshments."

"We provide that service in this section sir."

Martin placed his order with the man and sat back down.

"It appears the theater provides us with a waiter as well Ella."

She was studying Martins face, and did not respond

right away.

"I've never seen you so smile so much. Happy?"

Martin put his arm over the back of the seat, lightly resting his hand on Ella's shoulder, moving a finger along her long hair.

"Very happy. Are you Ella?"

"Perfectly."

The usher passed out refreshments to those in the section who ordered. He disappeared as the lights dimmed. When the film reel began, the theater filled with sound. Ella squealed.

"This is the first time I've ever been to a talkie."

"Never seen the inside any movie house myself."

Martin placed his arm on the back of Ella's seat. This position kept her bare shoulders warm during the entire show. Ella held his other hand, rubbing her thumb on the back often. Except when munching on popcorn or taking a sip of her drink.

Ella tapped Martin's leg during the musical portions, keeping time with the beat. They spent more time trying to catch glimpses of each other in the darkened theater; than viewing the show. When the lights came back up, they remained seated until the crowd dissipated.

A short stout fellow in a red vest came up to Martin.

"How did you and the little lady like the show Mr. Hurston."

"We thoroughly enjoyed the movie, the service was splendid, and these comfortable seats are perfect."

"I look forward to reading your review in next weeks paper."

He caught me off-guard. What shall I say?

"I can assure you, my commentary will be excellent."

The fellow darted off to speak with another show patron. Once Ella and Martin were outside, he confessed.

"I'm ashamed to admit, but the owner's name slipped

my mind."

"You, not know someone who runs a business in your own neighborhood. Maybe you spend too much time playing detective at the wrong things."

Another surprise Martin did not expect.

I wonder what she meant by that comment?

"How much time do you have left Ella?"

"I hope at least fifty more years."

"Now you are the one acting silly. I mean tonight."

"I understood what you meant. Church tomorrow, so I can't be too late."

"I'm a little hungry and thought you may like dinner."

"Do you like Italian Martin?"

"Sure do, but I don't think an Italian restaurant is anywhere near here."

"The perfect little place is around the corner. Not far either. Beautiful evening Martin, we can walk."

"A restaurant is this close?"

"You don't remember much about this area, do you Martin."

"No, and I'm even more surprised you do."

Ella grabbed Martin's hand, and pulled him around to walk back toward the rough end of the entertainment district. Martin cringed.

"Don't worry, we are not going far Martin."

They walked only one block and turned north. Within seconds, Martin was awed by a street lined with shops and stores; a bistro, and two restaurants. Quiet little places, compared to those found along the main drag in the entertainment district.

Martin realized stores were up this way, as Jerome solicited many of them for advertising. However, he pictured the area otherwise. More like an old city area. Ella stopped while Martin was looking in a store window, and he bumped into her.

"Here we are!"

He pulled the door open and followed Ella inside.

"Miss Thornton, welcome. Glad to meet you too Mr. Hurston. Right this way please."

Martin recognized the man from Hattie's church. He took them to a back corner table.

"Thank you Mr. Russo, this table will be perfect."

"This truly is a surprise Ella."

"I think the military messed with your head Martin. You grew up here, and can't find your way around."

"I never had much reason to come up to the industrial area, and never ventured beyond. My stomping grounds as a teen was south of Dowbers Mill, near Leitjen's Grove."

"You seem well versed on the north area."

"I owned a car before I joined the service, and apprenticed at the Midtown Star Journal. They ran me all over the northwest, like an errand boy."

"I thought you worked for Mr. Blaine before the war? The way Mr. Blaine tells his story, you have always worked for him."

"Well, I did, sorta. I was a paperboy when I was in school. Rode my bike up here every single week without fail. I wanted to learn the business and run the presses. The only chance of ever doing so, was if I took a class at the trade school."

"Did you go to Thompson-Riel? My brother Earl is a graduate of TR."

"Yes, they are the only trade school in this area. They had a deal with Midtown, to let us gain hands-on experience. I never quit working for J.B., still sold papers on street corners, when he promoted me to inside work."

"I don't supposed you and Earl crossed paths, he took a short auto shop class. Then decided he didn't like to be covered in grease all day. He scrubbed his hands raw, so they were clean enough to work in the grocery store."

"No, I never met Earl at TR. I only attended class in the new west building for six weeks. The rest were held at Midtown two days a week. My lessons did not conflict with the days I worked at the Ash Brooke Citizen for J.B."

"And now you are the Editor in Chief of the newspaper."

"Well, I still consider it J.B.'s newspaper. There were some technical reasons he turned the paper over to me."

"Yes, the fancy new machine he spoke about."

"We are ready. Installation starts on Monday."

"Guess you won't be available for lunch with all the commotion going on."

"If I can, I will. I don't think I will be needed during lunchtime."

"Don't worry Martin, I will come rescue you."

"What a wonderful dinner, I'm stuffed."

"Mr. Russo brings several dishes to our church dinners."

"Seems like a long way for him to drive to do that."

"The church is less than five minutes from here. Many of the members live in this community."

"Seems I don't picture this area very well, or its relation to your aunts, or the church."

"If you studied this area on a map, the roads might make more sense to you Martin. Between Liberty and the Boulevard, all the streets in this section are at an angle."

"I remember the old town streets running on the diagonal, but never came up here much, because I get lost every single time."

"From your apartment, or the mill, we must go around the square to go in any direction. The long way around. But from here to aunties is right up Vine Avenue."

"I understand now, Vine veers left, which explains why I get so twisted around. I always went right to Ninth Street and turned left twice."

"Before the Twelfth Street extension, that was the best way to Hattie's."

Martin and Ella walked back to her car hand in hand. She stopped in the secluded dark spot behind the garment mill again. They snuggled together, listening to the faint music drifting from the entertainment district.

"I've enjoyed the most wonderful time this afternoon and evening with you Martin. Wish it didn't need to end so soon."

Ella grabbed a box of tissues, handed Martin a couple, then used some cold cream to wipe her face clean. She touched up a spot Martin missed on his face. Martin checked his wristwatch.

"Still early, did you save space for dessert?"

"No time, mom is expecting me."

"I wondered why you removed your makeup. You are still gorgeous without it. How is your mom doing?"

"Better than ever. She still loves Royce, and seems to get younger every day."

"I'll walk home from here. The restaurant is busy, so you won't need to turn around in their lot."

"Remember to be ready early for church in the morning. Auntie will like some help with the chairs again."

Martin walked around to Ella's side for one last kiss. He strolled beside the car as she pulled toward the front exit. Before she reached her turn at the corner, he crossed the street. Rather than going home right away, Martin spotted a car and walked down to the newspaper.

Chapter Thirty-six – Ella reminisces with Martin

Roland's car is parked in the street in front of Mike's. Martin observed no sign of activity, and went around back to enter the newspaper. Two police officers stood in the alley talking. One shined his flashlight between Mike's and Burrows Air Chute Company.

Martin started to walk toward them when Roland came from between the buildings. He held his hand up for Martin not to come closer, and motioned for him to wait. After speaking with an officer, Roland walked down to Martin.

"Didn't want you to contaminate the crime scene."

"What happened Roland? Anything newsworthy?"

"Probably not. I found no evidence of foul play. Waiting for Mr. Burrows to make sure. Until he gets here, I don't want anyone near the building."

"Out with it Roland, you always do that to me. I will never report anything you don't clear first."

"Only a broken window, Martin. The glass was shattered from the inside."

"They wouldn't call you out for that. What are you not telling me?"

"The officer found blood on the shards, and on the window sill."

"Well, with the glass on the outside, sure doesn't sound like a break-in Roland."

They heard a car door slam out front. The building lights go on, and Mr. Burrows can be seen walking to the rear of the factory. He unlocked the back door and let the officers inside. Roland ran to meet them.

Martin went in the newspaper, leaving the back dock light on, so Roland knows he is still inside. An old wall map, which hung on the wall for as long as Martin can remember; only showed their early distribution area. Covering a mere three blocks north of Liberty Street.

He rummaged around the reporter's tables and found a crumpled road map. The drawing of a horn along the margin obviously proved the map belonged to Kent. The south county map was useless to Martin, and only reached north to the river.

Martin turned out the lights and locked up. He stood on the dock facing Burrows. Their back lights went out, and he walked to the front of the newspaper building. Roland's car is still parked out front, and the officers were walking away from Burrow's on the sidewalk.

Roland came out the door. The lights went off and Mr. Burrows followed. They shook hands and Mr. Burrows climbed into his car. Roland walked to his car, where Martin met him.

"Was nothing Martin. Only some employees fooling around, and a buckle hit the glass."

"What about the blood?"

"Their maintenance man went to pull the glass out and board up the window. A piece fell and stuck in the top of his hand. He had to break more of the window to get his hand back through and remove the broken piece. He tossed the bloody shard outside."

"Is he OK?"

"Yes, Mr. Burrows took him to get a couple of stitches, which is what took so long for him to get our messages."

Roland had another call to attend, so barreled off like he usually does. His tires squealed as he sped around the corner off Pottery Row at Klein Avenue. Martin walked home.

He was ready and waiting when Ella pulled up Sunday morning. He checked his wristwatch and made a mental note of the minute hand. She leaned over to give him a kiss before driving off. When they arrived at Hattie's, he checked his wristwatch again.

The drive took six and one-half minutes. Hattie was on the steps waiting when Ella pulled up. Martin scooted over closer to Ella to allow enough space for Hattie to get in. He glanced around, she did have a small garage. However, the doors appeared they had not been opened in years.

Martin checked his wristwatch again, they were stopped for under a minute. It took four more minutes to the church. He did not see a street named Cook, nor the cut-off.

I need to buy a map and study this area.

They were the first to arrive at the church. Hattie unlocked the door and turned on the lights. Martin pulled the chair carts from behind the partition wall, and rolled one to the back of the church, behind the rows of pews.

"Keep the rows closer together Martin."

Hattie scolded, as she moved the first chair in each row closer together as a guide. Ella went to the front to change the hymn numbers on the placard. Martin noted she used the same hymns they practiced together.

Other men came in with their wives. The women, most in the choir, took a seat in the front pews. The men helped unfold and line the rest of the chairs in place. Despite adding two more rows of chairs, once again, only standing room remained.

The service was lovely as usual, and Hattie raved about Martin's mellow tenor voice. Ella's angelic singing from the loft, rendered a heavenly aura throughout the church. The chairs need not be stored after the service.

Ella dropped Hattie off at the hospital. Afterward she drove straight back past the entertainment district to near where they were yesterday. Martin could not believe the elapsed time. The drive took less than four minutes, to arrive from the hospital.

The road Ella used disoriented Martin, he had no idea exactly where they were. Nor did he know what direction they were headed; until they passed the intersection where they previously walked from to Mr. Russo's restaurant.

"Hope you like donuts Martin."

Ella stopped next to a small boutique. The aroma from a bakery filled the air, but its location eluded Martin. The tiny shop had a single door and only one small window facing the street.

The room was narrow and long, with glass pastry shelves lining one wall. The kitchen was all the way in the back. Ella pulled Martin by the hand. He followed behind her to the last cabinet.

"I always start back here and work my way to the front, so I don't miss anything."

The other customers did likewise, as if a normal routine. Martin spied a lemon filled on the way down, and waited until they were up front again, before making his selection. Ella grabbed a cherry topped coiled pastry.

"I can only eat one, you can help yourself to as many as you like Martin."

"One is fine for me also Ella."

While waiting in line to pay the cashier, a customer came in the door, and Ella turned quickly toward the wall. Turning slowly forward as he walked past.

Ella obviously recognized many folks in this area, but why did she avoid this person?

"We can enjoy our donuts in peace at a small playground down the street."

"You seem a little nervous, is something bothering you Ella?"

"Not exactly. Some of the jerks I grew up with live in this area."

"I suppose that's true of anywhere Ella, we had more than our share too."

Ella daintily nibbled on her pastry, for a long time after Martin finished his. She started the car.

"We have a few minutes, enough time left to swing by the fountain."

"Where's your tissues? You have a touch of cherry on the tip of your nose."

Ella leaned up to see her reflection in the mirror, and started giggling.

"Thank you Martin. I wouldn't want to go around looking like Rudolph now would I."

The small community fountain appeared unkempt, but attracted several who paraded around the perimeter foot way.

"Let's walk Martin."

Ella and Martin walked hand in hand around the fountain twice, before taking a seat on one of the stone benches.

"My father used to bring me here when I was little. An ice cream vendor stood under that tree. Dad could only afford to get one and always let me have the first bite."

A tear formed in Ella's eye. She turned toward the fountain, hoping Martin missed her use the napkin to blot her face.

"You really loved your dad, didn't you."

"Yes, deeply. He adored me too, I was his little girl. I miss him so much. He was a lot like you Martin."

"Were you still young when he passed."

"Happened when I was working at Platte's. Something gave way inside the flour mill as he drove past, and flour spilled out covering his car. Workers rapidly dug him out, but he only lived for a few minutes."

"Sorry you lost your father so young. Heartbreaking."

"What about your parents Martin?"

"My father died on February fifteenth, ninety-eight in Havana Harbor when the ACR-1 exploded."

"How tragic. Will wars ever cease?"

"Doesn't seem likely. I joined the service right after mom passed from a stroke. Another war seemed probable, and I signed up when my friends enlisted."

"I'm sure you were glad to get home."

"Thanks to J.B., and you, I am. If you have to pick up Hattie, we best be going."

"Not enough hours in the day."

Ella drove south, and turned on Liberty. Martin found this odd at first, since Ella did not like driving through the entertainment district. Although quiet on Sunday with nothing open, it still came as a shock to him.

She slowed the car as they passed the first of the far west end clubs and began looking back and forth at the buildings. All of a sudden, she pulled to the curb and stopped.

"What's the matter Ella?"

"This little group of whatever they are now, used to be dress shops, and a hair salon. Across the street, that green building was a shoe store, and ladies hats and bags next door. Dad brought the whole family down here to shop, as a special treat."

"I remember the shoe store, only place in town with quality school shoes. Now they are all run down and filthy."

Ella drove a little further, crossing Vine to the well kept east end.

"At least they keep this end in good shape, and are always renovating. I hate to think of what may go on behind those doors."

She sped up as we neared the theater, and did not slow

down until she reached Martin's apartment.

"I dread each time I come up to this area Martin."

Martin knew Ella never drove toward that section of town when she left work.

"We've never had any trouble around the restaurant Ella, and almost none between The Boulevard and Vine Avenue."

"Oh, I didn't mean down here by the garment mill. I like working in this section."

Martin did not question her further. She dropped him off with a quick kiss and hurried to pick up her aunt Hattie.

Chapter Thirty-seven – The Linotype gets installed

On his way to work Monday morning, a large truck passed Martin and stopped in front of the newspaper. As Martin walked around back to open for the day, several workers arrived in their cars or trucks.

He unlocked the front door and greeted the men who came to install the Linotype equipment. The room next door was specially prepared in preparation for this day. The workmen dropped a plumb bob from the center of the flue pipe opening and scribed a mark on the floor.

This was their key point all other measurements were made from. The men made several chalk marks on the floor, and measured out to the walls. Martin overheard one employee say.

"Appears we have an easy job for once boss."

"Yes, plenty of room in here, and nothing in the way. However, getting through that door may be a problem."

"I measured the span boss. If we remove the new trim back to the studs, the unit will clear OK."

Martin became intrigued as they carried each of the main components in and mounted them in place. Luella glanced through the door several times. Now she stood in the opening, hand on Martin's shoulder.

"Looks like a million pieces doesn't it?" Wait until the magazine and distribution components are installed."

"Appears complicated to me Luella."

"Yes they are, but they run beautifully, and fast too."

Martin returned to his desk, and Luella went about her daily chores. Over the course of the morning. Everyone who works at the paper, and a few curious neighbors; stopped in to watch the massive machine being assembled.

Martin slipped out to have lunch with Ella.

"How's the installation going?"

"Boggles the mind, how the men slide the heavy parts in place so easily."

"Will the next issue be run on the new machine?

"Unlikely, nor the issue after next. Supposed to take them a full week to install all the main components. Then another week to set up and load the magazine, run tests and make adjustments."

"Wish I had time to stop by, sounds interesting. We are swamped. Clarence sent a huge order from the north factory."

"Did I hear C.W. was buying another factory?"

"He mentioned going to look at a small glove factory last week."

"I thought his check was written to a pencil factory."

"Clarence didn't buy that factory, he only invested in the building. He's more interested in the glove factory, and altering the machines to make teddy bears of all things."

"I had better get back to the paper."

Martin no longer got the words out of his mouth, when the whistle down the street echoed among the buildings.

"What, no kiss?"

"Sorry, my mind was on work. Everything is topsy-turvy today."

Martin rushed to the other side of the table, out of sight of the employees entrance and exchanged a kiss with Ella. Crumpled their lunch bags, and tossed them in the large dumpster, as an employee dashed past. She held the door for Ella.

Installation of the new Linotype machine progressed

steadily. The newspaper was without electricity on Tuesday for three hours. The utility company installed the new large transformer, required to power the machine.

The constant disturbances drove Martin out the door with a client. They used Mike's diner as a place to work up an article. Martin was in and out of the paper Wednesday morning. He went to his apartment to edit the next issue in peace.

The banker came by the newspaper to take a gander at the progress. Luella showed him all the installed components and what they were for.

"Several large pieces will go clear to the ceiling Mr. Clepstein."

"I have never seen such a magnificent machine up close. I was glad to make the offer to Mr. Hurston, before others learned of the availability. He's lucky to have you as the operator."

Martin finished his work and dropped the papers off for Luella to begin setting the galleys.

"You just missed Mr. Clepstein. He stopped in to check the progress of the Linotype."

"Did he appear to be concerned about anything Luella?"

"Exactly the opposite. He is like the proud father of a new baby boy. Oh, I'm not going out to lunch today, so go get your kissy-kiss-kissies over."

"Do I sense a hint of envy coming from you, a married woman Luella?"

She rolled her eyes and returned to the new doorway. Martin ran to the mill and seated himself at the rear picnic table. When Ella came out, she appeared to be tired and a little upset. Her eyes showed a hint of red and a tad swollen, as if she were crying.

"Is something bothering you Ella?"

"Mom had a bad night last night. I stayed with her until she was feeling a little better and went home after she drifted off to sleep."

"Do you think it is anything serious?"

"Not at the time. They called Earl three hours after I left. He took her to the hospital. I only learned about her condition less than an hour ago. At first they said she had a mild stroke and would be OK, which is why Earl didn't bother me last night. Now they are not so sure."

"They run a wonderful hospital, I'm sure they will get her fixed up in no time."

"I hope so Martin. I'm having enough problems trying to work two jobs to keep up with her medical bills."

Ella bit her tongue, knowing she just made a slip. Martin saw her grimace and decided to pretend he did not catch her.

"I spotted another big truck pull up at the paper this morning. How big is that machine Martin?"

"The Linotype is huge Ella. Wider than our first press is long, and taller than the ceiling in the copy room."

"I can't wait to come and visit your new toy."

"Would you like to take a walk down there now? We have enough time."

"Can't Martin. I'm way behind as it is. I should get back inside."

"I guess I should get going as well. With all the commotion, not much getting done. Luella will start setting the galleys this afternoon, so we don't get too far behind schedule."

Martin dumped their trash, and walked Ella to the door.

"Do you want to get together on Saturday? They have not changed the movie."

"Depends on how mom is doing. I will pick you up on Sunday morning for church. Not as early, the chairs are still up."

"I'll be ready and waiting."

The rest of the week was hectic. Workers running in and out knocked a galley out of Luella's hand. Poured down rain on press day, so the presses had to run slow to give the ink more time to dry. Later, a paper cart snapped an axle on the first delivery, and dumped papers to the wet pavement.

Kent borrowed a flat cart from Miller and Crofts, and let Jerome use the large twin cart. During a break in the rain, the Linotype installers unloaded the rest of the cartons from their trucks. They lined them down the aisle, next to the presses, and left for the weekend.

When everyone was out of the building, Martin shook his head at the mess. He already decided last week, not to go to the theater. He spent the early part of the evening, moving the cartons over against the type cases.

The rest of the night he cleaned the presses. He came in early on Saturday morning to move the cartons back against the side of the press. Then began putting the cold type away in their cases.

Martin went home for lunch. He wished Ella would come rescue him, at least for an hour or two. But he knew she is with her mom, where she should be. Besides, Martin needed to finish sorting the type, because he wanted Luella to spend as much time as possible with the trainers.

He presumed they were close to adding the final touches and fine tuning the machine. Martin worked long past dinner at the paper. Tripping over so many boxes made each task take longer than normal.

A cold cut sandwich and glass of milk is all he ate for dinner, before bathing and going to bed. He awoke in the morning to Jim, the tenant in apartment number one, hammering away on something metal in his apartment.

Chapter Thirty-eight – Ella drops hints of her Secret

Sunday morning, Ella arrived at Martins apartment later than usual.

"Sorry I'm late Martin. I stopped to bring mother some clean clothes."

"How's she doing?"

"Earl will pick her up Monday and take her back to Royce's, to complete her recovery."

To Martin's surprise, Ella cut through the garment mill parking lot and turned left on Klein Avenue. She planned to turn north on Simmons Parkway, but changed her mind, and continued to Vine Avenue.

She turned on the Hancock Cut-off and sailed straight toward the church, making the trip in record time. This is the first time she had ever taken this route Martin learned so much about.

"You forgot Hattie."

"I brought auntie early this morning. She wanted to clean the church before the members arrive. You know what a mess carpenters leave."

"Carpenters?"

"You'll be amazed at what we did inside."

At first glance, Martin thought they only added a few extra pews in the back. An aroma of fresh shellac filled the air. After taking his seat next to Hattie in the third row, he found the pew no longer aligned with the window. The carpenters shifted all the pews closer together.

He figured they tightened the rows by about three inches each, which still left plenty of leg and standing room. They also added a modesty panel in front of the first pew. Hattie informed him, by moving the pews up they added seating for over one hundred, instead of only forty-eight.

The members of the choir used folding chairs in front, facing the membership. After the choir sang the two opening numbers, the pastor stepped up to the podium. He announced a fresh coat of shellac in the loft, as the reason the main choir sang from the front.

Hattie looked around for Ella. She usually sang a solo number before the sermon. Members of the choir kept vigil on a door that leads to the pastors study. Where Ella stood in the hallway, not moving. The pastor began his sermon.

Hattie quietly slid from the pew and inched her way along the outside wall, trying not to disturb the congregation. The heavy door creaked when she slipped inside. The sermon ended and the pastor joined the choir in song. Hattie returned to her pew.

"Is Ella alright?"

Hattie gave Martin the strangest stare before responding. She stammered a few times before snapping.

"She's fine Martin, only suffering from stage fright. She has never faced the congregation when singing before."

Martin knew it was more than that. Hattie did not convince him.

The music started, and the choir broke into a song Ella usually did solo. She walked from the side door hallway, behind the choir. They finally quieted, providing the background for Ella's solo. She walked forward.

Martin immediately recognized Rosie's walk, the way she moved her arms, and the way she held her pose while singing. For the first part of her number, she stared only toward the left side of the church.

Every so slowly, she turned to the right, glancing over the front row, then shifted her focus to the back of the church. Martin sensed she purposely avoided eye contact with him. The absence of her beautiful trill, gave Martin cause for concern.

Her first solo ended, without a trailing crescendo. The choir joined in lightly with her next number.

I caught her glance at me a few times, before she fixed her eyes on mine. After she stared at me, her trill partially returned. Or is she only nervous?

Hattie's cold stern face made Ella uncomfortable. She turned away and faced left. Martin caught a reflection, tears rolled down her face. The pastor stood to walk to the podium, and the music for the closing invitational started. Ella stopped him to talk.

He raised his hand toward the organist, the music stopped. The choir sat down. Ella's back faced the congregation. Her short conversation with the pastor ended, and he continued his walk to the podium.

"I apologize for our hymns running out-of-order this morning. Our soloist requested this opportunity to perform her opening number."

The choir stood, and began to hum softly. The organist held a single light note. Ella turned peering straight into Martin's eyes. She smiled, and a warm glow steadily grew on her face. She began with a full mellow trill in her voice.

I heard Hattie huff, but never took my eyes off Ella.

Hattie stepped from the pew and moved toward the back of the church. Rosie's trailing crescendo trade mark clearly evident, and beautiful. Ella disappeared in the pastors hallway, as the choir sang the closing invitational.

After services, Martin found Hattie sitting on a bench under the arch. She appeared furious. Martin knew to keep his thoughts to himself.

"There you are. Ella's solo was the most beautiful ever?"

"She's a fine girl, but gets carried away too easily. Church is not a carnival side show."

I wonder how little or much Hattie thinks I am aware of, she sure acts angry.

Ella pulled up to the curb. Martin held the door for Hattie to get in. She motioned for him to get in first. Hattie got in and slammed the door as hard as she could. Not a word was said on the drive to the hospital. Ella never took her eyes off the road, nor turned to glance at Martin.

After she dropped her aunt off at the front door. Ella waited for Hattie to go inside, where she visits patients every Sunday. After she pulled to the side of the hospital to park her car, she touched her eyes and face with a tissue.

I can tell both women are upset. Ella squeezed my leg a might bit hard when Hattie slammed the door. Best if I keep quiet until spoken to.

Ella turned and stared at Martin for a good two minutes, revealing a most inquisitive look on her face. Martin returned a shallow smile, but remained silent.

"I'm going up to visit mom for a few minutes. I would like you to come with me."

"I would love to meet your mother Ella."

Martin smiled the broadest happiest smile possible, without looking fake. Ella finally smiled back and took his hand. When they reached the room, they found Earl fast asleep in the corner chair. Adella looked up and smiled.

"Well don't stand there Ella Rose, come give your mother a kiss."

Ella frowned and made a face at her mother. She leaned down and gave her a big hug and kiss on the cheek. Ella whispered something in her mother's ear.

"I get to go home tomorrow."

"That's wonderful mom. I want you to meet

someone."

Earl woke when they came in the room, and joined Martin in conversation by the door. Ella turned and called Martin.

"Mom, this is the newspaper man auntie told you about."

Adella gave Martin a stern, judgmental good going over. Martin felt a little self-conscious until Adella broke a big smile.

"I'm pleased to meet you Martin. Hattie says you are the Editor in Chief of the newspaper."

"Yes ma'am, and I am pleased to meet you as well."

"Hattie is pleased you joined her church choir."

Martin had not yet joined the choir, however, Hattie is pushing him in that direction.

"They recently completed some gorgeous remodeling work. Now Hattie's church holds all the new visitors who come listen to Ella sing."

Martin did not mean to upset Adella. He did not think about the loss to her church. Ella jumped in to calm the situation.

"You need to get your rest mom. Auntie will be along in a bit. She's upstairs."

Ella gave her mom another big hug, and motioned for Earl to follow her to the hall.

"Hey big brother. Since you are lounging around here with mom, will you do me a favor and bring auntie home today?"

"Sure thing Runtella, go have fun with your beau."

Ella punched Earl in the stomach, and gave a playful uppercut to his jaw.

"If you weren't a girl, I would flatten you."

"Oh yeah, you and who else. C'mon Martin, before I have to knock his lights out."

Ella shot down Ninth Street to the Hancock Cut-Off,

up Liberty to Brooks Ferry Road and down to the River
Road. Martin glanced at his wristwatch, as she turned on
the gravel road to the picnic area.

*This is impossible. Takes twenty minutes to get to my
apartment from the hospital. Ella covered the same
distance in only seven minutes.*

She turned the car around and backed into a parking
space. Ella studied Martin's confused face for a moment.
Martin thought not to say anything, since she did not
speed.

"I feel like taking a long leisure walk Martin."

They walked hand in hand along the quiet riverbank.
Following a path worn by the many fishermen who make
their way to a gravel bar. After Ella noted no one fishing
today, a bright smile glowed on her face.

A large tree trunk crossed the wide part of the path.
Placed there to keep cars from driving beyond the picnic
area. A little farther down the narrow path, a second log
ran parallel with the path, facing the river's edge.

Ella sat down and patted the log beside her. Martin
sat down and put his arm around her waist. After a kiss,
and a nibble on her ear, he whispered.

"I am in love with you."

"Me too you Martin."

They kissed and snuggled, and watched leaves float
down the river. Cooed and cuddled, while birds sang in the
trees. Martin smelled a very light hint of vanilla behind her
ear. A car passed by, up on the River Road, it did not turn
down the gravel road.

"Was there a problem in church this morning?"

"Yes, no, well not really. The choir director did not
give the organist the music score, so my cue to come out
never came. Then she started on a different song. I got
confused."

"Hattie thought you had a touch of stage fright."

"Is that what she told you?"

"Yes, but I didn't believe her."

"Well, my nerves made me a little queasy. So many from mom's church reporting me to moms pastor did not help. I'm sure the tension showed."

"You were not your normal self at the start. But then you came through beautifully as always."

"I had trouble focusing, not having my mind on my singing. I thought of mom in the hospital and several other things."

"Did I see a tear before you sang your last number?"

"Just a tear of joy Martin, that's all."

Chapter Thirty-nine – Martin confronts Ella

An old man in a small wooden boat paddling downstream, set his oars inside, waved and beamed from ear to ear.

"Don't y'all pay me no mind, I'll be gone in a jiffy. Only baitin' this jug line here."

He finished his task, took hold of his oars and continued downstream.

"I was young once, ya kids all have fun now. Me and the missus sat about where..."

His voice faded away as he moved down river. Ella was staring at Martin smiling.

"You are one mysterious girl Ella."

"Why, whatever do you mean Martin?"

"You understand exactly what I mean. Folks can set their watch by your strict schedule. Yet I'm not aware of much about you at all."

"You join me at work, I've taken you to the neighborhood where I grew up, and some of the places I liked to visit. What else can I tell you?"

"In a comment you made last week, about my doing too much detective work. You said I sought out the wrong things. You also mentioned working another job."

Ella looked deep into Martin's eyes for a long time before giving her response.

"Yes Martin, I work a small part-time job. To help pay mom's medical bills. I don't blame you for being curious about me. At first, I thought you were only a reporter, looking for a scoop.

"After I realized your intentions were personal, I became mad at myself. Now that we are dating, I expect to tell you everything soon. I can't just yet though."

"Why not Ella? You don't need to hide anything from me."

"Martin, I fell helplessly in love with you, and I'm sure you hold the same affection for me. Which is why the things I've done turned into such a mess."

"I doubt if things are the mess you think Ella."

"Since we started dating, I learned a lot more about you than I let on. What I do is not illegal, or anything like that. At first, I played a stupid game between me and a reporter; which I let get way out of hand.

"I had no idea we would fall in love. Now that we are, I don't want you to think any lesser of me, for carrying on my charade for so long."

"Would you like for me to tell you the things I considered, even though many of them were ridiculous?"

"No Martin, absolutely not. I understand what you've been up to. Please give me the opportunity to tell you in my own way. It is important to me, to explain the why and how first. The what will make more sense to you, and you will see all is most innocent."

"If your other job is what I think, I'm only beginning to learn how you managed to pull it off."

"Don't think about it Martin. Please, please, please, let me explain first. You were getting to close, and creating confusing situations. I appreciate your trust, and what I do must remain our little secret."

"Your secret will be safe with me Ella. I will wait until you are ready."

"Promise you will forget everything you think you learned about me, and stop snooping around. I will tell you everything. But you must keep our secret between you and me."

"I do promise Ella, you can trust me."

Martin and Ella tossed a few pebbles, skipping them across the river. Afterward, they took a stroll down the path, past the car, to stretch their legs. They followed the river upstream a little ways, taking a path through the woods before turning back.

Coming from this direction, Martin recognized the service shed and bench where they stole their first kiss. Ella ran over, but the bench was damaged beyond repair. The shed leaned back, pulling the bench up, putting a strain on the mounting bolts.

Martin thought the park lie farther east, and did not realize how close they were to the river. He made another mental note of the twinned pipe centered under the bench. He sensed an importance in remembering the landmark.

They held hands and began walking back toward the car. At each grove of trees, they stopped for a few hugs and a kiss or two. Their conversation helped to ease some of the tension troubling Martin.

Her touch regained the spark which brought them together. They sat for over an hour in the car, and giggled at each other like two teenagers. A truck rumbled by, up on the River Road. Martin sat up straight and Ella started the car.

"I am in love with you Ella."

"Me too you."

Ella dropped Martin off at his apartment. On her way home, she stopped at her aunt Hattie's to enjoy a long talk; about her jobs and the feelings she held for Martin.

Hattie's laughter became a roar, at all the things Ella had done to throw poor Martin off the scent. She did her ruse a little too well, and was now sorry she ever pulled such stunts. About the time Ella was going to confide with Martin, things backfired.

Ella hurt herself deeper than she realized, playing her

silly game.   She feared hiding from Martin had affected their relationship. She figured Martin got too close, before she was ready, and recent events proved he had surmised the wrong conclusions.

"Oh aunt Hattie, how can I ever straighten out this mess I made?"

"Your little escapade at church sure didn't help matters one bit. If he's half the reporter I think he is, he pegged you a long time ago, and is keeping what he learned to himself."

"I'm sure he learned a lot auntie. I think he has some all wrong too, even though he never said a word, he does hint at things."

"Yeah, and lately you hinted right back. Way to strong too."

"When I realized I could trust him, I had to do something to get him to confess."

"Well dear Ella, this reporter fellow of yours cares a lot more about you, than you realize. Enough so it is high time you tell him about yourself, before you drive him away."

"I hoped you thought that way too auntie. I love you so much."

Monday brought turmoil at the newspaper.   Luella spent the morning with the Linotype installers, and Martin picked up her share of the days work. He found it hard to think, and tried to avoid thoughts of what Ella might say.

He summarized what he learned, and wondered how close he was to what Ella will disclose about herself. She obviously realizes her secret is exposed, but feels she needs to explain in her own way. Martin slipped out the door to join Ella for lunch.

"You have not said one word since you sat down. How's your sandwich Martin?"

"Is there a rating scale on cold cuts I don't know about Ella?"

"No, I suppose cold cuts are nothing more than bland

tummy filler."

"I guess Earl brought your mom back to Royce by now."

"He hasn't called yet. Hey, you'll be glad to know, mom thinks you are handsome."

"Am I supposed to smile, blush, or go give her a hug?"

"All three of course, you silly goose."

"Seriously, mom's been sick for a long time Martin; she's undergone many expensive operations."

"Is that why you went to work?"

"Goodness no. I started work at uncle Oscar's store when I graduated from high school."

"Platte's Men's Shop?"

"Yes, the only place I ever worked, until auntie sold the store."

"Why did she sell out?"

"Sales were in a slump after the men went off to war. I only have a couple of minutes before I must get inside, so let me finish nosy nose."

"OK, I'll only listen."

"During my eighth year at Platte's, uncle Oscar started getting stomach pains; they turned severe, so auntie took him to the hospital. They were unable to do much for him, so I took over running the store, hoping he would get better.

"He was proud of the way I boosted sales and profits. His last night in the hospital, I promised uncle Oscar I would always care of my favorite auntie."

"Blasted whistle."

"I heard. I'll tell you more on Wednesday."

Chapter Forty – Linotype first run day

Martin had tons of work to catch up on at the newspaper. He found it nearly impossible to get any work done in the office. The noise the workers made distracted him so much, he took the work home to his apartment.

He glanced toward the window at the garment mill. Ella ate at her desk on Tuesday's, and only took an occasional bite while working away. In the late afternoon, another truck passed under his window and stopped at the newspaper. Martin ran to meet them.

They had hundreds of bars of a special lead alloy to unload. Enough employees were present to help get the truck unloaded before closing time. The bars were placed in a shed on the new dock area behind Mike's.

"The new machine is taking shape. Many improvements over the one I learned on. Oh, my bus. Bye."

Luella dashed out the door, and ran to catch the bus before the driver pulled away. Martin waited by the door to make sure she got on. He locked the front door and walked to the new side room to study the monstrous machine.

I sure hope Luella can handle this octopus.

Martin thought the machine would never be ready in time for this week's paper. He remembered, when completed, the top will reach the ceiling. So far, the machine is only two-thirds of the way. He pulled the announcement page from the edits, and locked up for the night.

When he arrived at work in the morning, two installers were working outside. They were busy assembling a main part, which looked like a huge rake of sorts. Martin studied the strange piece for a moment. Bewildered at the sight, he removed his hat to scratch his head.

"Good morning Mr. Hurston, so glad you arrived early, we hope to have this magazine installed and loaded by ten."

Martin held the door for them to squeeze through, then stayed out of their way. They were extra careful not to bump the delicate object on anything. He smiled after the strange item was secured in place, and they started adding several more parts. Luella arrived as the men were unpacking the brass matrices.

"Wait until you see this thing run Martin, the machine sorts the type all by itself. The matrices use these teeth to distribute each matrix back in its proper place in the magazine."

Martin never let on that he also studied the machine, and picked up little tidbits from the trainers.

"Beware of those type lice Luella!"

She laughed so hard her knees buckled under her.

"And here I thought you knew nothing about Linotype slugs."

Martin studied Kent setting new galley's from the Linotype into the press. He made a few measurements, some block tapping, and removed them again.

"Why are you doing that Kent?"

"Only making sure everything lines up right boss; we will be using much less pressure on the typeface. Linotype is softer than cold type."

Martin had studied and knew how the presses needed to be set for using the soft type. He truly appreciated the fact Kent went out of his way to learn all he could on his own. Kent also handled part of Luella's work, and still kept the machines clean, besides his other duties.

Martin checked his wristwatch. He did not want to be late meeting Ella for lunch. Roland stopped Martin on the sidewalk with some more information about Ella.

"I'm all done with that Roland. My assumptions were proven wrong, so I dropped the notion. You should too. Forget about my earlier nonsense. Oh, I have been working on the case file you gave me."

"How are you doing with them? Making some headway, but I have an appointment I have to get too. I'll fill you in later."

Roland watched Martin cross the street and disappear behind the garment mill. He decided to drive down Klein Avenue to follow Martin. Spotted him sitting at a picnic table on a loading dock with Ella. He continued on to Vine Avenue where he stopped to jot a note.

"Look what auntie sent for us Martin."

She uncovered two huge slices of cake, and handed Martin a plate and fork.

"Think I'll eat mine first."

"Hope you don't mind if I do too Ella."

"With you interrupting me the other day, I forgot to tell you when mom started getting sick."

"I'm busy eating this delicious cake, so I'll only listen."

"Good, you do that. Two years before uncle Oscar got sick, they operated on mom to remove her gall bladder. No sooner than she recovered from that, she had other problems, and they cut her open again."

Ella paused long enough to take a bite, and wash it down with a drink.

"Mom wasn't that old yet, and showed signs and problems of someone twenty years older. She suffered from constant colds, and infections persisted ever since."

While Ella finished her cake, Martin brought her up to speed on the Linotype installation. Then dug his sandwich from the bag, and Ella continued her story.

"Mr. Deckett supplied the store with materials, so we knew each other fairly well. He owned this mill, and after being awarded a government contract for Khaki shirts, he needed extra help. When he learned auntie had the store up for sale, he invited me to prepare his orders.

"As soon as she closed the store, and I was not needed any more. He immediately upped my workload to include everything I managed at Platte's. He purchased another garment factory on the other side of town, and made me supervisor of this store."

"I'm sure you were pleased the promotion came along when needed the most."

"I sure was, and it came none to soon either. Taking care of auntie's bills were enough strain, then mom needed another surgery, which took the last of her savings. Auntie used the money from the sale of her building, the next two times mom was hospitalized.

"Financially, things were not looking good. I felt badly enough after auntie paid mom's medical bills, and I learned she was broke. Auntie took in some ironing, not enough to cover her normal expenses. To keep up, she started selling some of Oscar's prize collections."

"Is that when you took on another job?"

"Not yet. I already worked all day, and took care of mom. I had no time for another evening job. One of the maintenance men here at the mill up and quit. His job was simple, and Clarence was overpaying the guy. I asked Olin to take over his duties."

"Mr. Wagner is an old friend of our family as well. He learned to cope well with his many serious birth defects."

"Olin is a hard worker and loved getting promoted. Clarence informed me, he has not missed a day of work in over twenty years. He learned right away how to maintain the machines, and keep up with his other duties."

"I'm sure he is a valuable asset to Mr. Deckett's

company."

"He's a dear friend to most of the employees; all the ladies love him. Clarence understood my circumstances, and offered me a substantial raise. A big help, but we were still falling behind. If mom needed hospitalized again, she would lose her house for sure."

"She still has her house, so things appear to be running smooth now. You succeeded in pulling everything together."

"Not really Martin, things did take a turn for the worse. Mom spent one night in the hospital, shortly before you arrived home from the service. My brother held a sale at his grocery store, and used his small savings to cover her costs."

The whistle blew and Ella asked Martin to meet her after work. With press day tomorrow, he had to decline. So they agreed to spend Saturday together. As Martin neared the newspaper, he heard the new machine running outside.

He entered the paper to find half of the employees watching the machine through the side door. On seeing him, they hurried back to their duties. Luella sensed Martin was in the building and rushed to ask him for tomorrows copy.

"No sense in wasting the test on useless samples. Is the copy ready for tomorrow? Might as well get some of the work done on the new machine during testing."

Martin handed her the copy. She glanced through the text, and sat down at the keyboard. She gave the trainers a few instructions. They set the dials and levers to match her request.

Luella began typing away. Martin stood in the doorway and stared at the machine in awe. The Linotype churned out slug after slug of galley ready lines of type. They poured out of the machine faster than Kent could load the chases. Jerome joined him, and called another worker to help.

The test run only lasted for about ten minutes. The installation men and a company operator, checked over each gear, clutch and rail. In that short time, Ella produced an entire editorial page on the Linotype. A job which normally took close to three hours.

Even at that speed, Ella was too slow to give the machine a proper testing. The company operator pulled a long tray out on the machine, and took a seat at the keyboard. He turned the copy page and studied the layout for a moment.

With him at the keyboard, the machine ran so fast, Martin could not follow the slugs as they shot on to the tray. He checked his wristwatch, only four minutes elapsed before the man stopped. Kent loaded the chases and handed the galley to Martin.

Perfectly justified and locked tight.

"I'm amazed Kent, thank you."

The company operator ran each galley strip within the same time limit. Martin smiled. Luella worked with Jerome to get the headlines set; while the company operator ran the machine through some features Luella had not yet familiarized herself with.

"Luella, didn't you tell me tomorrow is press day?"

"Yes sir, it is. But I have most of the galleys finished. Only this page and... Martin, where is the announcements page?"

"Coming right up Luella."

Martin fetched the page and handed the copy to the machine operator.

"Looks like some of this will need case pulled. Please send Luella back in here, we can do most of the work on this new style machine."

The man pulled a pica gauge from his pocket and told an installer to make a few adjustments. After sending one line of text, he asked for the slug. The worker lifted the item and when he went to give the slug to the operator, he jerked his hand back.

"Do you take me for a fool, let the line cool on the tray first"

The slug cooled fast. He took the strip and showed Luella. He let Luella run the rest of the announcement page. Jerome finished the headlines, and Kent blocked the galleys on the press. He yelled over the noise.

"Ready to check the proofs boss?"

Martin glanced up at the wall clock, double checked the time on his wristwatch.

"Are you telling me, here it is only four O'clock and the presses are ready to roll?"

"Sure am boss!"

The installation workers cleaned up and hauled their tools out. The company operator stopped to talk with Martin.

"I will come by tomorrow morning, in case a galley gets dropped and needs redone, accidents happen."

"Much appreciated."

"You haven't seen the last of me yet. Let Luella practice on the machine as much as she can before Tuesday. I will come to teach her some of the new features found on this top of the line model. I'm sure you are aware, practice does not waste materials."

The operator slipped out the door, and Martin announced.

"I think everyone deserves to knock off early tonight. Press day tomorrow, be on time."

Martin did not have to say so twice. The employees hit the door faster than greased lightning. All except Luella, who had to wait for her bus. She told Martin she would wait next door at Mike's. Martin locked up and ran to meet Ella, he knew she would not be expecting him.

Chapter Forty-one – Ella tells Martin her Secret

Martin sat at the picnic table outside, and watched Ella through the window. Her face remained tilted down as she focused on the work on her desk. Intuition made her glance out the window at Martin.

From outside he did not hear what she said to the girls, but all the machines powered down almost instantly. Martin checked his wristwatch. Olin looked up at the wall clock confused. Quitting time was not for forty more minutes.

Ella stopped him from his nightly chores of emptying waste containers and disposing of the trash. He came out the door and began starting the girl's cars. Within a few moments, several of the women came out, yelling thanks to Martin, as they headed for their cars.

The lights went out, and Ella appeared at the door, waiting. Olin rushed not to detain her for too long, but wanted to get the trash cart out of the building. Ella locked the door behind him, and he went about emptying the cart into the dumpster and placed in storage.

"I'm so glad you came Martin."

"Didn't relish sitting around work twiddling my thumbs."

"Does that mean you are ready for press time tomorrow?"

"Sure does Ella. Not only is the new machine fast, but Luella don't need to clean and re-case type anymore.

Other than a few headline fonts."

"I'll bet she love's you to pieces for buying the new machine."

The last car left the parking lot. Olin stopped at the table, to make sure it was OK for him to leave. Ella assured him everything was fine. He smiled at her, then reached out to shake Martin's hand. He turned and disappeared behind the mill.

"I can only spare one hour Martin. So I want you to listen, without interrupting me, or I'll be answering questions before I should be getting to them. Like happened Monday."

"You have my undivided attention Ella."

"I'm sure you learned this already, but our family belongs to a very strict church. After I took a job at the garment mill, mom became upset at my wearing a skirt and jacket. When mom became unable to attend church, our pastor stopped by our home several times to visit. Mom thought he would be mortified if he caught me dressed like this."

Ella paused to look around, she checked to make sure Olin crossed the street and not stopped to eavesdrop. She reached across the table and took Martin's hands, and gazed into his eyes.

"Mom got worse, so we set a twice weekly schedule for the pastors visits. On these two nights, I would stop by aunt Hattie's to change out of my work clothes before going home. Auntie would also fix a dinner, and we sat together to eat and talk for a while.

"She always had a plate ready for me to take home to mom. Do you remember my mentioning our financial condition over lunch?"

"Yes, didn't sound to good."

"Now don't jump to conclusions or say anything until I finish."

"I promise."

"Auntie is a close friend of Mr. Wilton Stoddard. She invited him to come to Blessed Hope to hear me sing. At the time, he owned an exquisite restaurant with an after dinner pianist, up in the posh west side. Auntie did not realize they had a small dance floor, and served liquor."

"I'll bet learning so shocked her."

"Just listen Martin, please; this is hard enough for me to say."

"K."

"Aunt Hattie owned some gorgeous full-length evening gowns. She fitted them for me to sing in church, wearing perfectly proper attire. Mr. Stoddard offered a sizable sum of money for me to sing at his restaurant.

"Hattie was most strict about the arrangements. She said I was a professional, and should be treated as a star. She ordered Mr. Stoddard to never to reveal my identity to anyone. Auntie asked Earl to fix Oscar's old runabout for me to use.

"He needed a name to announce, so we agreed on Helen Bright. Aunt Hattie feared I may be recognized, so she went out and bought some mascara, lipstick and face powder. Auntie appeared confident no one would recognize me.

"I arrived at seven, stood next to the piano, performed two songs, then departed. The night of my first performance, I felt like a painted up clown. She assured me, no one expected a member of Grace Miracle Church; be caught dead wearing makeup, or singing in a public place.

"Sounds like the perfect cover Ella."

"Yes, the restaurant patrons had no idea. Good thing too. I recognized a few members from our church, which made me nervous. I never told auntie, some were drinking heavily."

"Best you never told her."

"She worried enough about the dancing, even though I

left beforehand. I never disclosed Mr. Stoddard added a comedian at eight. Who later persuaded him to add a short vaudeville skit at nine.

"He charged for the late shows, but restaurant patrons were allowed to stay for the first of my two solos. This allowed me to take a short break; while the pianist played the same after dinner song every single night. Folks without tickets, must leave before he finished.

"Restaurant sales continued to drop, even though patrons packed the place. Mr. Stoddard cut back on the menu, and removed several tables. He added a foot high platform and theater type seating. Business boomed for the shows.

"After the government declared war, the owner of the Eagle Theater decided to sell out. With no takers, he kept dropping the price, until Mr. Stoddard found the deal too good to pass up. The restaurant remained packed solid for the shows, even after some men left for the service.

"His only fear of moving the show so far south, he thought he might lose most of his customers. From talking with customers, he learned most already headed south to the entertainment district after dinner, or after the shows ended."

"Always a big crowd up the street back then Ella."

"With the theater so close to the garment mill. He assumed I would walk over after work, sing two numbers, and walk back to my car. I refused, because everyone in the area recognized me and my old car.

"Mr. Stoddard gave me an advance to buy another used car. I bought the Monroe, which I kept hidden in auntie's garage. This way, I could leave work, go to aunties to change clothes, and she would put on my makeup. I would then drive the coupé to the theater.

"My first night in the theater was a disaster. The announcer messed up my introduction and almost blew my cover. He forgot to use Helen and called me Rose. After adding Night, he repeated my introduction as Rose Night.

"I recognized many who arrived before the lights dimmed. I was so nervous and shaking, I made a few horrible mistakes. The following week, the placard showed my name as Tea Rose. Needless to say, I was furious."

"Did he sell the restaurant when he bought the theater?"

"Not right away. For a short time, I sang at both places. We hospitalized mom twice while Mr. Stoddard still owned the restaurant. Singing four solos each weekend, I earned more than enough to cover her hospital bills.

"Mom had seen my paychecks from the mill many times, and understood I didn't make the kind of money needed to cover her medical expenses. She stewed and fretted over what I might be doing to make so much.

"Aunt Hattie broke the news to her gently, by telling her I sang professionally. To ease this shock, she also told her I wore the same gowns as I did in church to sing. Auntie only told mom, I sang at a posh dinner restaurant with a piano.

"Even though auntie told her to keep what I did to herself, we didn't have to worry. Mom would never tell a soul her daughter dared sing in a public house."

"I'm sure the news hurt her deeply Ella."

"She understood how badly we needed money, so never acknowledged I did anything other than work at the garment mill. Everything ran perfectly smooth, until this reporter fellow returned home from the service.

"Shortly after he moved directly across from the garment mill, my fears became real. Several rich tenants moved into the building, and took him to the theater with them."

"I wish you wouldn't talk about me in the third person."

"Sorry Martin, I must, because I had not met you yet, other than in passing."

"OK, I'll forgive you, this time."

"Mr. Nascent rented space in the building long before you showed up. After he gave you the keys, we met and talked often. You were always so helpful, especially when you helped several of the girls with things they needed.

"I admired you a little more each time we met. I also sensed you watched me like a hawk, and studied my movements about town. The way you examined my face, I feared you figured me out. The thought terrified me. Will I become another scandal in the newspaper?

"I discussed this new problem with Mr. Stoddard. He figured if he moved my schedule up, and provided a makeup team, it would throw this reporter off my back. I didn't want to cut the schedule so close, especially with my old unreliable car.

"Mr. Stoddard went out and bought me a brand new car. This worked out perfect, because you did not yet learn how I arrived at the theater. The bright Saxon stood out, the ideal car for a star."

"So you are Rosie, I knew it!"

"Yes Martin my love, I am, however, you must let me finish."

"K."

"Before we started seeing each other. I became so scared, I began doing everything in my power to throw you off the scent. Clara's comments alerted me, and I thought you were much closer than I imagined.

"You showed a sincere interest in me as Ella, and I must admit, I liked you too. Perhaps a little more than simply like. Thrilled by how much you loved to hear me sing, as Rosie. I looked forward to seeing you in the theater.

"Deep inside, I wished we knew each other better, before you began closing in on me. So I had a chance to at least straighten out all this mess before I started doing such horrible things."

"I don't consider it a mess Ella. I'm proud finally to know for certain. I felt badly about hurting Rosie by not going to the theater any more."

"I'm not finished, and you are ahead of me again. Just listen, I only have a few minutes left. After I learned Luella worked at the newspaper, and she invited you to the wedding; I almost called off singing for her."

"I was certain you would recognize my gown, and without my gaudy theater makeup; if you spotted me, my career would be over. I would become a disgrace in the town. A quick change of plans, placed me in the loft behind the choir, where you might not see me."

"I recognized your voice, and started digging deeper."

"I realized you did, and is when the awful games I began playing started. You even had me confused, because you never once mentioned going to the theater to me. For a short while, I thought perhaps I played my cards right, and you finally stopped thinking we are the same individual."

"Well, to be honest, I did concede, which is why I quit going to the theater. While I thought you were Ella, I could not possibly miss you sing. After you thoroughly convinced me otherwise; and because of how I adored you. I considered myself doing wrong.

"To me, I considered myself two-timing. The only way to be totally honest with Ella, is to not keep another girl in the wings, who I admired. I had to cut Rosie off clean, and only focus on you. I still hoped I was right, but couldn't take the chance. So I erased her from my mind."

"I cried myself to sleep that night Martin. Not seeing my biggest admirer in the theater broke my heart. All I could think of was what a mess I made of things."

"You could have told me long ago Ella, I would have understood."

"I am madly in love with you Martin, and discerned I had to come clean. After the stunts I pulled, I thought you would never speak to me again."

"Nonsense Ella. Now that you told me, I won't miss another one of your performances."

"So, will you forgive me?"

"Forgive you? You have done nothing you need forgiven for. If anything, I should be on my knees asking for your forgiveness."

"What on earth for Martin?"

"Where should I start? Hunting you down like a criminal, spying on you, trailing you, having feelings for Rosie."

"You better have feelings for Rosie, she has a beautiful voice."

"Simply charming! But the east side twang must go."

Amid the giggles and kisses, Ella pushed herself away from Martin.

"I'm late, I must go now. Promise me, not a word to anyone."

"I'm relieved to find out I wasn't two-timing. Your secret is safe with me."

"Oh, Clara knows absolutely nothing. In fact, she is mad at me, because you don't meet her after the theater any more. Do not say a single word to her about us."

"How do I explain coming back to the theater again?"

"You're a reporter, come up with something. She is not aware of Ella, so does not have any idea we are dating."

"Woohoo, so, is it official now Ella?"

"Martin, sometimes you can be such a silly goose."

"Can I date Rosie now too?"

"No you cannot. In fact, you can't even talk to her anymore. You broke her heart, remember."

"All her fault Ella."

"Touché, now I have to get going."

"One last simple question Ella."

"Shoot, and make it fast."

"Your aunts garage door looks like it's not been opened in years."

"Her garage also opens from the back, I use the alley side."

"Thanks, now scoot."

Ella's taillights disappeared around the corner. Martin looked into the window toward her vacant desk, then glanced up at his apartment window. A grin, followed by a smug smile appeared on his face. He slapped the top of his legs before standing.

Martin you devil, you were right all along, and can't even brag about it to anyone.

Chapter Forty-two – Special newsboys' initiation day

The presses sang a lighter less labored tune. No longer required to maintain the higher pressures they were accustomed to. Befitting for the joy which filled Martin's heart. Luella winked at Martin.

"What is written all over your face today Martin? You look like the cat who swallowed the canary."

"I'm just happy is all Luella."

"Out with it Martin. I can read you like a book. Your face tells a more interesting story."

"Well, I've been seeing Ella. Last night she called our rendezvous a date. I asked her if that means we are officially dating, and she sealed it with a kiss."

"A real kissy-kiss-kiss? Martin's all kissy-faced, Martin's all kissy-faced, kissy-kissy-kissy. Sorry, congratulations boss."

Kent, Jerome and the others did not hear Luella's teasing over the sound of the presses running. They realized something was up, by the way Luella kept teasing Martin. After the presses stopped, Luella rolled one of the desk chairs to the back, sat down, and propped her legs up.

The boys loaded the paper carts, including the three new ones delivered last week. They ran an extra wheel of paper, knowing sales would be up; with folks wanting a copy of the new Linotype issue.

To surprise Martin, J.B. called a special newsboys' initiation day for the event. The Ash Brooke Citizen will be sold on every street corner. From the river to beyond the new trolley tracks, and up to the new bridge.

Luella, still leaning back in the chair, placed her hands behind her head. She watched Kent and Jerome preparing to wash down the typefaces.

"Kent stop, don't waste cleaner washing the slugs. Only clean the galley headlines set from cold type. Jerome, you can save me a lot of work by stacking them on the lead shelf next to the new machine. No sense my moving them from behind the presses later."

Kent pulled the headline chases and set them in the cleaning tray. Luella did not move until some paperboys came to retrieve another cart and she was in their way. She almost hit J.B. as she rolled the chair back to the front.

"What do we have here? Where have you been with my chair Luella?"

"Took a short break Mr. Blaine."

"You'll miss your bus if you don't get hopping."

"Plenty of time. Only a few headlines to re-case."

"What about the galley's Luella?"

"What about them? They are all done."

"Impossible, takes two days to put the type away."

"Not any more. We reuse the lead to make new slugs each time."

"I don't understand these newfangled machines, but certain we needed one."

"They are truly a blessing. I'll get busy and put the cold type away now."

J.B. gave Martin a funny stare when he came wafting through the press room, searching for Kent. He found him in the Linotype room, holding a service manual, and cleaning the magazine rails. Luella followed, saying she wants to practice a bit before her bus comes.

"You can go meet your kissy-kiss-kissy. J.B. will lock up tonight, after the new newsboys turn in today's take and he squares away with them."

"I'll do just that smarty. J.B. sure is on his toes. I never dreamed our readers would be so interested in this issue."

Martin came close to missing Ella. She pulled out on Liberty to drive home, and barely caught sight of him waving from the sidewalk. She stopped and Martin ran to her door. Roland came from the other direction. He stopped on the opposite side of the street and yelled.

"Hey Martin, I have something for you. Ran across one of your friends yesterday."

Ella motioned for him to go find out what Roland wanted, said she would wait. Martin walked across the street and leaned in Roland's window.

"Pipe down will ya Roland. Got a scoop for me?"

"No, but I talked with Clara yesterday. Man is she mad at you."

"I'm sure, but don't worry about her, I'll get everything ironed out tomorrow night."

"She may not talk to you. Want me to be the go between?"

"I said I can handle it Roland."

"Appears you solved your case."

Roland nodded towards Ella's car. Martin smiled.

"Exactly what Clara is upset about. Rosie and I won't be talking anymore, and I missed the last three theater nights. I will attend tomorrow night, as always."

"Told you to listen to me, when I said you were barking up the wrong utility pole."

"I must admit, you were right Roland. But hey, I still ended up with a wonderful gal. Ella and I are now dating. Now what do you think?"

"I'm glad you finally cleared all the nonsense out of your head, and quit chasing those chorus girls. Ella will keep you in line."

"That she will Roland. Gotta run."

"What did he want Martin?"

"I think I'm going to need your help to solve a problem Ella. Well, not your help, but Rosie's help."

"What on earth can Rosie do?"

"I don't think Clara will talk to me, unless Rosie tells her something like, she won her favorite fan back. Roland said she is so mad at me she's about ready to kill me, because of how I hurt Rosie."

"We can't be seen together. I mean, I cannot talk to you any more after the theater. How much do you think the detective uncovered?"

"Roland didn't figure out much, and I'm glad he quit pursuing dead ends."

"Good. I have a few tricks up my sleeve to appease Clara. Sit in your usual spot when you come with a tenant. Clara will remember the solo I sang specially for you. I had never sung it before or since. I will do that number while smiling at you."

"Do you think she'll pick up on the song?"

"I'm sure she will, and I'll tell her I invited my favorite fan. It can't miss."

"If you get a chance to talk to Clara, ask her to meet me at Curt's."

Friday night, Martin arrived when the doors opened and sat in the loge. Ella waited until her second solo to sing the number, and poured her heart out to her favorite fan. Clara had no trouble seeing the joy in Rosie's eyes once again.

Martin never told Clara he is dating Ella. Each Friday night when they go for dessert, Clara tries to play matchmaker. She would like nothing better than to get Rosie and Martin together. She even pushed Rosie, trying to make her and Martin join them for a double date.

Ella and Martin had several good laughs over the

antics Clara pulled to get he and Rosie together. Rosie continuously refused to talk to those dangerous reporters, ever again. Relief finally came when Dale proposed to Clara, and after their wedding, she quit the theater.

For the next several months, Martin and Ella kept a low profile. They still ate lunch together twice a week; ate dinner out a few times, and spent most of the day on Saturday's together. Martin never missed going to the theater on Friday nights.

To all of their acquaintances, they were only a regular dating couple, each holding demanding jobs. Ella and Martin often met with Luella and her husband. They were also invited over to Roland's house a couple of times for dinner.

As more friends learned they were dating, they teamed up for couples activities. Mr. Deckett and other area business owners, now accepted Martin; Editor in Chief of the largest newspaper in town; like one of their own.

Ella and Martin were having the time of their lives. Attending numerous parties and social functions. However, some friction arose due to their declining invitations to special events. Martin attended several events without Ella, and their excuses began to draw a little too thin.

Chapter Forty-three – J.B. and Roland become suspicious

Luella mastered the Linotype, and learned to perform several functions the newer style machine offered. Kent maintained the machine with the same meticulous care Martin treated the presses. Without telling anyone, Kent completed a touch-typing class in the evenings.

"Will you let me do some of the work sometime Luella, I can type pretty good?"

"Why of course Kent. I can use a break. Miller and Crofts ordered an ad listing their sale goods. It will be perfect for you to cut your teeth on. Don't worry if you make a mistake, just retype the line and discard the bad slug."

"I learned how to do all the settings manually. But you'll need to show me how you do them from the keyboard."

Luella taught Kent the few things he did not already learn how to do. She felt a little envious he mastered the machine and all the settings, while she understood so little about the mechanics. Kent surprised her, when he displayed the completed galley.

"This is perfect Kent, but how did you get the header lines bold like that.?"

"Simple Luella, I used double space bands."

"No I meant so large."

"The auxiliary setting for the headline font matrices."

"That can't be Kent. The auxiliary produces italics."

"Tsk, tsk, Luella. The company trainer showed you how to change the auxiliary rail on the assembler. I learned how to do it by hand, but not from the keyboard."

"Dang you Kent, why didn't you show this to me months ago. I've been hand setting the smaller headlines all this time."

"I tried twice Luella, and you ran me off each time. Remember, you said you preferred to do all the headlines by hand, and to leave you alone."

The bit of friction between Kent and Luella finally ceased. Kent taught her more about the manual settings of the machine, and she gave him more copy to run. If the paper had not grown so large by that time, she almost worked herself out of a job.

Patron's of Mike's diner, disgruntled from waiting so long for a table, began complaining about the noise from behind the wall. Mike added a second wall to muffle the noise from the Linotype machine, but the sound transferred through the floor.

Martin, aware the newspaper must find a larger building soon, placed a bid on the deep brick building west of Burrows Air Chute Company. The only available place large enough in the area, and more than triple the size of the newspaper.

Mark tried to buy the building previously, and learned it was not for sale. So he was furious about Martin's acquisition. The shape is perfect for a restaurant, but a little too narrow to house properly a newspaper.

After a lengthy conversation with Mark, Martin agreed to trade the new building for the stores adjoining the paper, currently housing Mark's diner. When this transaction completed, the newspaper now owned the entire strip mall.

Martin ordered a second Linotype machine, and expected to add a daily edition after completing installation. To become a daily newspaper was J.B.'s lifelong dream. He also learned of a modern press coming up for sale soon, and spent weeks in bargaining.

Roland bowled on Friday nights, and his wife thought Ella sat home while Martin attended the theater. She did not understand why they never dated early on Friday nights. Mrs. Pease tried to invite Ella several times, but she is never home or always busy.

After Rosie's solo, if the play did not interest Martin, he walked up to the bowling alley and sat with Roland.

Being aware Ella belonged to a strict church, and how much Martin loved the theater. He often mused, if Martin and Ella ever got married, they will fight like cats and dogs over his carousing. Martin always went along with ribbing.

Roland's wife asked him to learn from Martin why Ella would never join her while the men were busy.

"Martin, if I were still single and dating such a gorgeous creature, I sure wouldn't be leaving my gal alone on a Friday night."

"You know she is busy Roland, and it's not every Friday. We often go to the late movie, or come over here to the bowling alley to watch you finish up your last game."

"When the restaurant held a surprise dinner birthday party for your thirty-eighth, you and Ella did not show up until after eight. Everyone finished eating and many left, tired of waiting."

"Hey, not fair, everyone understands Ella can't come before then on a Friday. Those who stayed had a wonderful time."

"We had fun all right, and after J.B. danced a jig, Kent had to take him to the hospital. You missed the action, because rather than joining us, you were camped out at the theater. I don't think you've decided who you love more, Ella or that showgirl Rosie."

Martin jumped from his seat.

"I've had enough of your snide remarks for one night Roland."

The league play finished, Roland stepped outside the

bowling alley, and saw Ella's car pull away from Martin's apartment. Her hair is down. He had never seen her not wearing a bun. His curiosity piqued, he attempted to follow them, but was too far behind to note where they turned.

When Roland arrived home, Ella, Martin, and two other couples were sitting in the dining room, having cheese and crackers with his wife.

"About time you showed up. Did you forget I invited the men over after the baby shower?"

"Who's having a baby?"

"Men, they are all alike. Why Luella of course."

The small party continued to almost midnight. The women talked about doing something together on the night the menfolk bowled. We should start a card club, one offered. Someone else remarked, playing cards is against Ella and Julie's religion.

After the party ended, Ella dropped Martin off at his apartment.

"I'll pick you up in the morning, lets say around ten. Appears we need to talk. Word got back to auntie that the women are getting nosy about my whereabouts."

"Yes, and I've been getting drilled from Roland, Luella and J.B., ever since my birthday party."

Ella brought a picnic lunch, and they drove down to the river park. Several fishermen worked their way up and down the bank, then moved farther upstream. Others who were fishing since sunup, loaded their gear in cars and left.

"I'm sure glad the city installed picnic benches down here."

"Not the city Ella. They are compliments of Mr. Clepstein. George's dad."

"Well tell him thank you for me."

"I will. You are the one responsible?"

"What? How can that be Martin?"

"From your conversations with Marie. What ever you talked about with her. I presume you said something about us, and she took it to heart."

"She only asked if I knew of a quiet little outdoor place nearby, away from everything; where she and George could sit and talk, while the baby is at grandmothers. I may have said we were here in the park, when we shared our first dating kiss."

Martin blushed. George mentioned something to him about constructing a pavilion. He had asked Martin where he and Ella first met as lovers. Marie probably passed to her husband what she learned from Ella, and why George confronted him

George and Martin drove down to the riverfront park. The log by the river, was too close to the water's edge. After George disclosed the boundaries of his land. Martin showed him the twinned pipe, formerly centered under the park bench.

"This is the exact spot Ella and I shared our first kiss. The shed and bench are now gone."

He measured the area and made several notations in his notebook. On the drive back to the Menton Building; he only stated he would ask his surveyor to do a feasibility study. George said nothing more about his plans for several months.

While at the park with Ella, Martin became curious if George's contractors visited the site yet; since he talked about possibly building a pavilion. Martin was unsure of what George's additional plans for the area may include.

"Would you like to take a little walk Ella? Let's go this way."

They stopped where a grove of trees shielded them from the road. They stood holding hands, staring into each others eyes, until they began giggling like teenagers. They embraced, kissed, touched noses and played with each others ears.

"Oh Martin, remember the first time we stood in this very spot? When you kissed me I felt like I was melting. I would have fallen if you didn't hold me up."

We were seated on the bench, not standing.

"How could I forget? That old shed used to stand right here, and the bench sat in this very spot."

Martin squeezed her tight against him, lifting her feet off the ground. He decided to test her memory.

"Look Ella, I didn't notice this before."

He pointed to a pair of trees growing close together up the hill; then pointed to a large tree across the river, and at the large boulder behind her.

"Wow, I remember. A car passed on the River Road, and the headlights shined between those two trees and lit up your face. We are standing in the exact spot where I realized I was madly in love with you."

She said standing, again. I remember clearly we were seated on the bench. We did share a more memorable and tender kiss after we stood back up.

Martin smiled. He wished to share the upcoming surprise, but had to wait. After a few more kisses, they walked back to the picnic tables to eat.

"We must come up with what I do on Friday nights Martin, something believable."

"I don't think you meant the way you sound. My Ella would never tell a fib now would she. You are correct, saying you are busy isn't cutting it any more."

"Hattie thinks perhaps I should say I'm working a part-time job. She bit her tongue when she said, up north, because that would not be truthful."

"A few weeks ago, I told Roland you were practicing voice lessons. He mentioned a few things similar to my early thoughts. He's been to the theater enough times himself now, he too is finding a resemblance."

"Last Friday after work, I saw his car up on aunties

street. I parked the coupé in front of the garage as usual and went inside. But had to wait until he moved, so he could not view the alley, or the Saxon pull from the back door of aunties garage."

"I wonder if he is talking to J.B.? He cornered me the other day and asked about the Rosie case I once worked on. I told him I dropped my nonsense long ago, impossible as he said."

"What are we going to do?"

"One thing would help. We need to appear earlier at Friday night functions. Early as possible to appease most of them."

"Mr. Stoddard is changing the routine again. I'll ask him if I can do my two numbers back to back for the next couple of months. I'll clue him in on what's going on. He'll understand."

Chapter Forty-four – Martin proposes to Ella

Martin hired a prominent area contractor, to renovate totally the four unit strip mall. Their architect designed a beautiful new front, befitting the home of a major newspaper. The project included resurfacing and enclosing the rear dock.

To ease the transition, the sections formerly housing Mark's Diner, became the new front office. The original offices were transformed to add space for a new modern press. A soundproofed wall separated the journalists and reporters desk area from the Linotype area.

A new entry from the dock, will allow for easy installation of a second Linotype machine, scheduled for delivery next week. J.B. will man the 'city desk,' with a receptionist in the front, and 'feature desks' to each side.

During this massive renovation project, Martin and Ella attended every function, including Friday night functions; arriving at most between seven and seven-fifteen. This added socializing brought other folks together with them, some who attended Hattie's church.

Within the month, word got around among the industrial district's business owners, that Ella was a soloist at Blessed Hope Baptist Church. Shortly thereafter, her being raised attending the strict Grace Miracle Church, became common knowledge.

Blessed Hope grew fast, as area businessmen and their families started attending. The church outgrew their newest addition almost immediately. Building fund donations poured in, to build a massive extension.

Everyone loved to hear the garment mill manager sing.

Ella was careful to maintain a mellow tone, totally devoid of flourishes. Rosie on the other hand let out all the theatrical stops. She also managed to accost Roland outside the theater a few times, laying on her east side twang; trying to make him her fan too.

J.B. is a better detective than Roland. His lifelong nose for news, combined with Martin's early research and sharing of clues; led J.B. down the same path as Martin. He was closing in, and fast. Martin was certain of J.B.'s confidentiality, but thought best to throw him off for now.

Martin previously pinpointed the spot he would like George to build the pavilion. He questioned Martin again about the significance of the twinned pipe, and asked for Ella's initials. His construction crew took special care to ensure the new concrete floor was centered perfectly.

Work started on the pavilion while the new Linotype installation took place. After the floor set, George picked Martin up to view the new slab. He pointed out the pipe and said he will leave an indent in the floor, forever to mark the spot.

After Martin shared he planned to propose to Ella, George smiled.

"Martin, I wanted to surprise you with something today, but now I thought of a better way. I will place a layer of cement dust in the divot. During your proposal, wipe the dust from the indent to expose my gift to you and Ella."

"You must give me some idea of what the gift is George."

"I asked my crew to leave your special pipe in place. A cap was required, so I ordered and engraved memory marker. More fitting now, if I let you and Ella expose the cap together."

"You didn't do something to embarrass me did you George?"

"Would I do that to you Martin. I'm sure you will be pleased. Don't peek, and good luck."

Martin drilled George unsuccessfully on the drive back to the newspaper. George convinced him the engraving was simple and something both will enjoy. He suggested the spot be wiped clean after the proposal, regardless of which way Ella responded.

From the car window, the activity around the new modern press drew Martin inside. The normal Friday proof edition of the paper was running. The machine appeared to function properly. Kent ran to the office to meet Martin as he came in the door.

"Mr. Blaine thought best if we used this press for the upcoming daily newspaper editions."

"What? This is our primary edition, not a daily."

"Better talk to Mr. Blaine. He wishes to reserve the old trustworthy presses for an oversized weekend edition."

Martin had not planned for a weekend addition at this time. Kent returned to the press, and Martin went to speak to J.B. He insisted the paper start a weekend edition come next Saturday. Martin hoped several things would take place first.

For the first ever Saturday Edition to carry the information Martin desired. He must confide with Luella about his plans, and tell her to set a separate front page in private. Plus set the regular front page as a backup, and a second copy if the front page moved inside.

This presented a problem. Luella had not yet learned all the manual settings on the Linotype, and loud mouthed Kent. He could never keep from blabbing if his life depended on same. The only alternative was to ask the Linotype companies trainer to stay one extra night.

He was from out-of-town and stayed in a motel. He agreed to help Luella, and even give her a ride home after they finished. This also gave her a chance to use some of the newest features added to the second Linotype machine.

Together they turned out the most beautiful front page eyes ever beheld. She asked Martin to come in, lock these galleys in the safe, and close up for the night. Luella and the trainer did not go straight to her home. They stopped at Jimmy's for a late night dinner.

The dinner was perfectly innocent, as neither had eaten. Luella called home to tell her husband she was working late, and called again later; to tell him where she was and with whom. She was seen by a couple of her neighbors and gossip spread in north town.

The trainer left for home in the morning as planned. The only person who caught anything amiss in the newspaper was Kent. Four galleys were missing from the shelf. Luella had to tell him she set them after work and they are locked in the safe.

"Why would you lock the galleys in the safe Luella?"

"They contain pending sensitive information, which is nobodies business."

Time was running out for Martin. Rain poured down on Monday, so he did not ask Ella to the park. Tuesday she took the time cards to Mr. Deckett and visited her mother.

Can I possibly get her out of work early on a Wednesday?

Martin relied on Luella for several of his duties over the past few weeks. From setting the alternate front page for the newspaper, she was aware of what Martin planned. The information bugged her to no end, not being able to blab the news to her friends.

But she promised not to say anything to anyone. She understood the beautiful announcement page may never run, if things did not turn out for Martin as he hoped. Familiar with Martin's routine, she offered to lock up so he may get out early.

Ella was busy at her desk when Martin arrived at the mill. He stood to the side of the window first, out of her sight, trying to ascertain how much she had left to do. He saw her close a folder and drop it in a drawer. She closed the drawer without pulling another folder.

Martin stepped in front of the window and tapped lightly to get her attention. Ella looked up and her face beamed like the sun. She grabbed a whistle and blew hard. The machines instantly began powering down. Poor Olin cranked his head around to see the clock.

The girls realized what was coming down, and to help Olin get out faster. When each stood from their station, they picked up their waste cans and dumped them into his cart as they raced for the door. Olin beat them outside and started a few cars, before the girls shot out.

Several of the women yelled a thank you or we love you to Martin as they passed. One even gave him a hug. Olin retrieved the cart and pushed it on to the dock as Ella doused the lights and locked the door. Martin gave Olin a wink and he and Ella walked to her car.

"I hope I don't get you into trouble for shutting down early."

"We were done for the day Martin. I'm glad you rescued me."

"The evening is so pleasant, how would you like to drive down to that little river park before dinner."

"I don't want to get stuck Martin, the path will be so muddy."

"George had several dump trucks of gravel delivered for the road. He also covered the picnic area with a new layer of crushed pecan shells. I've not seen the park yet, but he told me all is done."

"Well, since he went to all that work, we should at least go have a look."

Ella did not believe her eyes. From the foot of Brooks Ferry Road, in both directions on the River Road, the drive was covered with white limestone. The walking paths were redone as well. Light tan river gravel led to the picnic tables and along the river.

A few new pole mounted benches added for fishermen to sit at water's edge. Ella was a little uncomfortable walking on the pea gravel. She ran to the picnic benches to feel the soft pecan shells through her thin soles.

"This is beautiful Martin. George really went all out down here."

"The credit actually belongs to his father. But you haven't seen the half of it yet. He added more picnic benches at the other end. Let's take a walk to our little hideaway."

"Can we wait here for a few more minutes Martin, at least until that family of ducks paddles by."

Martin moved to the other side of the bench with Ella, to watch them pass.

"They are so cute Martin, little ducks all in a row."

"I believe they are called Teal, but I may be wrong. I'm not familiar enough to be certain."

"Well, whatever they are, they sure are cute. I wish I changed shoes, these thin sole dress shoes are not made for walking on gravel."

"Are they in the car? I'll be glad to run get them for you."

"No, they are under my desk at work. I wore them to get through the puddles."

"I have some good news, I made the last payment to Mr. Nascent on the Menton Building."

Ella was so excited for Martin, she jumped from her seat and pranced around the picnic table. She loved how the soft pecan shells compressed under her feet. She grabbed Martin's hand and they trotted down the path away from the picnic area.

When Ella saw the new pavilion, she forgot all about the gravel, and danced all the way. She stepped up on the concrete floor and after she checked the twin trees and split rock, she stopped on their spot.

"Can you believe this Martin? Our special place is dead center under the pavilion. And look, a dent in the floor to remember the spot by. What are the chances of that happening?"

"Seems pretty amazing?"

Martin knelt down on one knee, and glanced at the dent in the concrete. He removed a handkerchief from his pocket and set it between them over the loose cement dust in the divot. He reached up, took Ella's left hand, and gazed into her eyes.

"Ella my love, if you can put up with this nosy reporter. He would love to take the best soloist in the whole wide world as his lovely bride."

Martin fumbled around in his pocket for the ring. Ella stood motionless, frozen. A sense of terror raced through her for a split-second. She forced a smile, a tear raced down her cheek. Martin squeezed her hand and pulled it closer to him.

"I'm asking you to marry me."

He held the diamond engagement ring in front of her finger and waited for her response. A teardrop landed on his hand. Ella took a deep breath and spoke.

"I can't... - I am madly in love with you... - I can't... say no... - Yes Martin, I will love to marry you!"

Martin slid the ring over her finger. But before standing, he took his handkerchief and brushed the cement dust from the dent in the floor. This exposed a bronze medallion. Ella knelt and gave Martin a kiss, before she looked at the floor.

"Martin, it has MTH and ERT engraved with a heart around our initials. It's beautiful. You scoundrel. You asked George to build the pavilion here, right in this place, on purpose."

"Hey, all George's idea. I only went along with his plan. Well, yeah, he did let me pick the spot."

"You sure took a chance guessing my initials. I don't

have a middle name, and how did you learn about my double first name?"

"Remember when you took me to visit your mother the first time?"

"Yes, but you couldn't have overheard her, you were still behind me in the hall."

"The way you frowned at her. How could I not pick up on that?"

"The medallion is beautiful Martin. You are so special. My knees are killing me."

"Sorry, I'll pull you up."

Martin stood and helped Ella back to her feet. They embraced, kissed, hugged and kissed some more. Ella held her hand up to admire her ring.

"You sure went all out Martin. I don't ever want to take it off."

"Well, I don't want you to wear the ring after work on Friday's until late evening."

"No, I guess that would not be to wise. I am considered a respectable lady."

Ella cracked up after making her comment. Martin failed to resist the contagion and roared with her. Their laughter was broken by someone farther down the bank.

"Hey you two, I'm trying to fish down here. Go somewhere else with all that cackling, before you scare the fish away."

"I guess we should get going Ella, a dinner is waiting for us."

Martin swept Ella up in his arms and carried her to the white limestone, where he stopped fast and set her down.

"Something the matter Martin. I didn't feel like you were going to drop me."

"We're not married yet, so I can't carry you across that line."

"Oh you silly goose. The things you come up with."

When Ella pulled out, she made a right on Liberty.

"Forgot to tell you, we need to go the other way."

"Through the entertainment district? Whatever for?"

"I made reservations at your favorite restaurant, Russo's."

"No problem, I can get their faster going this way."

Ella found so many short cuts through town, it boggled Martin's mind. She shot up Simmons Parkway to Klein Avenue, and past the back of the theater. When she reached Brooks Ferry Road, she pulled over to the curb.

"Why did you stop Ella?"

"We're here Martin. Russo's is only half a block away. We can't take the car any farther."

"I thought we were in east town when we came to Russo's?"

"You sure don't understand directions do you Martin. Remember? We walked to dinner from the new movie house."

"With so much on my mind, I guess I didn't pay attention, and I misjudge distances when riding in a car."

They walked down the little corridor from the opposite direction. Martin recognized the restaurant and held the door for Ella. She could not resist showing off her ring to Mr. Russo and a couple of long time neighborhood friends.

Chapter Forty-five – The Ash Brooke Citizen goes daily

When Martin arrived at work Thursday morning, Luella was all over him like a rash.

"Well out with the news Martin. C'mon, I can't wait, did she say yes? Did she, did she?"

"She might have, then again maybe not, or she may still be thinking about it."

"You liar. Confidence is written all over your face. I'm sure glad I don't need to disassemble the best galley I ever set. – Um, I don't do I?"

"No Luella, your work will appear on the front page of the new Saturday edition."

"Woohoo! Hey everybody; Martin's gettin' married, Martin's gettin' married."

Everybody made a big fuss over hearing the news. J.B. congratulated Martin, then stood back eyeing him while rubbing his chin. One could almost hear the rusty old gears in his head grinding over.

"OK troop, party's over. Let's make music pour from the presses."

"J.B. said we must run the daily on the new press."

Martin stared at J.B. puzzled.

Has their lifelong only issue now been reduced to just a daily. What has J.B. been doing behind my back now?

The new modern machine spit the paper out faster than greased lighting, and with two-thirds less noise.

Martin checked the paper.

No smaller than our normal run. How can we keep a daily this size?

J.B. knew what was going on in Martin's mind. But he covered everything.

"Martin, come up front to my desk, I will show you what I planned now for well over thirty years."

Martin pulled a chair over while J.B. was dragging ratty old notebooks from his bottom desk drawer. He yelled back to Kent.

"Please ask Luella to bring the daily layout up front. Beginning on Monday Martin, The Ash Brooke Citizen will officially run a daily. You already filled most of the columns for the next few months."

"I did? How can I possibly not realize what is going on."

"You stopped paying close attention to my activities, when you started dating the mill manager."

"She's my fiancée J.B., please refer to her as Ella, or Miss Thornton."

"No offense Martin. I kept things to myself, until I was sure my plan was doable. I did make you the boss, but if you study these papers, you will agree the paper is ready for a daily."

J.B. opened his notebooks and continued to talk about his vision. Commenting often about how times changed, and the appearance of the paper from the old days. Martin examined the schedules J.B. worked on for decades, adjusting and polishing them, until they were flawless.

Luella came in carrying dozens of folders. Each containing a layout section of a daily paper. She beamed from ear to ear as she opened and presented each to Martin. Seeing everything only hours away from being ready to roll was staggering.

The layouts only lacked the daily headline and article, plus a few journal columns. All the article pages were filled for the next three weeks, with only a few blank galleys later in the fourth week. J.B. cleverly worked out a uniform paper, and had enough articles backlogged to carry them for a good four months.

Martin checked his wristwatch when the press powered down.

Two-thirty, did something go wrong?

The carts were filled to capacity and Jerome pulled the first few galleys from the press. Kent noticed Martin coming and tapped Jerome on the back.

"Hi boss. Still need to run several ad fliers and a side-paper for West Towne. We should be done by four."

"Ad fliers? West Towne? What are you involved in now Kent?"

"Hey, don't blame me boss. Ask that crazy marketing director you hired."

Martin returned to the front office. J.B. sat grinning from ear to ear. He overheard Kent filling Martin in. Luella made a kissy-kiss-kiss face at Martin from behind J.B.'s back before speaking.

"While you were out playing Romeo, we've been busy Martin."

"Appears so Luella."

"I have another surprise for you. Kent can run the new Linotype faster and more accurately than the trainer, and keep it humming too. He's also been teaching Jerome and two of the pressmen as backups."

J.B. stood and talked about not letting working hours be wasted doing idle busyness.

"I asked the marketing director to pick up a few loose ads, and up he pops with some high paying sales fliers. He lives over off Twelfth Street and the printer doing their little West Towne Community Bulletin shut down. We took over most of their accounts."

"Well J.B., I'm grateful you are staying on top of

things. As I said, you are still my boss."

Luella presented the folder for the Saturday issue to Martin, and returned to the Linotype room. Martin sat down with J.B. to go over the new large weekend edition. J.B. detected the folder contained two front pages, with one set as page two.

"I don't understand this second page Martin, Luella's never made a mistake like this before."

"No mistake J.B., the front page we are using is not in this set."

"The face is right here Martin, same as always."

"Turn around and open the safe J.B., be careful you don't knock the galleys off that narrow upper shelf. A few copies of the front page are sitting on top of them."

J.B. pulled the galley proofs from the safe and spread them out on his desk. He is so captivated by the new highly ornate Ash Brooke Citizen logo, he cannot take his eyes off the scroll work. He read the lead headline announcing Ella and Martin's engagement.

"I can't think of a better headline for our first weekend paper Martin. Congratulations. But how on earth did you manage this fancy new header?"

"Do you remember the artist you hired to paint our logo across the top of the building?"

"Of course I do Martin. He's done admirable work around town for years. Hard man to track down and find time to do our building."

"His brother is the master engraver who made most of the city's official seals. He replicated the design you selected for the building; added some flourishes and asked George to slip them under my apartment door for approval."

"Well, I must say, this is a most attractive header. The only problem with doing something like this Martin, the fine lines will wear out or break. Folks will be disappointed seeing the old header back when that happens."

"No worries J.B. They are cut from steel and hardened, not the usual soft copper. He made us four weekend plates, six daily plates, and dig this; as a gift, he cut two small plates to run letterhead on our stationery."

Luella sent Jerome to get the special Saturday edition galleys from Martin. To start setting the main presses to run the new weekend paper on Friday morning. Luella secretly held a couple special front page articles for the occasion.

She kept them hidden from Martin, and used an alternative when Kent ran the proof copy. Kent was in on the surprise, and ran a proper proof copy for Luella to double check. The beds were in place, and the presses ready to roll.

The new press powered down for the third time that day. Martin checked his wristwatch. Three-fifteen. A pressman pulled the small cart near the front door. Four bundles of the West Towne Bulletin sat on top.

"I didn't realize their little community paper was so large."

"Only a split four sheet boss, appears bigger than it really is. They are supposed to pick up the bundles at four sharp. Easy as pie to run on that new press."

Martin took the time to go thank each of his employees, starting with those in the back working areas of the newspaper. He often made these rounds after the days press work was done and the building quiet.

Tonight he spent a little more time than usual with each of the newer employees. He wanted to listen to each of their thoughts on the paper going daily. His goal, to discover if they noted any problem areas or improvements needed in their departments.

He also spent more time talking with J.B. about the direction the paper is moving. Although Martin loved the paper as much as J.B., he still had a lot to learn about the overall newspaper business.

Chapter Forty-six – The new weekend edition

Martin awoke on Friday morning to the sound of three local factory whistles announcing the start of work. No time for breakfast, he was due at the paper an hour ago. Martin forgot Luella and Kent both carried all necessary keys.

He dressed in a flash and ran all the way to the paper. The two old presses were already rolling. They sang in tune, but without the heavy rhythmic beat Martin became accustomed to hearing.

Martin wake up, Kent runs the presses lighter now.

Luella breathed a sign of relief, when Martin arrived late. The face of the special front page lie face down in the racks. When collated, bundled and stacked on the carts; Martin would not discover her changes until too late to do anything about them.

Everyone, except Martin, is aware of Luella's changes, and helped keep Martin busy. They came to him with one thing after another until near lunchtime. Luella taunted him to go meet Ella for lunch. She almost needed to shove him out the door.

"What a surprise for you to come visit on a Friday Martin."

"Luella tossed me out on my ear. I sense she's got something cooked up."

"You worry too much. I'll bet the paper can run without you hovering over it like a mother hen."

"J.B. decided yesterday, all subscribers will get our

first weekend edition free. He also called in the extra paperboys again, to work every street corner."

"I don't doubt Mr. Blaine is exactly certain about everything he is doing."

"I'm sure he is Ella, and am trying to learn as much as I can from him. He showed me his personal notebooks. Things about the paper he spent a lifetime working all the bugs out."

"Oh, do me a favor. Please sit in one of the front rows tonight. I'm going to sing a special song, just for you, and announce our, I mean your engagement to Ella."

"Do you think doing such is wise Ella? Many who attend the theater are unaware of my presence, and none ever met Ella.

"Auntie and I talked at length, and we have a wonderful idea. She's sharp as a tack at confusing people and throwing them off-guard."

"She may be, but I worry about you Ella. Whatever you cooked up sounds mighty risky to me. Time I get back to the paper."

"No need to worry, everything will be perfectly OK, you'll learn why soon enough."

Martin returned to work, the presses still filled the air with their glorious music. The journalists kept him from getting to the back room. By inundating him with sample copies for the rest of the week.

Kent started the power down process shortly after three. The only sounds from the back, a squeak from cart wheels moving about, and the strapping machine. The journalists crowded tighter around Martin to block his view and burst into song.

"For he's a jolly good fellow, for he's a jolly good fellow. Congratulations and congratulations again, for he's a jolly good fellow."

Luella, J.B., Kent and Jerome, each took a turn speaking.

"Mr. Hurston, congratulations on your engagement, kissy-kiss-kiss."

"Martin, congratulations. Without you my dream would've never come true."

"Hey boss, thank you for being the best ever. Go Citizen.

"Congrats on the weekend paper Mr. H., and to your Miss T. as well."

The pressmen rolled a cart with two large cakes in to the center office. The first said; 'Congratulations, Martin and Ella.' The other; 'The Ash Brooke Citizen, Daily and Weekend.'

J.B. had a tear in his eye he did not want anyone to witness, and slipped into a corner desk. Martin turned around to say something to Luella, and found Roland in his face.

"Hey bub, I'm placing you under arrest for disturbing the peace. I heard the racket up on Coventry Street. Don't you realize detectives sleep from two to six?"

Roland brought a laugh as usual. Everyone talked, shook hands, and slowly trickled out to go home from work. Martin pulled a chair up next to J.B.

"We have a fantastic staff, thanks to you J.B. I'm sure they can manage the load with ease. Can I say congratulations to you, for all your hard work, and sharing your business with me?"

"Martin, I learned the first year you worked for me, you had ink in your veins. I was so close, and the blasted war started and ruined everything. I still remember clearly, the day you returned home, walked in the door and dropped your duffel bag on the floor."

"Yes, and all these years I've wondered, why do you hate your middle name.?"

"My father's name reminds me of a not so happy childhood Martin. He would come home drunk and slap me around, then turn on mother. On my tenth birthday, I tried to stop him from hurting her and he came close to killing me.

"Sounds awful J.B., but you went on and made a name for yourself. A shame too, you are the kindest man I ever met."

"Hard for me to get ahead for a long time, unable to work after that beating. My grandmother kept me for three months to heal up. Father moved out before she brought me home, and afterward our lives changed drastically.

"I never finished school, and immediately went to work in the brickyard. Mother's health declined rapidly. She died when I was only twelve Martin. I lived in hiding for four years, to avoid reform school, until I turned sixteen.

"Found a cellar in an abandoned house, where the bank now sits. Earned enough eating money selling left over newspapers by a car plant at night. When I came of age, the newspaper offered me the corner, and enough papers for all shift changes.

"The two brothers who ran the small newspaper, continually fought with each other. The rougher brother left the business, which lifted a heavy burden from the older brother shoulders. He took a liking to me and offered me a job inside. I worked hard and saved up my money.

"Over the years, he taught me everything about the newspaper business. I caught many things he no longer did well. Like I am now, he grew older, getting up in years, and his mind started to go.

"He did a lot of crazy things which cost him many lost subscribers. For no logical reason, and unable to afford them, he turned around and ordered two new presses. They were sitting on a rail car the next city over, when a fire swept through the entire city block.

"I presume he paid for them, because the bank held no lien against the presses. He disappeared, and the storage bills from the freight yard started coming to me. I went to get the manufacturer's name from them, and they told me I had to move the presses.

"After I sent a letter of inquiry, they replied with a bill of sale in my name. I took this to the freight yard and paid the storage fee, and had them delivered to this building. My lifelong savings barely covered the rent and all the acquisition expenses.

"Did you pay attention to the wall next to the back door before we remodeled?"

"I remember some unusual wear marks, and often wondered what caused them."

"Martin, with no money to spare, I slept on a cot against that wall as I got the paper off the ground. I only had the presses, and acquired everything else a little at a time. Took more years than I care to remember to afford a place of my own.

"I had to do everything myself, and with only two font cases. Two people should man each press, but I worked alone at first. I was blessed though Martin. An old master pressman came to work with me.

"He only requested a small share of what little we made. With his expert help, the paper grew rapidly. He retired at the age of eighty-one, and I hired a young lad to help me. I'm sure you recognize him, he now owns The Ash Brooke Citizen."

"Even though he never faced the many hardships you have J.B., he loves the paper as much as you do."

"I know Martin, I know. You had better get going, almost curtain time at the theater."

Chapter Forty-seven – Rosie has a surprise

Martin ran all the way to the theater. The lights dimmed as he found a seat in the second row. He caught Clara peeking from the edge of the side curtain. When she spotted him, she emoted a broad wipe across her brow.

The choreography went through its normal new routine, except they replaced the platform with the staircase from a previous months show. When the spotlights narrowed and the curtain opened, Rosie walked down to the middle landing and did her first solo.

Rather than continuing down the steps to do her second solo. She stepped back on the landing, allowing four chorus girls to surround her; one in each corner of the platform. The rest of the girls lined both sides of the staircase.

"Ladies and gentlemen, in our audience tonight is a special friend, who only missed two of my many performances. I dedicate this next song to my favorite fan, the Editor in Chief of The Ash Brooke Citizen, Mr. Thomas Hurston."

As Rosie began her special number. The four girls on the platform took turns holding up large placards; announcing the newspapers new weekend edition, hitting the streets tomorrow. Near the end of the performance, the signs announced the paper is now a daily paper.

Although many folks already subscribed for the daily paper. The Saturday edition was supposed to be a surprise to the community. Only those who advertised in the newspaper were aware of the weekend issue. But Rosie had an even bigger surprise for Martin.

One which shocked him so much, he almost passed out from the scare. From her platform, Rosie announced; she would like the following audience members to come to the stage; to enjoy a special solo.

After she made the announcement, the chorus girls formed a heart on the lower stage. Those on each side of the stairs ascended the steps filling the platform. Their fans formed a large star shape. The girls and the fans partially hid Rosie from view of the audience.

"My fans, I offer some wonderful treats for you tonight. The first lovely couple from our audience, Mr. and Mrs. Sunderleigh, please come up. When their baby comes; Luella will be the first employee of The Ash Brooke Citizen to bear a child."

Martin almost choked, Rosie just called Luella and Patrick to the stage.

"I would also like to announce the engagement of our very own showgirl, Clara Mae Remmert to Dale Fenston. Many of you meet with Clara and Martin at Curt's Over The Under Corner Deli after the theater. Clara tried to hook me up with Martin, more than once."

After the laughter subsided, Rosie made her next announcement. Martin came close to having a heart attack. The showgirls on the platform held up a copy of tomorrows weekend edition of the newspaper, while Rosie read the front page.

"The staff of The Ash Brooke Citizen daily newspaper; are pleased to announce the engagement of their Editor in Chief; Martin Thomas Hurston to Ella Rose Thornton. Will you three couples please join me here on stage for my final solo."

Martin's legs turned to rubber. Male stage hands were notified ahead of time, to usher him up to center stage, after the two other couples were shown their positions. They only walked him as far as the side steps and waited until Ella appeared.

From the theater floor next to the orchestra pit, at the opposite side of the theater. Wilton Stoddard, walked with Ella up the stairs and across the stage. Martin started walking to his spot. Like a proud father, Wilton ushered Ella to center stage and placed Ella's hand in Martin's.

Ella wore her best business skirt and jacket, and her hair was in its usual bun. The chorus girls lined behind them like a backdrop. The soft music playing this whole time, transitioned into Rosie's solo.

Rosie's voice filled the entire theater in song. The spotlights were on the three couples. Ella was smiling, staring into Martin's eyes. Her solo ended with a pronounced crescendo. The spotlights moved and broadened on the chorus girls, who began their choreographed routine.

In the shadows, Wilton motioned for the couples to leave the stage. He took Ella's hand and they exited the stage on the left. Martin was directed off the stage to the right, but was detained behind the curtains for a short time.

A stage hand met him there and passed a message from Ella to meet at his apartment after her next solo. The note also suggested Martin use the side or stage door, rather than go through the theater. The choreographed routine brought the girls to the side of the staircase.

As those on the platform moved away, the spotlight tightened on Rosie, who began her fourth solo for the evening. Martin stayed to enjoy Rosie's song before leaving the theater. He returned home and waited about fifteen minutes before Ella pulled up in her Monroe coupé.

Martin, still in a state of shock, asked a bundle of questions. Ella was back in her business suit again. The same outfit she wore on stage, her hair in a bun and no makeup. Martin hopped in the car.

"I asked Mr. Stoddard to send out special invitations for certain guests to appear at the theater for tonight's performance. I checked and all invited were there, except my mother."

"Dare I ask to whom you sent invitations and why?"

"We must be back at the theater in thirty minutes, so we can spend some time together. We are expected at Russo's to meet friends. Let's go up to your apartment, I've never seen inside."

"I'm sure you are hiding something else Ella. I don't think I can take any more of your surprises tonight."

"This hallway is beautiful Martin. I never dreamed inside is so posh."

"The tenants hired professional designers. Here we are, please excuse the mess. I do most of the editing up here where it's quiet."

"Your apartment is gorgeous Martin. I love your choice in furniture, and so organized."

"Not my doing, a surprise gift from my tenants. What about those invitations?"

"I invited certain nosy guests to put those snoops in their place. I asked my brother Earl to bring mother, and aunt Hattie. I also invited Mr. Blaine, and Mr. and Mrs. Pease."

"You invited Roland? What if something went wrong? A mighty dangerous risk Ella?"

"Was it? You should have seen the look in your eyes when Rosie sang her solo to us."

"Rosie sang alright, I can recognize her voice anywhere. How did you do it?"

"I told you not to ask. I will tell you later when we are alone, away from any earshot."

"Roland and J.B. both are asking way to many questions."

Especially Roland, he cornered Clara with several trick questions. She got suspicious and is even watching me now."

"But inviting them to the theater. You took an awful

chance Ella."

"We had better get back to the theater now."

"Why are we going back there?"

"It is only an outside reception line. All six of us will greet the patrons as they leave. I will be wearing my stern, I don't like being here face, so don't let that worry you."

Ella started the car and pulled through the garment mill lot and circled back on Liberty. She found a parking space three rows back, and we walked up to the front of the theater. Luella and Patrick are already outside with Wilton.

He is busy showing them where to stand. Clara and Dale came up behind us. Quick thinking Clara pretended she was talking to us as we walked. Wilton showed Martin where to stand, and pulled Ella off the sidewalk to the street.

The ushers made sure J.B. and Roland were among the first group to leave the theater. As soon as the door opened for them to exit, Wilton pretended to coerce Ella to the sidewalk. She is adamantly refusing to go nearer the theater.

Wilton motioned for Martin to come closer to them. Martin realized what they are doing and begged Ella to step up on the sidewalk. She started arguing with Wilton in a moderately loud voice, then picked a spat with Martin for bringing her to this horrid place.

Roland stood at the door listening when the charade started. He moved behind Martin and tapped him on the back.

"Lover's quarrel, eh Martin? You should'a never brought her here. She'll never forgive you, hah, hah."

"Don't worry Roland, I'm sure this will be the last time too. Luella persuaded her to come listen to Rosie sing, and promised we would leave before any skits started."

"Hah, hah, you can't fool me. I didn't miss Mr. Stoddard drag Ella up the steps and pull her across the stage. She definitely did not want to be up there, not even for you, loser."

J.B. leaned against a pillar, enjoying Roland's comments to Martin.

"Well Roland, I guess our curiosity is settled."

"Settled what John?"

"We are now certain Ella is Ella and Rosie is Rosie."

"I did not see Rosie while Ella was on stage."

"She was up on the platform singing, I noticed her behind the fans, twice."

"I saw somebody up there John, but how can I be sure it was Rosie, could be any one of the girls."

"Ella was on stage with her mouth shut, looking at Martin, and I watched both of them."

"Now that you mention it. From my angle, Ella stood behind the curtain, plain as day. Wilton still holding her hand, like a vise, while Rosie was on the platform singing."

No sooner than they finished speaking. J.B. jerked Roland by the shoulder, and pointed toward the Klein Avenue exit. Rosie's Saxon was pulling out of the parking lot. Martin caught Wilton wink at Ella.

She gave Mr. Stoddard a big kiss on the cheek, and gave Martin a bump with her rear end, pushing him closer to J.B. On seeing Rosie's car leaving so much later than usual. Clara unknowingly sealed the deal for Ella, with the most ingenious comment yet.

"I sure am grateful with Rosie for taking my place in the skits tonight."

J.B. rolled his hat down his arm, his trademark for the end of a long intriguing story. He and Mr. and Mrs. Pease parted company, and walked to their cars.

Appears Ella convinced J.B., I hope Roland is as well.

Martin, Ella, Luella and Patrick, met some of Ella's old neighborhood friends at Russo's. Where their friends held a late dinner and engagement party. Clara and Dale were not invited. Clara, only privy to part of the nights arrangements, had no idea about Ella's secret life.

Chapter Forty-eight – Ella protects another Secret

Martin arrived at the newspaper shortly after five, to make sure the new Saturday edition hit the streets early. Unaware, one week prior J.B. pushed starting time up to four-thirty, in preparation for the paper going daily.

Before J.B. hired more newsboys, Kent and Jerome ran the presses and made all deliveries. Afterward, he promoted the boys to full-time work in-house. As the newspaper grew, paper delivery passed to a distribution department, overseen by the top newsboy.

Per Martin's request, Mr. Blaine continued to manage the affairs of the paper. Martin still considered J.B. his boss, and the transfer of the paper to him only a growth necessity. J.B. made a single step down at first, and began teaching Martin the ropes.

Long before J.B. showed Martin his notebooks, Martin's duties grew along with circulation. Becoming a daily paper exceeded the limits of what one man could tackle alone. So J.B. stepped in to oversee the new additions to the operation.

Along with arranging the building renovations and setting up a new press; J.B. organized the hiring and established necessary departments to maintain a daily paper. Martin, aware of J.B.'s efforts, approved each without question.

He became concerned about Luella's pregnancy, when she would need to leave, and if she would return. Luella loved the paper too, and taught Kent, who in turn taught Jerome how to typeset. Kent also trained Jerome on the maintenance of the Linotype machines.

Without Martin's knowledge, J.B. secretly worked with these two men. He is teaching each how to fill in for Martin, as he learned more of J.B.'s duties. Mr. Blaine realized the day would come too soon, when Martin will have to fill his shoes.

The team purposely hid the new altered Saturday edition from Martin. All the paper carts were already out on deliveries when he arrived. The bus passed, and a moment later Luella appeared in the door. She pulled Martin to the center of the office.

Kent and Jerome ran to the front, carrying a normal copy, and a special edition printed on linen, as a keepsake. J.B., Kent, Jerome and Luella, plus two other upper management employees, surrounded Martin.

Kent handed Martin the first Saturday edition, with the special engagement as the front page. Jerome stepped forward to present him with the linen gift copy. Tears welled up in Martin's eyes, and he retreated to the same desk J.B. did only a few days earlier.

J.B. went to him and mentioned a speech is in order, your team is waiting. Then returned to the group. Martin followed a few moments later.

"What do I say? Words cannot describe the wonderful work each of you have done. J.B. should be given most of the credit, he's the one who put everything together. This is the most beautiful edition I have ever seen. Thank you."

J.B. could not resist telling the story of how he founded the paper, and when Martin began as a paperboy. He mentioned Kent and Jerome following in his and Martin's footsteps. He also raved over Luella's amazing abilities as a master typesetter and Linotype operator.

The clock struck six and the phones started ringing off the hook. Business owners arrived to their offices and read the Saturday edition, with the announcement of Martin and Ella's engagement. He had the phone glued to his ear all morning.

Martin promised to call Ella at ten, and the time is now a couple of minutes before noon. She understood he might be busy with the new weekend paper. But after reading the altered front page, and not able to reach him by phone, she drove to the paper.

Ella burst through the front door and ran right up to Martin, who promptly stood up. They embraced and she smothered him with kisses in front of the entire staff. J.B. shoved the couple out the door.

"You two scram so we can get our work done. We have a Monday edition to print. Martin, I do not want you back in the office at all today."

Ella beamed with excitement, and jumped from the curb into her car without opening the door. She bounced across the passenger seat and dropped down in her own.

"Auntie is expecting us for lunch. Mind your manners, she invited several of her oldest friends from church. But don't worry, none are as strict as from mother's church."

"I don't think I have time for all that Ella, we're a daily now."

"You heard Mr. Blaine, he doesn't want you back again until Monday morning."

"Do you know they hid today's paper from me?"

"The copies we read at the theater were exactly like today's inside page. So the front page is a surprise to you too?"

"Not completely. I planned the announcement page, but Luella and the team made changes. For the better I might add."

"Well, I hope you don't get cold feet. Now that the whole town's been informed, you can't weasel out."

"Aw. C'mon Ella, would I ever do that to you?"

"Here we are, now behave yourself."

When they went inside, all the women suddenly became quiet. Martin instinctively realized the topic of their conversation. They most likely were talking about he and Ella. Hattie hopped up.

"Here's my niece now, and her handsome beau, Martin."

Hattie introduced him to each lady in the parlor, and two husbands in the sitting room. After the introduction, Martin joined the men, and the women helped to set the tables. The men raved about the paper until Hattie called them to lunch.

A house full indeed. Eight sat around the dining room table, Martin, Ella, Hattie and five women. The two men, their wives, and two women sat around the kitchen table. Hattie shared what the ladies talked about earlier.

"I explained to the girls what the theater looked like inside. More elegant than I imagined. We didn't stay for the show."

Ella picked up on her aunts cue.

"We left right away too auntie. I was most uncomfortable in that horrid place."

"I owed the owner a big favor for letting us use his sound equipment. I mentioned you and Martin are engaged, and he insisted on making the announcement. Plus telling his patrons about the newspaper going daily."

"I was certain someone would spot me, and probably spread it all across town."

"We are sure the theater is beautiful. But you will never catch any of us inside, or at that end of town."

Only one lady made the comment, and all the rest nodded in agreement. The topic then shifted to the morning paper for the rest of the luncheon. All the guests left after lunch and Martin posed the first question.

"How did you get home from the theater last night Hattie?"

"Mr. Stoddard arranged my getting home Martin."

"I think Martin wants all the details auntie. Turned out different from what we planned. Why didn't Mr. Stoddard bring you home in the Saxon, like we agreed?"

"He couldn't, so asked one of those hussies to bring me home. I thought you were the driver at first."

"Sure risky, what if she tells someone Hattie?"

"She won't, because Mr. Stoddard didn't tell her anything Martin. He came by later to put the car in the garage, and told me why he changed the plan."

"I thought as much, and who drove my car too. Patsy snatched my gown after the last solo. I'm sure all he told her is to hide Hattie and get her home. Wilton you old rascal."

"He told me to duck down in the seat, and inform the driver I am hiding from church folk. Mr. Stoddard asked her to wear your gown and wait three-quarters of an hour before leaving. She parked in the alley and drove his car back to the theater."

"My suit and gown got a workout last night. Patsy wore both of my outfits. The gown while I was on stage with Martin and my suit behind the curtain with Mr. Stoddard. During the solo, she stood on the platform, behind the feather fans, with her face hidden"

"Looks like Wilton's idea of using a double to drive your car away late worked perfectly."

"I sure hope so. Even if Clara learned of our plans, she could not have come up with a better line."

"I'll never forget the look of disbelief on Roland and J.B.'s face. They were standing near Ella and I, when Rosie pulled out of the parking lot in the Saxon."

"While you are here Ella, you may want to turn your car around. Mr. Stoddard pulled in frontwards, and you normally back in."

"I will before Friday rolls around again. We should get going."

Ella helped Hattie do the last couple of dishes before

they left. Martin put the top up, because Ella wanted to run up to North Towne taking the Boulevard. She pulled into a parking lot a mile before her planned stop.

"Let's take the new trolley Martin, I've never ridden on one."

"Sounds like fun, lets."

They walked around the shopping district for an hour, before the next trolley cycled back to her car. Then drove down to riverside park via the Hancock Cut-off.

"I'll never figure out these streets up here Ella. Some seem to go in circles and others, well, whatever it is they do."

"Martin, you are the only person I've ever met, who can get lost inside an empty building."

"I must ask, how did you sing while standing on stage with me. Wasn't a double, nobody can duplicate your voice."

"You are absolutely right Martin, no one can and no one did. That was I you heard."

"Impossible, I never took my eyes away from you, the entire time you stood in front of me."

"Oh, it is possible, you witnessed it yourself. But I promised Mr. Stoddard I would not tell you until he says I can."

"You always seem to keep one more secret from me."

Chapter Forty-nine – A larger apartment

In the six months since Ella and Martin announced their engagement, many new businesses opened in Ash Brooke. Lured to the area, by the newspapers unique and highly successful, coördinated advertising program.

Ella's boss constructed a new three-story factory on Klein Avenue, with offices overlooking the garment mill. The restaurant in the Menton Building, where Martin and Ella meet daily for lunch, expanded after Mr. Deckett released their rented storage room.

Clarence combined the products from his northern factories, and migrated their operations to the new building. He sold every old building, except the garment mill, and used a small first floor office, rather than the lavish penthouse.

Blessed Hope completed the massive new wing started last year, larger than the original church. They converted the first addition to classrooms. Ella picked Martin up for church early every Sunday, because Hattie prevailed in getting him to join the choir.

For Clarence seventieth birthday, Ella and Martin held a large party at the restaurant. All area businessmen who provided products or services during the war effort were invited. Plus Mr. Deckett's north county friends and neighbors, Martin's tenants, and Mr. Stoddard.

J.B., the senior newspaper staff, their spouses, and Wilton invited Ella's aunt Hattie. Martin felt something suspicious, but could not put his finger on the reason for his concerns. He had not announced their wedding date, because Hattie insisted it be held on a Friday.

Martin's tenants did not spare any expense, or cut any corners, and served the best they had to offer. The birthday party progressed normally, so Martin enjoyed the dinner and entertainment. He and Ella unaware of what is soon to transpire.

George stood and tapped a glass for attention. Wait staff brought out the cake. Clarence made a wish and blew out the single candle. He made the first cut, then the staff divided the cake into slices and served all the guests. George struck the glass again, and Hattie rose.

"On behalf of Ella and Martin, and for our wonderful hosts who provided this fine dinner. My first wish is to our guest of honor, Mr. Deckett. All present here wish you a Happy Seventieth Birthday. Noisemakers whirled and bells rang.

"My friends, I am standing here, not to diminish Mr. Deckett's birthday, but to add to this joyous occasion. We have several important announcements to share with you this evening. Mr. Deckett has two to make. Mr. Deckett."

"No Hattie, you make the first announcement, I'll save mine for last."

"It's your party, but since you insist. Friends, we are all curious about a certain wedding date. We expected an official notice to appear in the paper. For lack thereof, we set the date."

Martin turned to Ella and shrugged his shoulders. She shook her head, equally surprised as Martin. Wilton came up behind Ella and whispered not to worry, he worked everything out.

"My lovely niece Ella... Martin will take your hand in marriage, at Blessed Hope Baptist Church. On the first Friday in June, the second day of the month, at six o'clock in the evening. A reception will follow right here in this beautiful restaurant."

Amid the cheers, whistles and congratulations, Hattie

took her seat. George tapped his glass, and asked tenant Jim to make his announcement.

"Mr. Deckett, on behalf of George, Dan, Douglas and myself.   In   consideration   of   your   timely   recent transactions. With Martin's approval, we have renovated apartment number two, in this building, as our birthday gift to you."

Doug held the keys high and carried them over to Clarence, who stood to thank each tenant by name. Martin noticed he seemed a little irritated by Jim's words. George tapped his glass.

"Martin and Ella, all the renovation noise you heard was not only in apartment number two. Our contractors are also working in apartment number six. While you and Ella are on your honeymoon, we will complete the final restoration, doubling the size of your apartment."

"Now, how will I be able to afford the rent in my own building? You all will do anything to keep me under your thumbs. Thank you for such an extravagant wedding gift."

"Don't pay attention to him, we will love living across the hall from you and Marie. Won't we Martin. You are supposed to say yes."

Mr. Deckett stood. He managed to break the glass with his knife handle.

"They don't make these things like they used too, do they."

A server quickly cleared away the broken glass shards. Clarence, still holding the knife, walked from the head table to the center of the room. He handed the knife to George.

"Here, take this thing, I'm to dangerous with it."

George took the knife and leaned over to whisper something in Clarence's ear. He motioned for Mr. Blaine. The wait staff brought out three chairs, and helped Mr. Deckett sit down, then J.B. waited for Ella and Martin to take their seats.

"Martin my boy, my son. Clarence only has a few years head start over me, and he's in better health than I. I've appointed Kent as the managing editor of the newspaper. He will assume your duties so you and Ella may enjoy your honeymoon.

"As the Editor in Chief, it is high time for you to fulfill that title. In front of all present, I say you long held the capacity and are fully qualified to fill my shoes. I will work in a minor capacity for as long as I am able, but on your return, consider me retired."

The room fell silent. Everyone knew Mr. Blaine turned the paper over to Martin years ago. But he is a landmark at the paper. Surely he is not retiring. J.B. glanced at the amazed faces around the room.

"Don't look so sad folks, I think you got the wrong idea. I'll still be behind my desk. My retirement cottage, my home, my place. You can visit me there, but don't ask me to do a dang thing."

After a long pause, the room filled with cheers. A few stepped up to shake his hand, saying they would stop by more often. George helped Clarence to his feet.

"Ella, you and Martin please sit back down. Seems hard to keep things secret these days. Many of you don't know me very well, since I lived so far north. It appears I will be your newest neighbor now, and I would like to personally meet each one of you.

"But I'm not here to talk about myself. I want to tell you about a young girl whom I have admired for years. A proper young lady who had a hard life, and despite her many hardships, cared for others first.

"You never see her out and about, because she is busy working. She toils from morning well into the night. After her uncle Oscar passed away, on top of all her other duties at Platte's Clothing. She took over the business so her aunt Hattie could keep the store open.

"Men's suits were an unaffordable luxury during the war and Hattie closed the store. I was a most fortunate man when Ella agreed to come work for me. Times were hard, her salary low, yet she worked like a slave, and never failed to smile.

"Only out of necessity, did I place her in the dusty old garment mill. I would rather kept her working beside me. But she was the only one qualified, whom I could trust to make sure everything was managed properly and orders completed on time.

"At my advanced age, there is a reason I built a new building, and on the specific site I chose. I did not take the first floor office because of the stairs. But because I reserved the penthouse for our new CEO.

"The office overlooks Liberty Street, and from the large windows many sites can be seen. It was not by accident, my design was on purpose. I want our new officer to keep an eye on her home, and on her man.

"Miss Ella Thornton, I hereby appoint you as are our new CEO. Congratulations, and believe me when I say, you've earned it."

The whole room erupted in cheers, whistles and clapping. As Ella was hugging and squeezing Mr. Deckett, he handed her a large sealed envelope. He whispered in Ella's ear.

"Place in your lock box unopened. A gift for you and Martin, to open after I'm gone."

Mr. Stoddard also had an expensive new gift for Rosie, one which would benefit Martin as well. For reasons obvious only to himself, Martin and Ella. Wilton could not present the gift at Mr. Deckett's birthday party.

Chapter Fifty – A Friday night wedding

Martin worked extra hard, side by side with J.B. to learn aspects of the newspaper industry he would soon face alone. Kent already did more than one-half of the editing, and Martin stopped checking his excellent work over a year ago.

First thing Monday morning, J.B. moved his old desk near the front door. So his visitors would not disrupt the working members of the newspaper. He promoted Jerome to fill his position at the city desk.

When the lunch whistle blew, Martin ran down to the restaurant to meet Ella for lunch. She came out the garment mill's door, rather than from the front door of the new building.

"I though you would be settled, up in your new fancy office."

"Not yet, I chose to stay in the mill to train a new supervisor. I told Mr. Deckett I wouldn't move into the penthouse office until we returned from our honeymoon. He admitted he had a hunch I would not, and was pleased with my decision."

"About your aunt's announcement. Shouldn't we choose when we set our wedding date? I thought a Friday night was totally impossible."

"We can't talk here. Wilton and auntie have the specifics all figured out. He will fill me in, on the finer details this Friday."

"You also promised to tell me how you sang and didn't

sing at the same time."

"Meet me after work and we can drive somewhere quiet, where I can tell you better."

When Martin arrived back at the paper after lunch. He was not met with the usual dozen or so journalists shoving papers in his face. Kent was at his desk, looking calm, and not a bit frazzled. Martin pulled a chair up to his desk.

"Is everything going OK in your new position as managing editor Kent?"

"Sure is M.T., not a single problem arose."

"M.T. eh, what brought that on?"

"I hope it's OK. I mean, you call Mr. Blaine J.B., so I figured it was a term of endearment."

"Perfectly fine with me Kent. Never been called M.T. before. But shouldn't it be M.H. For Martin Hurston?"

"Oh yeah, right you are M.H. M.T. sounded a little freaky and demeaning."

"I came over here to ask if the journalists showed you their mornings work for approval."

"All except Larry, he is not back from his appointments yet. I edited their work and they are making the changes now."

"How could you do so much editing in only an hour?"

"I simply asked the team to turn in their columns, as soon as each was ready. So I'm not hit with all of them at once, and they will be checked by the time they get back from lunch."

"Sounds like your method works well. You had lunch?"

"Not yet. I planned to go when you returned, but I'll wait for Larry first."

Martin rolled across the floor in his chair, over to J.B.'s desk. Martin managed the business affairs since J.B. turned the paper over to him. J.B. has tons of notebooks he wrote over the years, and amended versions in new books, to pass to Martin.

Kent rang a counter bell on his desk, then he and Jerome slipped into the press room. Within a minute, Martin heard the new press power up, and returned to his desk to get some work done. Luella stopped at his desk and handed him a copy of Tuesday's paper.

She only waited long enough for Martin to read the front page, then went back to work. Before he finished reading, he heard the new press power down. He checked his wristwatch. Two-twenty and tomorrows edition is done.

A few minutes to three, he heard the press power up again. The machine only ran for about ten minutes and was turned off. One of the new young pressmen roll a cart next to J.B.'s desk. Martin got up to go take a look. A one page, quarter folded, and a cut ad flier.

"Fabulous layouts J.B., the new accounts you picked up sure help."

Ella pulled up outside to wait for the paper to close for the day. J.B. waved his arm for Martin to leave, and held up his keys as a sign he would lock up. Both Linotype machines were running, but Martin didn't stop to ask why, certain everything is under control.

"You're early."

"Mr. Deckett asked me to let the new supervisor lock up. He want's to watch her from his office."

"After only one day of training. Seems a bit unusual to me."

"She's worked with me for years Martin. Locked up many times in the past."

Ella drove straight down to the river park. A fisherman was below the pavilion area, so they sat at the open air picnic tables.

"Mr. Stoddard was talking to Mr. Deckett when I left. He doesn't know anything about our little secret, and I've never seen them together before."

"Wilton had his crew help move Mr. Deckett into his new apartment over the weekend. From what I understand, they are old north town friends."

"I forgot. When I dropped off the time cards, there was a picture in Mr. Deckett's old office of two young men shaking hands. Which is something I don't need to do any more. Payroll is now a part of my new job duties."

"Hey, before we leave for dinner, you were going to tell me how you pulled off the song."

"You would not believe how many times they made me sing the same song. Mr. Stoddard brought a machine he called a Rubber Line, he experimented with in his home. He thought using the theater sound equipment as the feed would work. It didn't.

"Two weeks later, after visiting a movie studio, he had their crew come by the theater. This was the Wednesday I told you I must practice a new routine. I was scared to death of the cameras. Mr. Stoddard assured me they are only used to record my voice.

"I believed him, because they set this big round thing with a tall screened box in the center; right smack dab in front of my face. Apparently this was some recent invention called a Phonofilm. We started over several times, before the adjustments were correct.

"The more Mr. Stoddard paced the floor, the more I shook from fear and being tired. I'm sure this crew cost him a pretty penny. One man hung a black piece of curtain material over the huge microphone.

"After making several tests with metal forks which made tones. A man came up and told me to stay a foot away from the curtain when I sang. Also to focus on him and only him while I sang, and as he raised his hand up or down as cues. He rolled off his fingers, three, two, one."

"I'm sorry they made you nervous. Whatever they did, your solo sounded perfect."

"May have sounded perfect to you, I felt I was dreadful. I sound nothing at all like what they played back. The crew and Mr. Stoddard said I did. One of them told me a person does not sound to themselves what they think they sound like."

"Amazing machines they make these days. I guess the new machine is how the movies render audio. Although the movies do not sound as good as you did Friday night. You were perfect."

"We had better get to dinner Martin."

Over dinner they talked about their upcoming wedding. Hattie is controlling almost everything, except for Ella's dress and the flowers. The lady who made Luella's magnificent gown offered her services. Martin and Ella would visit the florist next Tuesday together.

The days before their wedding whizzed past. Seemed nothing would be ready in time, nor can they be attended to on Fridays. With Clarence now living down the hall from Martin, he and Doug joined him for the theater.

Everyone in town learned Mr. Stoddard bought a brand new 1922 black four-door Duesenberg Touring Car. One reporter for the paper discovered Wilton purchased two cars from the dealer. The second a cream colored Model-A Fleetwood two-door coupé.

After Rosie's solo, the last Friday show before Ella and Martin's wedding. Mr. Stoddard presented the new automobile to Rosie as part of the choreographed program. The Fleetwood was so bright, anyone in town would recognize the car instantly.

Martin met Ella after work on Wednesday night. The last time they would meet together, until she walked down the aisle in her wedding gown. They drove to Russo's for dinner.

"Mr. Stoddard will pick you up at your apartment at four-thirty in his old car. He will park his new car at the church around four. After the wedding he will drive us to the restaurant. We will use Rosie's Saxon for our honeymoon."

"Had I not learned of Wilton's shrewd plan to protect your secret. I would never have agreed to using Rosie's car. He advertised the Saxon Roadster in the daily newspaper for a full week. Later, he announced Mr. Deckett bought the car for you to chauffeur him around."

"I hope folks do not notice us in Rosie's car and think I am her. Oh, Mr. Stoddard asked me to give my Monroe to Luella, instead of to you. The car never gave me a problem."

"Luella truly needs a car. Patrick tries to bring her as often as he can, so she don't need to ride the bus. I wonder what else Wilton is pulling off? He advertised Rosie for Friday."

"Yes, I read the paper. Rosie will be singing."

"Is he doing what he did last time?"

"No, this time he hired another person from out-of-state to take Rosie's place for one night. He can get by with his stunt, because all our friends will be at the wedding and reception."

"He seems to be getting a little too brave with your reputation at risk."

"Since he will be at the wedding, he thought about closing the theater. But with it being the first night for the new vaudeville act, and two-thirds of the tickets sold. He can't."

"Well, no one can sing as beautiful as you Ella. I hope his plan works."

"He selected a new set of songs, I am familiar with each, but never sung them before in the theater. By the next Friday we will be back to the usual show songs."

"Let's take one last drive down to river park before you take me home. I would like to hold you close, under the pavilion on our spot. For our first and last dating kiss together."

"What a wonderfully romantic idea Martin. Let's go."

Later, when Ella dropped Martin off at his apartment, they agreed not to kiss. They both chose to preserve their special moment, over their token bronze coin. They will kiss once at the altar, and not kiss again until after the reception, under the pavilion, on their way to honeymoon.

Everyone worked like crazy at the paper. To finish the weekend edition and side orders, to close at four. Martin asked J.B. as a witness. Kent, Jerome, George and Roland as groomsmen. Ella asked Luella to be her bridesmaid, and Wilton to give the bride away.

While standing at the altar, before the preacher spoke, a soloist in the choir loft began a soft hymn. In shock Ella and Martin turned and peered up, then stared at each other in disbelief.

"She sounds like Rosie, but cannot be her. For we are standing right here. Soon to be we."

The solo finished, and their vows shared, tin cans and old shoes danced behind the car. The red carpet they walked led to the head table. The party was grand, but not a tune played or a dance step made; until Ella's mother and friends from her strict church left for home.

Our newlywed couple ducked out early, a special first kiss to share over their medallion. Where they shared their honeymoon is their little well kept secret. They arrived home to find their apartment, now double, was fully remodeled and furnished, most extraordinaire.

In the Monday morning daylight, they noted a new addition to the parking lot. A valet moved the Saxon to a parking space clearly marked Mr. Clarence Deckett. Martin walked Ella to her new penthouse office.

She could not believe her eyes. Clean and crisp, everything new, like their apartment. They held hands and viewed the landscape from the massive windows.

"Oh look Martin, you left your hat on the desk."

"I'll fetch my cap on the way to work."

Martin glanced toward the newspaper.

What on earth did they do down at the paper?

"They added something big and shiny on top of my building."

Ella smiled and gave Martin a hug and big kiss.

"I'm not the only one with a new office Martin. Why don't you run along now and go explore my present to you. I have a whole weeks worth of work to catch up on."

Martin retrieved his hat from the apartment, but before leaving for work, he walked through every room. A tear came to his eye as he admired all the ornate workmanship and the new furniture.

He tapped softly on Marie's door. No answer. He met Jim on the stairs.

"I can't believe what all you guy's did in my, I mean our apartment. Ella and I thank you from the bottom of our hearts."

"We don't get all the praise Martin, we only contracted for the renovations. Your new furniture is a gift from Mr. Blaine and the newspaper team."

"Speaking of which, I had better get down to the office."

"Don't be too shocked, Ella hired the same contractors and designers we use."

I wondered what her and Marie were cooking up.

Martin trotted all the way to the paper. He glanced at the Monroe parked beside the building.

Ella didn't drive past me. Oh yeah, Luella.

He entered the building and all the employees swamp him at the door. They won't let him around them until Luella arrived from the back.

"I want to thank you and Ella. I truly needed a car. So gracious of you and Ella to think of me. Her brother Earl cleaned and polished the heck out of it. Looks brand new. Thank You."

Luella gave Martin a big bear hug. Martin then

thanked everyone for their gift of new furniture. They step back to give Martin viewing room. The desk area is completely changed around, and a new reception counter greets patrons who come in the front door.

"Wow, this place feels like a New York lawyers office. Where is my desk?"

"Come behind the counter and look up boss. All Ella's idea. J.B., Jerome and I bought some new office furniture and cabinets for you."

Martin did as Kent directed. Spanning the entire width of the center office area, a wood railed loft hovered over the front counter. The side of the new roll-top J.B. gave him a few years earlier sat like a monument to the industry.

To build the floor, the former twelve foot high ceiling was now only nine feet high over the lobby. The roof raised, surrounded with glass windows, and the loft extended to about midway over the new front counter.

"How do I get up to my office Kent?"

"Well boss, they couldn't put the stairs where we wanted them, because the walls need to hold up the floor. So the stairs enter from both sides, in the press room or in the Linotype room. Easier for you to sneak up on the employees too."

"I never sneak up Kent."

"No you don't M.H., only added the comment for fun is all."

Martin went into the press room. The new modern press was turned lengthwise, and the staircase hugged the wall. He went upstairs where new filing cabinets, visitors chairs, and tables greeted him. Nothing on his desk appeared disturbed, exactly as he left things.

He gazed out the huge plate glass windows. Ella was standing at her window peering in his direction. She waved and threw him a kiss, then sat down at her desk again. Martin walked out the other door and glanced down at Luella typing away.

The matrices flying down the Linotype magazine captured his interest. No one noticed he was up high on the landing watching them. He stepped back into his office and over to the railing to observe everyone at work. He realized he had not seen J.B. yet.

Martin went back downstairs. J.B.'s desk is to the left of the new counter, in the lobby area. It seemed out-of-place by the door, and would not blend in with the new desk area either. Kent glanced up from his desk and caught Martin staring at Mr. Blaine's desk.

"J.B. is at the womens' union rally, or I should refer to them by their new name; the garment workers local rally."

"Does Mr. Deckett know about this?"

"Sure does, and he's in their favor. Said the union will make running his business much easier, and they will never be shorthanded."

"Strange for a business owner to be on the side of a union Kent."

"I thought so at first myself. We ran an article in Wednesday's paper, and an interview with Mr. Deckett in Thursday's. The benefits far outweigh the small demands. A copy of each paper is on the corner table in your office."

As they were talking, a paper flew past Martin, headed airborne up to his office, and landed on the desk Kent mentioned.

"What the heck. What is this new contraption Kent?"

"Something Jerome rigged up. J.B. said no one is allowed to go up to your office. So Jerome made this delivery system from some leather belts he got from Miller and Crofts. Come into the press room, I'll show you how it works."

Kent picked up an envelope, stepped on a pedal and the belts moved around two flexible pulleys. He put his hand in, to show the mechanism cannot do harm. Then he slipped in the envelope, it rode between the belts and dropped at the other end on the corner table.

"Neat-o ain't it boss?"

"Isn't Kent.   I must compliment Jerome on his inventiveness."

J.B. came strolling through the door and dropped down at his desk. The counter girl waved at Martin, and pointed toward Mr. Blaine's desk.   Martin entered the office area.

"Welcome home Martin. I hope you and Ella had a good time. Where did you go?"

"None of your business where we went J.B. Appears you've been more than busy while I was gone."

"No more than usual. A bit noisy and dusty in here for a couple of days."

"I bet.   Thank you, everything is perfect.   Much appreciated."

"Clarence told me what is in the envelope he gave to you and Ella.   Now that you two are back, he thinks I should tell you the contents. Not the details though, just what important documents are inside."

"Why would Mr. Deckett give us something so important it must be locked up J.B.?"

"I must tell you and Ella together. I can assure you, he is offering something wonderful. We worked on the details together, right after our first Saturday weekend paper issued."

"So you are aware of the contents, but can't tell us. Sure is odd J.B."

"Are you meeting Ella for lunch?"

"Sure am, at the restaurant. You are welcome to join us."

"I will, but only for a moment. I won't stay for lunch."

Lunchtime arrived before Martin finished catching up on the past week. John walks a little slower these days. Ella crossed the street before they were half way to the restaurant. She seated herself at their usual table with only two chairs.

She moved to a larger table, when Martin arrived with Mr. Blaine.

"No need Ella. I'm only relaying a message to you and Martin, then I'll be on my way."

They moved back over to their normal table. J.B. spun a chair around and sat down to whisper to them.

"Ella, Clarence asked me to tell you and Martin what is in the envelope he handed you at the wedding reception. He does not want you to do anything other than keep it safe. No prying or opening to see the contents either."

"We understand Mr. Blaine, we are good at keeping secrets."

"I'm sure you are Ella. Us old timers understand a lot more than you give us credit for, and we are wise enough to keep things to ourselves."

"I hope some day to possess your outstanding wisdom J.B."

"You grasp more now than I do Martin. I may not understand those newfangled machines, but am happy about how they improved the paper."

"They sure did J.B., and you had the wisdom to push them into operation."

"The waiter will be bringing your food, so listen. The envelope contains the Last Will and Testament of Mr. Clarence Deckett, and is not to be opened until after his death."

"Why would he give his Will to us J.B., shouldn't such a document be in the bank's vault?"

"A duplicate copy is in the bank, and a couple of other places as well Martin. You are not the only beneficiaries, but that is all I can say. Don't say a word about the envelope. Clarence felt he could trust you enough to learn the contents, but not what is disclosed in his Will."

J.B. hopped up and put his chair back under the other table when the waiter approached.

"Martin, do you think he learned about my Friday nights?"

"I don't think so Ella."

"Certain comments he made indicate otherwise."

"He does fish out of habit when digging for a scoop, to get folks to say something they would not otherwise. He is a sly one."

"Well, he is aware of what is in the envelope."

"He did say he worked with Clarence on some of the contents months ago. Oh, my office is beautiful. Thank you. Where on earth did you get the money?"

"I'll never tell. Perhaps I've not told you all my secrets yet."

"I know you too well now Ella, you are plumb out of secrets. Besides, Mrs. Hurston would never keep anything from her husband."

I wonder what other secrets she harbors under her beautiful long blond hair?

THE END

* * * * *

To learn more about Dutch Rhudy, please visit

http://home.comcast.net/~dutch-rhudy/

* * *

Other Books by this Author
Non-Fiction Short Stories:
Boot & Milk Balls (Plus three additional short stories)
Lady Buff & Yardstick - The Three-footed Kitten
Fiction Short Stories:
The Elusive Smoking Gun
The Vanishing Corn Mystery

# # #